The Queen Must Die

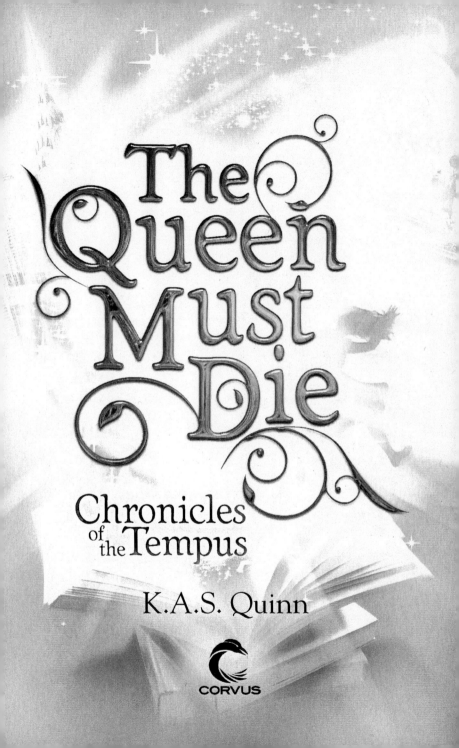

The Queen Must Die

Chronicles of the Tempus

K.A.S. Quinn

CORVUS

First published in Great Britain in 2010 by Atlantic Books,
an imprint of Atlantic Books Ltd.

This paperback edition published in Great Britain in 2011 by Corvus,
an imprint of Atlantic Books Ltd.

3 5 7 9 10 8 6 4 2

A CIP catalogue record for this book is available from the British Library.

ISBN: 978-1-84887-052-9

Printed and bound by CPI Group (UK) Ltd, Croydon, CR0 4YY

Corvus
An imprint of Atlantic Books Ltd
Ormond House
26-27 Boswell Street
London WC1N 3JZ

www.corvus-books.co.uk

To Stephen, William and Lorcan Quinn

The Visions

Was she going insane? The visions were appearing with greater clarity and ever more frequency. Just yesterday, Katie had turned the corner to find a tall man in a black silk top hat. He seemed to be searching for someone amid the chaos of the 86th Street subway station. He was deathly pale, with creased, almost dusty skin – his pallor emphasized by his strange close-fitting black garments. The only colour about him was his eyes. They glittered green in the sun as he reeled around and strode towards Katie, raising his walking stick as if to strike her. He opened his mouth, but no sound came out. Instead, the word '**SEEK**' formed in the air before him, floating above his head like the message of a sky-writer. And then he was gone – disappearing through the steam of the subway.

He wasn't the first. There was the girl with the grey eyes and serious face. Katie had thought she might just be some new neighbour. But then Katie had noticed the long starched skirts, the high, buttoned leather boots and the ridiculous fur muff. She too spoke in these silent smoke signals. '**I will serve**,' she declared, looking so kind and grave that Katie longed to hear her voice. Afterwards came a series of children. The one in rags, the tiny urchin girl, so pretty and so timid – '**I will sacrifice**' hung over her like a pall. Such a frightened child, but Katie could never quite reach her. And then there was the small smug boy in velvet shorts and a ruffled shirt. Katie recoiled from his message: '**I will slay.**' These children, these visions, whatever they were, they weren't just in the wrong neighbourhood; they seemed to be in the wrong time. They had something to say, but Katie didn't know what, or why. She tried to shake it off, shrug her shoulders and ignore it all, the way New Yorkers blank the freaks and weirdos of life. But today's episode had changed everything.

Walking home from school, she'd come face to face with a small plump woman in fancy dress – pink satin swept off the shoulders with six inches of silver lace and an abundance of diamonds. The little lady's pigeon eyes twinkled with pleasure as she talked and laughed with someone directly behind Katie. But when Katie turned around all she could see was a businessman talking on a cellphone.

'Not another vision,' Katie thought, her stomach lurching upwards. 'There must be a rational explanation for this. Was it performance art? A carnival? A commercial?' Katie scanned the streets for a camera.

Suddenly the little woman's eyes bulged. Her mouth opened in a silent scream as she backed away and slid down the side of the building. Katie ran towards her, and then took a step back. A bright crimson stain was spreading over the bodice of the small woman's pink dress. The woman held her arms out, as if pleading for aid, and then her eyes rolled back in her head. She slumped; lifeless in a heap of satin and blood. 'Help,' Katie cried, 'help!' The passers-by looked briefly at Katie and, deciding she was just another crazy person in the street, turned away. They kept walking, talking, drinking coffee out of paper cups and looking at their watches. One man, reading the newspaper, actually stepped through the woman and the growing pool of blood. And then the woman was gone, the sidewalk clean where there had been gore. Katie's legs buckled, she'd have to sit down – right there on the sidewalk. She wiped her forehead. This habit of seeing things. This was not good. She'd have to tell someone, but who?

Chapter One

Under the Bed

It was filthy, sitting in the gutter, and the old Greek guy in the shoe repair shop was giving Katie suspicious looks. She got up and wiped the muck from the skirt of her school uniform. If Katie had been part of a normal family, she'd have rushed home to tell her parents. But Katie's family wasn't normal. Could she really tell her mother Mimi? Katie doubted it. Mimi was far too busy with her latest boyfriend to care about her daughter's visions.

Katie Berger-Jones-Burg's mother liked to get married. Katie had accustomed herself to this. It only really got to her on the first day of school. Calling attendance, the teacher ploughed through Alcott, Allen, Applebaum, Bayle... The class held their breath as the teacher paused, trying to string Katie's names together in the correct order. In year two Miss Grant had got it spectacularly wrong and christened her 'Boogerberg'. It had stuck for years. 'Why doesn't Mimi just live with them?' Katie wondered. 'Why do they all have to marry her? And adopt me?' It had to do with morals, family values, Mimi had explained. And then she'd wept, embraced Katie tenderly, exclaiming at the great wonder of having a daughter, more like a sister, that she could always talk to. 'Yeah, talk about yourself,' Katie thought. But in her role as listener and number one fan, it wasn't part of her job to actually say anything.

Katie's mother had once been quite famous as a member of an all-girl pop group – Youth 'n Asia. They'd worn long black Chinese braids down their backs, and no one over the age of twenty was allowed into their concerts. Mimi was used to being the centre of attention and wasn't about to give up this position. Katie thought about the meal Mimi would make of the visions: the visits to new age 'doctors', the consultations with therapists, the interview with the *Pop Times*. Perhaps most frustrating of all, it would stop being Katie's problem and start being Mimi's problem. Katie could just hear Mimi wailing away to some glossy magazine. 'Had *she* failed Katie as a mother? As a friend? Perhaps the visions were visions of Mimi, in her different roles in Katie's life?'

'No,' Katie sighed. 'I just can't bear the Mimi factor in this. I'll talk to Dad next time I see him.'

Dad was the 'Berger' in 'Berger-Jones-Burg'. Danny Berger had been her mother's high school sweetheart. 'We married young, very young,' said Mimi, showing Katie a photograph of the two of them at a rock festival: Danny staring adoringly at Mimi, while Mimi stared adoringly at the camera. Katie thought her mother looked about the same – a bit thinner now and a lot less happy, but about the same – blonde hair, white toothy smile, turned-up nose. But the Danny Berger of Katie's childhood looked nothing like the one in the photograph. The humorously thin young man with curly black hair had put on weight and lost his hair. He now looked old enough to be – not just Katie's father, but Mimi's father as well. 'It's because of the huge amount of money I have to pay to keep you in your posh private school,' he griped. Katie sighed again. Now that Dad was remarried and had a new young family, he was tired all the time. Cranky, too. She'd have to keep the visions to herself for now.

The Greek guy in the shoe repair shop was now tapping on his window, so Katie moved on towards home. Mimi liked to keep her busy, as this kept Katie out of her way, but for once Katie didn't have ballet lessons, tennis lessons, yoga or t'ai chi. She ducked under the awning of her apartment building, nodded to the doorman and punched the elevator button for the eleventh floor. As she turned the key in the lock, the sound of a Spanish soap opera greeted her, loudly. Mimi couldn't possibly be home, if Dolores had the sound up that high. 'Hey, Dolores,' she called to their long-time housekeeper 'Qué pasa? No Mimi?' Dolores had set the ironing board up in the kitchen. In front of her was a small television, making big amounts of noise. On the screen was a young woman with a serious hairdo and lots of eye shadow. She was crying and screaming as two solid, expressionless policemen led her away. 'What's the crime?' Katie asked. 'Did she rob a bank? Or murder her boyfriend?'

'This show is not for you,' Dolores said, without taking her eyes off the screen. 'It's for grown-up people who know about these things. And don't go saying "hey" to me. Hay is for horses. Mimi says you're way too slangy.'

Katie looked in the refrigerator: macrobiotic crackers, Swedish seagrass yogurt, freeze-dried salt cod, and a jar of Mimi's face cream. Turning from the fridge, she rummaged through Dolores's handbag and found a Snickers bar.

'Mimi's not here,' Dolores added.

'That's obvious,' said Katie, 'we're both having way too much fun. So where is she?'

'Well, baby,' Dolores said. This was not a good sign. Dolores only called Katie 'baby' when she felt sorry for her. 'Mimi's gone.'

'Gone?'

'To Acapulco. You know that therapist she's been seeing, Dr Fishberg? You know how she's been saying, at last here's a man who understands her? Well they seem to have become real good friends, and...'

Suddenly the Snickers bar didn't taste that great. 'Oh Dolores, she can't run off to Acapulco and get married again!' Then something even worse dawned on her. Katie Berger-Jones-Burg-Fishberg. Picking up her rucksack of books she fled to her bedroom. This one she could never live down.

Katie's room looked nothing like Katie. While Katie was tall and awkward with her father's bushy black curls, this was a room designed for a very different child: a small, delicate golden-haired child – the child of Mimi's imagination. 'Think pink!' had been Mimi's motto when briefing the decorator. The carpet, the lampshades, the curtains, the cushions spanned the hues from candy-floss pink to sunset rose – or, as Katie saw it, from pale vomit to inflamed sunburn. Katie could have lived with it, except for the wallpaper. Hundreds, but hundreds of whimsical fairies fluttered across Katie's walls. These fairies were very busy indeed: waving their little sparkling wands, hovering over large (pink) flower blossoms, standing on tippy-toe and giving each other big wet kisses. Katie had spent endless hours, throwing a baseball against the wall, attempting to knock out the fairies one by one. While many of them sported a black eye or a broken wing, Katie had barely made a dent in their sweet little world. She looked at the carpet. It might be pink, but at least it didn't have a bunch of fairies kissing on it.

'Now, this Dr Fishberg,' Dolores was yelling from the

kitchen, 'he doesn't seem half bad. At least he's not that yoga instructor she was mooning over last year. Breathing. All he ever talked about was breathing. As if we didn't *know* how to breathe. We wouldn't be alive if we didn't *know* how to breathe.'

Dolores was right. Mimi's men were as wide-ranging and temporary as the rest of Mimi's enthusiasms. There had been the tennis pro, the enema expert, the guy with the flotation tank and then the professor upstairs – the one who went on and on about parallel being and the temporal psyche of history. But still – Fishberg!

Katie crawled under her bed, massively high, with a canopy, netting and the inevitable pink ribbons. Katie thought it was almost as bad as the fairies, but what was underneath her bed made everything else in the room – and her life – bearable. Because of its height, there was lots of room underneath. She called it 'The Library' and it was the only place in the whole apartment she could call her own. Mimi knew nothing about it, and Dolores left it alone – she wasn't much interested in cleaning, aside from ironing in front of the television. The Library consisted, along with a great many dustballs, of a Peter Rabbit lamp left over from Katie's baby nursery, a flashlight (just in case), her diary, a cardboard box filled with her treasures, a pillow and a crochet blanket from her grandmother – now dead. And, of course, the books – it couldn't be a library without books. There were stacks and stacks of them, lining three sides of the bed. It was getting pretty cramped down there, but Katie couldn't bear to part with even one of them.

Katie's books were carefully organized: fiction, non-fiction, topic, author – and then that special category, importance to Katie. She didn't share this interest with any of her friends. Dolores was told as little as possible. Mimi didn't ask. Weak as her social antennae might be, Katie knew her book obsession was about as riveting to others as those boys at school who could tell you the exact subway route to get anywhere – yes, anywhere – in New York City. This was not the hobby of a popular girl.

And it got worse. It didn't really matter what the books were about: *Catcher in the Rye*, *The History of the Bee*, *Harry Potter*, *The Essays of Emerson*, *The Life of Jim Morrison*, *The Letters of Queen Victoria*, *Putt Your Way to Golf Perfection*. Katie would read anything. 'Why?' her father had once asked her, years ago. 'Reading's a great thing, Katie-kid, but why so many books?'

Katie struggled to explain. 'It's like, like a trip away,' she said slowly. 'It's like I'm really going someplace, I'm flying in my head, a journey, just me, my own mind. It belongs to me – I make it happen. And I get to make new friends – not just the people in the book, but the person who writes the book too, and the story, and…' And then the phone rang. Her father left the room. When he returned, he'd forgotten what they were talking about.

Despite the books under the bed, Katie wasn't really that

much of a student. Her interests and that of her school just weren't the same. The Neuman Hubris Progressive School was modern and cutting edge, with a vegetarian, anti-toxin cafeteria and interpretive dance during recess. They didn't do a lot of books. Mostly it was internet stuff – downloading, Googling. When they did get assigned an old bulky, tree-destroying book, it had to contain some very current message. Neuman Hubris was all about the here and now. Dusty classics? Faded history? Face it – that was the past. Racist, sexist, Imperialist drivel. She pulled her satchel underneath the bed and took out her assigned reading. There on the cover was little Mashaka. His village had no water and he had to walk seven miles, barefoot, to school. Inadequacy flooded through Katie. How selfish was she? Here she was, with everything in the world she could possibly want, and she couldn't even take the time to read about little Mashaka. Katie was not an uncaring person, and Mimi had drilled charity into her. She brought tinned goods to school on 'Stop Poverty Now' day. Her discarded toys and clothes went to charity shops. Mimi had once made an appeal on television with Youth 'n Asia:

> Hold 'em
> Feed 'em
> Show 'em that you need 'em
> You gotta adore
> the poor…

Mimi had sung, tears welling in her luminous blue eyes. Katie hadn't known whether to laugh or cry. She wanted to stop poverty too; she just didn't see stopping poverty as a leisure activity.

She put the book back in her rucksack. Mashaka would probably get water and a ride to school by the end of the book. (Katie's teachers were all for edgy realism, as long as it had a happy ending.) Instead she took out her own diary. Katie had been reporting on her life since she could string a sentence together in wobbly capital letters. There were half a dozen volumes of 'The Life of Katie Berger-Jones-Burg' under the bed already – dog-eared notebooks filled with the victories, defeats, joys and sorrows that made up her fairly average life. She flipped back several months, just as a kind of monitor to see how things had been going.

8 January

Mimi is smoking again – and it's only a week since she gave it up. I found her in the kitchen with her head halfway out the window – puffing away. It looked like she had three cigarettes in her mouth at once. I mean it was snowing and she had her head out the window! She begged me not to tell Dolores. Said I couldn't understand because I didn't have a passionate addictive nature. Mimi thinks I'm boring because I don't smoke or drink or take drugs or make out with boys. I really would, if I thought any of those things would be fun, but I just don't see the point. And I know I'm boring, but when I try not to be, it doesn't work, I just go all silly. 'Get a grip,' I told Mimi – 'and stop leaning out the window, the neighbours will think you're going to jump – and you've just had your streaks put in – you're totally messing up your hair.' That did the trick. Saw strange man in the street again today. I can't figure him out. It's like, he sees me, but he doesn't see me. He's looking for something. What is it? Really weird guy. I'm so creeped out.

11 January

Went to Phoebe Schneider's birthday party. Their apartment is so big, they had a pony ride in the playroom – with a real pony. Phoebe had a hissy fit – says she's too old for ponies and what was the party planner thinking? There was lots of cake – which the boys ate and the girls didn't – and games and really good prizes – but right in the middle of the whole thing I said 'I'm lonely'. Out loud. I didn't know I was going to say it, but I did. A couple of other girls stared at me and moved away. I don't blame them. What's wrong with me? I've known everyone at school since I was really little. And it's not like anyone picks on me. I mean, I'm not a cheerleader, and I'm not going to be class president – but I'm not the school lowlife either. I just feel so separate from everyone now – like there's a big wall between me and the rest of

them. Went home and looked in the mirror. My nose
is definitely growing. Again.

13 January

'Your eyes are like really nice when you laugh.' That's
what Jonathan Cohen said to me today. He's OK,
Jonathan Cohen, even if he is really awful at baseball –
he throws like a girl. Michael Fester ruined it by adding
'if you can see them past her big nose'. I loathe Michael
Fester, and I know he copies my algebra papers. We had
a test today, so I wrote in all the wrong answers, waited
until he'd copied them and then at the very end of the test
period, crossed them out and put in the right ones. I do
have OK eyes. I just wish there were more things that
made me laugh. I used to laugh with Mimi, but not
anymore. I kind of hate to write it, it sounds so stupid,
but I'm seeing the people again. The girl in the costume
followed me home from school today. It's not like she's
scary or anything, she looks really nice. I wish she was
my friend. She's trying to talk to me, and her words
appear, but not her voice. It's like she's following me,
but doesn't know it's me. What's with these people and
these costumes?

14 January

Mimi's worried about my weight, well, not so much my
weight, but my bones – she says my bones are so big that

they make me look heavy. She's right. Between my big
bones and my big nose I look like a horse. And not just
any horse. Those horses that pull the big carts. Mimi
thinks we should go on a diet together and jog together.
Well, she'd jog, I'd have to trot. More weird people in
weird clothes. A little boy in velvet shorts and a teenie
tiny velvet jacket. Totally dorky outfit. And long blond
curls to boot. I'd have killed Mimi if she'd dressed me like
that. He looked really angry too, and shot me such a
look. Like total hatred. It almost hurt me when he looked
at me. Right behind him was a small girl with black curls.
She was dressed in rags – but not homeless street rags.
No – she was in dress-up rags – but the dirt on her
clothes and face looked real enough. Poor thing – she was
crying. Is this all going on in my mind? Or are these real
people? I've just about had enough.

27 January

Spent the day with Dad and Tiffany and their new baby
Angel. Angel! What a name! I wouldn't ever tell Mimi,
but I like Tiffany. She's no brain box, but she's, well,
she's nice – and is nice to Dad and thinks her baby is the
greatest thing ever. Tiffany just seems to like being herself.
I'm a lot smarter than Tiff, but I would like to learn what
she knows – how to be happy being me. Is it possible?
Mimi pounced when I got home – wanting to know
everything about Dad and Tiff. She got out a calculator

to figure out how much all the baby things have cost him
– was furious that I didn't know what 'brand' the pram
was. Jesus.

Katie had to admit, aside from the people in strange clothes, it was not a riveting life but, flipping the page, she wrote in today's date.

1 February

I've really had it. Turned around today and what do I
see? A woman – dressed in old-fashioned costume –
covered in blood. Well! I am sure now that they're not
real people, that it's a mental problem. It's confirmed: I
AM GOING INSANE. I'll try to cover it up as long as
possible, live as normal a life as I can until… well, until
total dementia sets in. To make things worse, Mimi has
run off with fish-face Fishberg. I should have been
watching her more closely, looking for the signs. I've had
such a good track record lately – saved her from the
tennis instructor, yoga master, I.T. guru… it's those
damned visions I've been having. I took my eye off the
ball and now she's bolted… Everything is a mess. What
is the point of me?

Katie chewed on the end of her pen. The thought of herself as a gibbering lunatic in a straitjacket was bizarrely comforting. She wouldn't have to worry about her nose or her heavy bones, or what the other kids at school thought of her or how to guide Mimi through life with minimum catastrophe. She'd just dribble and shriek. Bliss. Stuffing her diary back in her rucksack, she took a look at the rest of the week's school reading.

She found a book with a singularly striking cover. 'Mummy, Say No!' was emblazoned over a photograph of a child taking a hypodermic needle from her drug addict mother. This story did interest Katie. She was fascinated by illness and medicine. It was one of the things she liked to read about. Her library was peppered with books on disease. Typhoid, typhus – 'not the same thing' Katie would explain to anyone who would listen – cholera, dementia, haemophilia, and consumption could be found in her stacks. Katie was not just a nerd, she was a morbid nerd. One of Mimi's boyfriends, the professor who rabbited on about parallel histories and healing and time – was it Professor Diuman? – he'd actually been interested in what Katie read, and gave her lots of books. Letters from hundreds of years ago, doctors' essays, ancient newspaper clippings – it was fun, at least for Katie, and it was an easy relationship for Mimi, as he lived at 23c. But he made Mimi yawn, and then she'd found someone new, a mountaineer. It was Katie who had to break the news to the professor: Mimi was gone, this time to Everest.

Katie pulled a book from the pile propped against the wall. It was the letters of Queen Victoria's daughters.

Wasn't there something about drug addiction in these letters? A letter to the Crown Princess of Prussia? Was it Von Bismarck? Was it morphine? Katie opened the book at random, and was immediately absorbed in a letter. It was from the Princess Alice, Queen Victoria's second daughter, to her older sister Vicky, the Princess Royal:

My dearest Vicky,

Your journey to the North sounds so interesting. How lovely for you to be able to travel with your fiancé. I know that Mama and Papa find Frederick William to be everything a future son-in-law should be. A marriage of dynasty AND love. You are so fortunate, and will make a most wonderful Empress of Prussia. But I weep at the thought that you will be leaving us for foreign lands. We are all destined for such a future, though you are the first to fly the nest.

I was alarmed by what you said of Frederick William's young nephew, Felix. It is terrible that he should develop such a high fever. I but hope that the fever will drop. Perhaps the boy should be sent back to London, though I have the highest confidence in your household's attendance upon him. What are the doctors saying?

The tours of the new mills must have been most enlightening. To learn of the actually 'doings' of our people is so important. I look forward to hearing of your trip to the coal fields.

Last night we had ever so much fun. Our only sorrow was that you were not here to join in. After supper in the nursery, we were all brought down to Mother and Father. The poet Tennyson was there and had composed rhymes with each of our names in them! It ended in disaster though, as Bertie sneaked up behind me and whispered:

'Poor dinky little Alice
Hates living in a Palace
She wants to live in a hovel
The palace fills her with malice.'

I couldn't stop giggling and was sent to my room in disgrace. Today I am confined to the nursery as punishment, with Fräulein Bauer dozing at the door as sentinel. It is raining and so stuffy and the nursery still smells of new plaster. I think I will have to slip away just to stretch my legs. No one is ever in the North corridor flanking the quadrangle at this time of the day, so I should be safe there. But if Lehzen catches me… she's already in such a temper…

It was stuffy under the bed too, and Katie became dozy as she read. Did the bit about drug addiction come before or after this letter? She had a fuzzy memory of reading it before. Poor young Felix was sent back to London, but died of scarlet fever on the way. Vicky did marry the Prussian

Crown Prince Frederick William for both love and country – but that too had a tragic ending. And Alice, what could she remember about Princess Alice? From what she wrote, she seemed like a nice girl. Katie read the letter again, and everything around her – the bed, the books, the pink shag carpet – dropped away. The letters drew her on. She could see what she was reading. There was Princess Alice: skipping back and forth in the palace corridor, pausing on tiptoe and pushing back the green satin curtains to look out of the window at the rain-sodden courtyard, where the servants were unharnessing the horses, steaming from the rain and their fast trot… Alice is bored with the rain outside, she twirls on the polished floors, navigating her way between the many small tables, large urns and potted palms; she gets down on her knees to peek under the carved legs of a sofa… Katie's eyes became heavy… she really was very sleepy… 'I could use a nap,' Katie thought and her head drooped into the book…

A ray of light from the setting sun flashed under the bed and woke Katie. 'I've got to stop disappearing into my books. I can't mess around with Princess Alice all day,' she thought, shaking her head at her childish imaginations. 'I've got tons of homework and I haven't even started.' As she turned her head, she realized the floor was cold under her cheek. And the dustballs were gone. Had Dolores actually cleaned under the bed? The television must have broken. Raising her head, she practically knocked herself unconscious on a wooden strut. The bed was high, but this was low. 'What's going on?' thought Katie. At the sound of a small cry, she turned her head to see two serious grey eyes, wide with astonishment, staring directly at her.

Chapter Two

Who Are You?

The grey eyes narrowed. 'Have you come to kill my mother?'

'Kill your mother?'

'Yes, an assassin. Are you an assassin? Why else would you be hiding under the sofa? The last one was about your age. The boy Jones. Tried and tried to get her. They had to ship him off to Australia in the end.'

Katie spoke aloud, to herself rather than the girl peering at her. She thought she knew who that girl was, and she definitely knew this was impossible. So Katie said as slowly, deliberately and loudly as she could, 'I am not loony. I am under my bed, having a dream. I've been reading too much and am under some stress. I will now wake up and go into the kitchen and have a glass of milk. I will skip my home-work and go directly to bed. No reading. Tomorrow everything will be OK.'

'Oh please do keep your voice down,' said the girl with the serious grey eyes. 'If Lehzen finds you you'll be marched off to Newgate prison in no time. And for your informa-tion, if you are an assassin, insanity is by far the best plea. It will keep you from hanging. They would probably flog you and assign you to hemp-picking, which is not too taxing, though it does make the fingers bleed.' She backed away from Katie slightly. 'Do *not* think I am trying to help you in your devilish plot. I love and revere my mother with all my heart. But I can tell by the look of you that you could never, ever have carried it out. You're not English – what a strange accent you have. Are you part of a gang? Are they holding your family hostage and forcing you to act in this dreadful manner?'

Trying to still her panic, Katie opened her mouth to protest, but a sudden noise made them both stiffen. Foot-steps were coming towards the corridor. The girl slid under the sofa next to Katie. 'Shhhhh, Lehzen,' she warned, 'and MacKenzie too. This is double trouble.'

The footsteps rang across the marble floor – a man's boots and a woman's slippers appeared inches from Katie's nose. Twisting her neck, she could see the two people, grotesquely foreshortened from her position. 'I don't think they'd look much better from any position,' Katie thought.

They were a most unattractive couple. The woman was in her sixties, but was dressed like a giddy young girl. She wore a long pink and lavender gown bunched awkwardly with ruffles and ribbons from the waist to the toes. Her dyed black hair was divided into three enormous puffs, one on the forehead and one behind each ear. Each puff was decorated with lace, bows and artificial flowers, which trembled and bobbed above her craggy features and yellowed teeth. 'Mutton dressed as lamb,' was Katie's verdict, making a mental note to talk to Mimi about dressing her age.

The man was younger, but certainly no better to look at, with small mean eyes set low in a receding hairline. What hair he had looked as if it had been sewn into his skin, high atop his head. Though smartly dressed in striped trousers and a cutaway coat, the extremely tight fit of his clothes made him a figure of fun. He was not just round, but corpulent to the point of bursting. As he turned with a strange rolling walk, Katie could see the perspiration falling from his bright red face – he looked as if he'd been boiled.

'And what is the Queen's complaint?' the man asked.

'It is not the Queen's complaint,' the woman snapped indignantly. 'That gentle and gracious person does not complain, Mr MacKenzie. It is the Prince Albert. He is the one that does complain. He says there is the noise in the corridors late at night, that the movement in the Palace does keep him from sleep.' Her English was awkward, with a deep German tinge, and she pronounced the words 'Prince Albert' with a guttural contempt.

MacKenzie rolled from one foot to the other. 'As the husband of the Queen, the Prince has every right to complain,' he replied stiffly. 'But the sounds he speaks of must be in his imagination. Or perhaps it is the plumbing... I knew no good would come of indoor plumbing. Please inform the Queen and the Prince that we will flush through the pipes.'

'Do the pipes speak?' asked the woman, 'because he is hearing the voices, and scuffling and doors that are banging.' She had been chewing something throughout the conversation, and now turned her head and spat a stream of brown liquid on to the floor. MacKenzie stepped aside in distaste.

'I assure you, Baroness Lehzen, there is no irregularity in the Palace,' he said, nodding his head emphatically. 'It is the plumbing, and that is all it is.' Baroness Lehzen shot MacKenzie a suspicious look. The man seemed more and more uncomfortable. What was afoot?

'There is, perhaps, an easy answer, yes?' she replied. 'As the Master of the Royal Household, Mr MacKenzie, all servants are to your charge. And this corridor. It is popular – yes – with the lower housemaids. They play the game of sliding on the polished floors.' She moved her tasselled slipper across the surface, detecting an imaginary scuff mark. 'I will have the furniture replaced along the corridor to discourage games, and they will gif the floor polish in the morning. For your part, Mr MacKenzie, I think you need to keep your eye sharp on your staff.'

From under the sofa, Katie saw Mr MacKenzie suddenly relax. Mopping his brow with a large handkerchief, he replied: 'Baroness Lehzen, you have got it in one... the under housemaids... acting up... absolutely correct. They shall be severely reprimanded. I cannot think how the Queen would survive without you. But then you have nurtured and protected her since she was a wee babe...'

Lehzen's suspicions grew. Compliments from Mr MacKenzie always boded ill. But her next question was silenced by the sound of horses in the courtyard. 'The Queen, we must go.'

Katie had been clutching the sofa leg so tightly, her hands had gone stiff and cold. She unhooked her fingers and let out a long breath, 'Thanks, thanks a lot.'

'I haven't done anything.'

'You didn't give me away.'

'My motives were not entirely charitable,' the girl said. 'Can you imagine the trouble I would have had with MacKenzie? And Lehzen? She might have spat her dreadful caraway seeds all over me!' The grey-eyed girl got up from under the sofa, and Katie looked her over. She had silky brown hair hanging down to her waist. Her delicate angular features and steady calm gaze gave her an extremely grave look. She was wearing a long starched skirt and high, buttoned boots – just like all the other times Katie had seen her on the streets of New York. Katie turned pale, and then flushed, but the other girl smiled and held out her hand. 'That floor cleaning will be happening soon. You'll be discovered and put on the first sloop heading for Australia. Unless you want to be seasick for the next six months, I suggest you come with me.'

As Katie crawled out from under the sofa it was the other girl's turn to flush. 'Goodness,' she cried, 'did they take your clothes away?' Coming close she took Katie's hand and whispered in her ear, 'Are you some kind of slave? I have heard a bit of this, but I don't quite understand…'

Katie was wearing her school uniform: grey pleated skirt rolled up at the waist to minimum shortness, long green knee socks, and a decidedly soiled white blouse. With her thin legs and large bony knees, it was not a good look. And compared to the layers and layers of clothing worn by the girl next to her, she did appear practically naked. 'No, no,' she reassured the girl, 'my clothes are OK. It's what we wear. It's a uniform.'

'Well, now we have twice the reason for no one to see you. You'd be arrested for exposing your limbs in public. Quick, come along.'

Leaving the splendid corridor by a side door, they entered a long low passage. Going upstairs and downstairs, turning corner after corner, and darting past a smoky room filled with soldiers, they finally arrived in a simple suite of attic rooms, prettily papered in blue and cream flowers.

'We'll be safe here,' the girl whispered. 'I've had my supper and because I'm being punished I won't be called down to the drawing room tonight. Leopold is next door, but he's bedridden, poor dear.'

Katie sat down on the edge of the bed. Dreams were usually not this long. And she couldn't remember ever being so tired. She looked at the girl with the grey eyes. 'Who are you?' she asked.

'I am the Princess Alice.' Despite her modest demeanour, the girl could not resist a toss of her head.

This information made Katie go cold. She stared hard at the girl. 'I've, like, seen you before,' she said in a low, strained voice.

'It's those engravings in the *Illustrated News*,' said Alice. 'I wish they wouldn't. Why should everyone in the land have the right to gawp at me? But Mother and Father say it is part of our national duty, to be seen by the people.'

'Your mother,' Katie added in a daze, 'is Queen Victoria. Your father is Prince Albert.'

Alice looked at her intently. 'Everyone knows that, at least everyone in England. Have you just arrived from a foreign land? Are you running a fever? You really do look queer. Perhaps you *are* a bit insane. I'd call Dr O'Reilly to look at you, but he's not to be trusted.'

Katie's heart beat quickly and she began to sway. 'You

know, I don't feel too good... I've got to lie down... to go back to sleep now.'

'I don't think it's wise to call for bedding. They'd wonder why I wanted it, and besides, it takes hours to get anything here. I'll share mine with you. I'm afraid you'll have to sleep under the bed as a precaution...' Alice took a blanket from her bed, and a fluffy toy sheep fell to the floor, uttering a plaintive 'Baa'. 'It's Woolie Baa Lamb,' the princess explained, giving the toy a quick hug. 'I know I'm too old for him, but I get so lonely. My older sister Vicky used to sleep with me, but she's been moved to another floor – promoted out of the nursery. Louise and Lenchen sleep down the hall, and Leopold is next door. I don't like sleeping alone.'

A flash of sympathy swept through Katie, as she thought of a certain doll secreted under a pillow on her own bed. 'Don't worry, I'll be OK under the bed,' she assured Alice. 'I've spent a lot of time there over the years.' She looked at Alice, busily settling blankets and pillows. 'Don't you want to know why I'm here?'

'Of course I do, but your health comes first, so explanations can wait until tomorrow. You're fatigued, and so am I. They've forgotten to send someone up to undress me again. That's a small favour.'

The bed springs squeaked as Alice climbed into the bed and Katie crawled underneath.

'Why *am* I here?' thought Katie. 'Here's the girl I've been seeing in those visions, and it turns out she's Princess

Alice, who I know from that book – the letters I was just reading. But then she's saying things and doing things that aren't in the book. So it's kind of familiar, but kind of strange too. And frightening. Really frightening.'

Katie's heart contracted as a new thought occurred to her – maybe she'd tipped over the edge, gone insane, and this wasn't a dream, but another vision – a hallucination that might never end. She lay under the bed and tried to think of practical things: the multiplication tables up to 1,000, how many subway stops to her Dad's apartment, how many calories in a cheeseburger... Eventually, though, fear gave way to exhaustion, and sleep weighed down upon her.

A terrible cry awoke Katie in the night. It ran up the scale, from moan to shriek, piercing the darkness around her. A high-pitched, thin, young cry. The cry of a child frightened and in pain. Katie started from her hiding place, but the sound of running feet held her back. Doors slammed and candles flickered quickly through the room. Alice's silky hair dangled over the side of the bed. 'It's Leopold, my brother,' she said in an agitated whisper. 'He suffers from the bleeding disease. He's had an attack. I do hope it's not a bad one. Dear Leo...'

Katie was pulled in two directions: she wanted to go to the suffering child but she also wanted to hide under her blankets and cover her ears. It was Alice who solved the dilemma. 'Stay where you are,' she ordered Katie, pushing her firmly back under the bed. 'I'd run to help myself, but they'll say I'm in the way and send me back to bed. Oh, but where is Dr O'Reilly?'

As if to answer her call, an authoritative male voice came from the next room. 'Quick, some water and ice – the bleeding is internal. We must tighten the veins.' The doctor had arrived.

'Mummy!' whimpered Prince Leopold, 'Mummy!'

'It is not necessary to wake the Queen at this point,' the doctor admonished. 'Though painful, this is a mild attack – a slight internal bleeding in the groin and upper thigh. Fill the bath with ice – the cold will contract the veins. And we'll need bandages – cambric soaked in perchloride of iron.' Raising his voice, he called to someone across the room. 'James, you will find cambric wrap in the adjoining nursery's wardrobe. Hurry!'

The door to the nursery was flung open and a boy moved softly and quickly through the room, stopping at a wardrobe just opposite Alice's bed. Katie held her breath as he opened one drawer after the other, searching for the cambric bandages. Alice turned slightly in the bed above her. 'Baaaa,' came the low growl, as Woolie Baa Lamb rolled to the floor. Katie reached out to grab the toy and ended up clutching a cold hand about the same size as her own. She froze, as did the boy, as they stared, stunned, at one another. 'Now I'm done for,' thought Katie, her heart turning over.

'James – the cambric!' the doctor called.

The boy hurriedly reached into a lower drawer and found the bandages. 'You stay there,' he hissed at Katie. 'One move against the princess and I'll shoot you myself. I have a pistol.'

Katie slid back under the bed, her nerves a-jangle. She was pretty sure he wasn't armed but one couldn't be too certain when it came to a gun.

Alice's upside-down head appeared again.

'It's Jamie O'Reilly. He's the doctor's son, and he certainly does sound angry.'

The cries in the next room changed from pain to protest as Leopold was lifted into an ice bath. 'No!' he cried repeatedly, until he couldn't speak through the chattering of his teeth.

'Do stop thrashing about,' the doctor ordered. 'You will only damage yourself further.' Leopold's complaints gradually petered out to incoherent mutterings as his lower torso and legs were wrapped in wet, foul-smelling bandages. But the worst was yet to come. 'Purge him with sulphate of magnesia,' the doctor prescribed to renewed protests, followed by gagging and vomiting. It was a lot for a small child to take; even Dr O'Reilly seemed to see that. 'A purge is never a nice thing,' he said more gently, 'but it must be done to bring out the humours. And now for a tincture of opium, three drops, every five hours.'

'Please, no,' Leopold appealed, still trying to catch his breath from the vicious purge. 'The opium makes me see things, frightening things that aren't really there. And then I sleep and sleep and feel terrible for days.' The strong dose of opium was administered nonetheless, and Leopold fell into a drugged slumber.

'Opium,' thought Katie. 'I understand that they don't know any better, but it is a kind of child abuse. The treatment might kill him before the disease does…'

She was angry at her inability to help Prince Leopold and very worried about her encounter with James O'Reilly. Gradually the rain began to soothe her and lull her into an uneasy stupor. She was finally dozing off when she found herself being pulled across the floor by one arm.

'Explain yourself,' said James O'Reilly grimly. 'And remember, I have a pistol.'

'You have no such thing,' said a surprisingly regal voice as Alice jumped out of the bed, 'and stop pulling Katie around the room by the arm. That is not a gentlemanly way to behave towards a girl.'

'Baa,' said Woolie Baa Lamb, as he rolled on to the floor again.

James looked as if he would die of embarrassment. He wasn't that comfortable with girls to start with. And now he was stuck in a room with a haughty princess in a night-dress and a half naked intruder – *both* girls. He thought about bolting, but the safety of the Royal Family came first. He bowed to Princess Alice but, still looking at Katie, repeated stubbornly, 'Explain yourself.'

Katie stood up and James looked at the floor. He could see her legs, way up past the knee. James had helped his father many a time, cleaning a patient who had died under his care. But this was worse than preparing the dead for burial. At least the dead weren't moving.

'I don't know how to explain, it's kind of hard.' Katie took a deep breath and, picking up Woolie Baa Lamb, reassured herself with a cuddle. 'If this is a dream, who knows how you'll react. If it's not a dream, I know you won't believe me. I'm not sure I believe myself. But here goes…'

There was stunned and total silence in the room, as the other two tried to absorb Katie's story. James's face was full of scepticism. Alice sat on the edge of the bed and bit the nail on her index finger, deep in thought. She shook herself as if to wake. 'Katie,' she said, 'can you think of any way to prove that your story is true? That you come from another time?'

'There is no way to prove it,' James cut across Alice. 'These are the ravings of a lunatic. I'd best call my father back, or the household guard.'

The Princess stood up. 'Funny,' Katie thought, 'how a short person can make themself look tall.'

'Jamie O'Reilly, you will not call your father,' Alice commanded, 'and you will certainly not call the household guard. This is my guest. I am a member of the Royal Family. You will obey my instructions.' She pointed to a footstool near the wardrobe. 'Now sit here, and give me time to think.' Turning to Katie, Alice gave her an encouraging smile. 'You simply must try to find a way to validate your story.'

Katie thought for a moment. Would her knowledge of the future be proof enough? She could talk to them about cars, airplanes and rocket ships – of radio, television and computers – fantastic inventions yet to come. But it could all be taken for fantasy. She had no proof. She couldn't exactly rustle up a computer out of thin air. And while computers and TV were great, some of the things in the future – well, they weren't that great. Conflict. And poverty. And pollution. Why should Katie be the person to tell them about these terrible things? She even knew bits and pieces of their own futures. Wars, looming in the decades to come, and diseases they couldn't cure, and death. Katie was discovering that it was pretty uncomfortable, knowing the future. Perhaps she should start with what she'd seen here, that night. Katie's nerdy interest in disease might just help.

'Do any of you understand what's wrong with Prince Leopold?' she asked.

'We know he has the bleeding disease, haemophilia, and that Dr O'Reilly is trying to find ways to strengthen his blood vessels.'

'It has nothing to do with his blood vessels,' Katie explained. 'It's the blood itself. It doesn't clot.' Alice looked confused, so Katie tried to explain in simpler terms. 'When you cut yourself and bleed, the blood quickly changes from liquid to solid. The platelets in your blood bunch together around the wound to form a kind of plug to stop the bleeding. Prince Leopold's blood doesn't do this. If he lived in my time, we could give him injections of the bits he needs to make clots in his blood, but I don't think you can do even the simplest blood transfusions in your time, I don't think you can…'

'Will we find the cure?' Alice asked, looking earnestly into Katie's face. 'Can we learn from you, and save him?'

Katie looked down at her green wool socks. She didn't like what she had to say.

'I don't know enough,' she replied finally. 'And you don't learn enough in time… the cure doesn't come in time…'

Alice's eyes filled with tears, but James's eyes showed only distrust and anger. 'Your diagnosis and analysis of the case are sheer foolishness,' he protested, 'made up words and total fiction. Like that book by that ridiculous woman, Mary Shelley – *Frankenstein* – it's all a lie. Dry your tears Princess Alice, it's a hoax. She is a foreigner, bent on badness. I really do insist…'

They were interrupted by a cooing cry followed by the soft slap of bare feet, as a very round-limbed toddler padded around the corner, laughing at the sight of James O'Reilly. 'Blast,' said James, 'the nursemaid must have dozed off again.'

'He obviously knows you,' said Katie, as the small child wrapped himself around James's legs.

James picked him up and hugged him tightly. 'This is my brother, Riordan O'Reilly.'

'That's a funny name,' said Katie, forgetting briefly that her own name was Berger-Jones-Burg.

'It's an Irish name,' said James. 'My mother chose it. It is a family name. Riordan Donnolly, that's her father's name. There's been a Riordan Donnolly in her family for over one hundred years. My father would have preferred a Charles or a William – something more English, less Irish – but he gave in on this.' James looked down and absently nuzzled his baby brother's curly top. 'It was the last thing he could do for my mother. She died soon after Riordan was born.'

Riordan laughed and wriggled in his brother's arms. Everyone else in the room was silent. James held his little brother tight to his chest and turned his face away from the girls. No one knew what to say. James's anger and distrust, Alice's hauteur and Katie's fear evaporated. They seemed petty and silly in the face of death. James O'Reilly might not be likeable, but Katie felt deeply sorry for this stiff, dour, motherless boy.

Alice broke the uncomfortable pause. 'First things first,' she said gently. 'Baby Riordan simply must be returned to his cot. It's very cold, and he's only wearing a nightshirt. Then Jamie, you must leave too.' She put up her hand as he tried to protest. 'We will all think more clearly in the morning. Katie and I shall meet you tomorrow. If her story is true, and I believe it to be so, then we must try to send her back to her own time as soon as possible. Your family must be frightfully worried.'

Katie thought of Mimi, drinking margaritas in her honeymoon suite in Acapulco. She didn't see the need to share this picture with the other two.

James bowed again to Princess Alice. 'I will settle Riordan, and then, should you need me, I will be in the corridor, directly outside your door. All night. One call and I will be at your side.'

Alice sighed. This wasn't how subjects behaved towards her mother. 'Fine,' she replied curtly, 'if you wish to spend the whole night in a chilly corridor that's up to you.'

Giving Katie one final, furious look, James shouldered his little brother and left the room. Alice turned to Katie. 'Now to bed,' she ordered, running her eyes over her new friend as if she were trying to remember every detail. 'And if you are a dream, as you say you might be, then let me tell you this before you disappear. This day has been the greatest adventure of my entire life.' And with that the Princess climbed into bed and fell fast asleep.

Chapter Three

Bernardo DuQuelle

Katie awoke the next morning flooded with relief. It had been a great dream, what with princesses and palaces, danger and mystery in the dead of night. But it was good to be home. Katie was no Victorian and she never would be. She wanted Diet Coke and central heating and Chinese takeaway and TV. But it had been fun to imagine. Best get it in her diary before she forgot. She looked around for her rucksack, but instead came face-to-face with Woolie Baa Lamb. Panic shot through her. It just had to be a dream.

'Good morning,' said Alice, kneeling down beside Katie, 'or should I say good afternoon. You've certainly had a long sleep. Travelling through time must be tiring. They came to dress me hours ago. I was terrified you would wake up and pop out from under the bed just as they were putting my stockings on. What a fright that would have given Fräulein Bauer.' Seeing Katie's fuzzy bewilderment, she patted her hand. 'We're both still here, so it's obviously not a dream. But don't look so worried, I promise to help you return to your family.'

Katie felt another pang at the word 'family': did Dolores even know she was gone? She probably hadn't looked up from the soaps on TV. 'Are we still under guard?' she asked.

'By Jamie O'Reilly? No, he's long gone,' Alice replied. 'His father found him slumped outside the nursery door and sent him off to treat one of the palace maid's toothaches.'

'He really doesn't believe me,' Katie said glumly. 'He thinks I'm a fraud, and a dangerous fraud at that. He might be calling the guards right now.'

'He wouldn't dare,' Alice replied. 'Jamie O'Reilly might be a grump, but he's as loyal a servant to the Crown as there is. Since his mother died, the Palace has been his only home. He's a fierce boy, but a fine one. With a bit of coaxing he'll do as I tell him. He's to meet us in the nursery after everyone's asleep to help send you back to your own time. He says there are a thousand questions you'll be able to answer if you really do come from the future. And he has some quite unique ideas about how to transport you. He's very interested in science.'

Katie was not crazy about becoming James O'Reilly's experimental guinea pig, but it was better than being marched off by the household guard.

They were interrupted by sounds in the hallway. Katie just had time to dive back under the bed when Baroness Lehzen entered, followed by a small woman in a black dress, her hair in grey braids wound around her ears like giant Danish pastries.

'Your father has come to see the Prince Leopold, and he wishes to observe the lessons you take. But are you working? No! You are playing with the toys!' A loud 'pop' reverberated through the room, as Lehzen boxed Alice's ears. 'Now go!' she ordered. 'To the schoolroom, and try to put the ideas into the little little brain you haf.' Alice ran through a door on the opposite side of the room, followed by the two ladies.

Curiosity overcame Katie's fright, and she crept back out from under the bed and to the door. Opening it, just a crack, she could see a long narrow attic room, whitewashed, with one of the walls painted black as a chalk board. The others were covered with maps, botanical drawings, dictation symbols, scripture quotes and an enormous diagram of the royal succession to the throne of England: from Ethelbert the Unready onwards. The two women were curtsying again and again to a tall man with blue eyes and silky brown hair like Alice's. This must be Alice's father, Prince Albert. Katie thought he looked silly, with his long sideburns and delicate mustachios, but she knew it was the style of the time, and that Prince Albert had been considered quite a heart-throb – at least by Queen Victoria. He turned to the table and began to leaf through some of Princess Alice's work.

'And with Vicky gone from the schoolroom, how do you get on with your studies?' he asked Alice, who was standing in front of him, trying to smooth her rumpled gown. His accent was softly German as he had come from the tiny state of Saxe-Coburg to marry Queen Victoria.

'She does poorly without the Princess Royal,' Baroness Lehzen interrupted, getting another curtsy in for good measure. 'The shining star is the Princess Royal, such a star! The liebchen Vicky. So like the dearest, sweetest mother.'

Annoyance flooded Prince Albert's face. Katie could have laughed, except that Alice looked so miserable, her grey eyes downcast. 'I try,' said Alice. 'I try to follow the classroom regime as closely as possible.'

'Ya,' interrupted Lehzen again. 'We keep to the regime. In the morning there is the study of the arithmetic, the poetry, the history and the dictation. And the afternoon does go to the geography, the scripture and the study of the royal progenitors.'

'And German,' added the small woman in the black dress. 'And the music, and the art, and the dancing…' Fräulein Bauer began to curtsy again, as did Baroness

Lehzen. Prince Albert rubbed his eyes and sighed. Katie noticed his hairline was receding and his face looked puffy and tired. Her own father often had this look, after a hard day at work, especially when Mimi was asking him for yet more money. Cutting across the two bobbing and grinning women, he turned again to Alice.

'Vicky was exceptional, and was given exceptional academic training. If you are finding the work too difficult, we can of course adjust the schedule.'

'No,' Alice answered, looking agitated. 'I must be able to do as well as Vicky. It's just…'

'She is without the application, the concentration, we cannot find it in her,' Baroness Lehzen plunged in. She lifted her hands as if to box Alice's ears again but catching sight of Prince Albert's face hid her hands behind her back and tried another curtsy.

As Albert began to speak there was a knock on the door. The Prince's Private Secretary, Bernardo DuQuelle, moved softly into the room to remind the prince of his other meetings and obligations. DuQuelle was a tall man with jet black hair and a strange pallor, as if his skin were powdered. His eyes were hooded and his nose was hooked. Despite his very English clothes, he had an air of the Orient about him. He wore a tight-fitting black frock coat and high black hat only emphasized his exoticness. Katie couldn't take her eyes off him. In the back of her mind she had known all along that he would be here. It was the tall man in the black silk top hat. The man of her visions. '**SEEK**' had swirled above his head as he had emerged from the subway in New York City. As he peered around the room, he still seemed to be seeking – lifting random papers from the schoolroom tables, and drinking in the words. She couldn't say she was delighted to see him.

Bernardo DuQuelle turned towards the Prince. He had a way of waving his elaborately engraved walking stick, and whispering in the Prince's ear. The Prince looked annoyed, and moved away from him, as if avoiding a bad smell. But there were half a dozen appointments left in the day, and Prince Albert knew DuQuelle was right. The allotted time in the nursery was over. The Prince took Alice's hand. She curtsied. Just like the others. '*Mein liebe*,' the Prince said, 'I am so busy at the moment, so occupied with my big project. We will talk soon, though, I hope.' He did not sound very hopeful.

As the two men turned to leave the room, they passed near Katie. She could just catch part of their conversation. DuQuelle spoke low, to avoid the curious ears of Lehzen.

'MacKenzie insists it is the plumbing, but the senior household steward fears a breach of security. We are getting word of a new underground movement of anarchists; coming from the Balkan States… they are, how would one say it, a particularly rabid strain of anti-monarchists and seem to be targeting the Royal Family… the children…' Albert turned to look at Alice. Katie thought he would have liked to have gone back and embraced his child. DuQuelle lifted his head and scanned the room; he almost seemed to sniff the air. Did he know of Katie as she knew of him? Shaking his head slightly, he hurried the Prince away.

As the door shut, Baroness Lehzen vented her anger, giving Alice a swift clip on the side of the face. '*Dumm-kopf!*' she spat.

'Perhaps the Princess needs help. I could stay to advise with her lessons,' Fräulein Bauer offered timidly, only to be answered with a matching box of the ears.

'You know what I have asked of you,' Baroness Lehzen snapped. 'Can none of you remember any of the things I say? Must I repeat every little word? You must follow Mr MacKenzie, watch him. We must find out what is the mischief he is doing.' The door banged shut, but the Baroness's scolding of Fräulein Bauer continued down the corridor.

Putting aside her own fears, Katie ran into the room and hugged Alice. 'How can you put up with that? Why do your parents let that horrible old hag near you?'

Alice gently shook off Katie's hug and squared her shoulders. She would not cry. 'The Baroness Lehzen was my mother's own governess when she was a girl. She fought for the Queen like a lioness for its cub, protecting her from the intrigues and power struggles of the Court. The Queen loves her like a second mother, and the Baroness's love for the Queen knows no bounds. She can't bear anything that gets between herself and the Queen, so she hates us, all the children, except my older sister Vicky. She thinks Vicky is just like the Queen. She particularly dislikes me – she says she cannot bear the turn of my countenance. And then there is my poor performance in the schoolroom…'

'I don't believe her for a minute,' Katie said, trying to cheer Alice up. 'I bet you'd be head girl at my school. No one looks as brainy as you do without some real brains behind it.'

Alice tried to smile. 'I am not unintelligent,' she admitted, 'I like my history and poetry lessons. And occasionally they let me read science. But the Baroness Lehzen has a point. I do not concentrate. I am no Vicky. I am no star.'

'But why?'

Alice thought for a moment, listening to the rain dripping from the trees outside. 'It's different for Bertie, he's to be King, but everything Vicky and I have been taught – the arithmetic, the music, the history, the languages – all of this is to prepare us for marriage. Vicky is bounding towards this goal. She is already engaged, and confident that she is making one of the greatest of matches to the highest of the European Crowns. She is sure that her marriage will be a stupendous success. Of myself I am not so certain.' She looked at her feet as if she were about to tell Katie a shameful secret. 'I don't think, well – sometimes I don't think I even *want* to get married.'

'Well, that proves you're brainy,' Katie reassured her. 'I don't want to get married either. Look at Mimi – my mother – she's been married three times and each time it's ended in disaster.'

Alice looked up, her face full of sympathy. 'But your poor mother, widowed three times! She must be prostrate with grief.'

'Oh no,' Katie said cheerfully. 'Not widowed – though she'd love that: lots of crying and in-depth touchy-feely interviews with the gossip magazines. She'd probably bring out a new single on the back of it. No, Mimi's a serial divorcer. My dad's the first one, followed by Dr Jones – plastic surgeon to the stars. She's just left Bob Burg, founder of Burg's Burgers. She's still in court about the payout, it's sure to be huge, though it's really messy, and it's just so embarrassing, because it's in the papers all the time.'

'Plastic surgeon? Burgers? Payout?'

'Sorry, Alice, forget what I just said. It's not important. And you might just make the brilliant match they expect of you.'

'I am the third child, of much less dynastic importance than Vicky and Bertie. And my looks and manners will hardly make up for this. I am too sharp-tongued, too quick-tempered, too serious. I have none of the qualities to attract a brilliant match.'

'If you could do something else, what would you choose?' Katie asked.

'There is no other choice,' Alice said with a trace of bitterness.

'But if there was?' said Katie.

Alice looked into the distance, as if she could, just faintly, see a different future. 'I'd like to learn things that I could use in the real world, the world outside the Palace. Then I could do something with a purpose – not embroider or dance or tell you who all my ancestors are: but maybe make sick people well. I'd like to know enough of medicine to be of real use. And I'd like to use this knowledge to help the lower classes, those poor souls who need the most and receive the least. But how can I be of use to them when I am trapped in the Palace?' She shot Katie a look of defiance. 'It is impossible, I know, but the profession of nursing, it calls to me. That is the choice I would make, but I can't. And sometimes it makes me angry.'

Katie had grown up with hundreds of girls. She'd sat next to them in class, gone to their birthday parties and heard their whispered whines about teachers and parents and boys. She'd liked some of them, ignored others, and disliked quite a few. But she'd never been close to any of them. The girls she knew seemed so predictable, so trite. Better adventures and more interesting conversation came from books.

Alice was still looking past her, to the life she dreamed of. Now, here was a girl, straight from a book, who interested Katie more than anyone she had ever met. Alice had everything her time could offer, but she seemed lonely, just like Katie. Unlike Katie, though, she had a goal. She didn't loll about under her bed feeling sorry for herself. Not Alice. She wanted to help other people. Katie thought with great guilt about the book in her rucksack – was it still under her bed at home? Or was it under the sofa in Buckingham Palace? Inside was that book about little Mashaka. Alice would want to read it. She would want to feed and clothe him, to find a way to get him to school.

'Poor Alice,' Katie said. 'Bertie's rhyme is right. *The palace fills you with malice.*'

Alice shot Katie a startled look. 'How did you know that?'

'Because you wrote about it in a letter to your sister, a letter I read over a hundred and fifty years later.' Katie was sorry she'd brought it up. It must be creepy for Alice, talking with someone who not only knew the details of her past, but also scraps of her future. Katie tried to remember more about the letters Alice had written to her sister. Did Alice marry? And if so, who was it? 'Perhaps,' she said carefully, 'you'll be able to do the things you want from a Palace. I think it would be easier to change the world from a position of power anyway. And face it, Alice, you're a lot better off than most girls in England at this time.'

Alice's face brightened. 'You're right, thank you, Katie.'

'Thank you for what?'

'For listening, and understanding. The only female friend

I've ever had is Vicky – and everything is so easy for her. She can't understand why it isn't for me. Follow your duty, she says, and I try. And the more she lectures, the more Lehzen scolds, the more disappointed Papa looks, the more I want to rebel. But you seem to know how hard it is for me, and for some reason that makes it easier. It has been indulgent of me to neglect my lessons, just because I can't achieve exactly what I want. And to let dear Papa down the way I have… He is perfect in every way. I must respond by trying harder and taking up every opportunity he provides for me.'

Katie hadn't formed quite the worshipful view of 'dear Papa' that Alice seemed to have, but she kept her opinions to herself. 'Alice,' she said, 'I have got to have something to eat. And then I might be able to help you with your lessons. Though don't ask me about the royal progenitors. I'd be totally lost by Ethelbert the Unready.'

Chapter Four

The Cloaked Intruders

When James O'Reilly returned that night, he was still in a sulk. To make things worse, he had Riordan in his arms.

'Why is that child never in bed?' Alice asked crisply. 'A baby needs to keep regular hours.'

'You'll have to discuss that with my father,' James said glumly. 'He's hired the damnedest – I mean the worst – nursemaid possible. She is the youngest daughter of Lord Twisted of Wastrel – she's been disappointed in love and has no dowry. She weeps and weeps, drinks like a fish, passes out and leaves Riordan to roam the Palace.'

'But why would he hire someone like that?' Katie asked. 'Your father's a doctor.' James turned a bit pink.

'She's the daughter of *Lord Twisted*. They were once a very grand family, it's an old title – even if they have fallen on hard times. My father thinks it might help him, the connection, you know, in court circles…' Seeing Alice look at him curiously, he grew even pinker.

Alice turned her attention to Riordan. 'He's half asleep now. Why don't we put him in my bed? That way we can keep an eye on him.' Taking the chubby little boy in her arms, she rocked him gently, murmuring snatches of lullabies. His round cheek drooped on to her shoulder and soon he was snoring, his baby mouth half open. Laying him gently in her bed, she wrapped him in her blankets and turned to the others. 'I believe a plan would be of great help,' she said.

'All experimentation must be with the physical object involved,' James pontificated. He was relieved that their talk had moved away from his distant, ambitious father. He wasn't comfortable with that particular topic and would rather cut off his arm than discuss his 'feelings'. He was on much firmer ground with science. That was solid. That was fact. That couldn't hurt your heart when you lay awake at night. James was still sceptical about Katie, but he couldn't close his mind completely to the idea. The innovators of his age had already wrought such wondrous things. The more he thought about time travel, the more excited he became. 'You say you found Katie under a specific sofa in a specific place? I suggest we return to the sofa and examine it minutely. If Katie is telling the truth – though I still think she is not – then the sofa will open to reveal another time and…'

'That's stupid,' Katie interrupted, 'a magic sofa is a lame idea.'

'Not as ridiculous as a time travelling girl—'

'You really can be an ass—'

Alice looked seriously nettled. 'We're not going to achieve anything by arguing. James, I have full belief in Katie's story and insist you have faith in her as well. Katie, I won't have that kind of language in the Palace. Since you don't seem to have any ideas yourself, I suggest you treat Jamie's with a bit more respect.'

Alice's sharp outburst brought the quarrel to an end. For the first time, James and Katie smiled at each other: blood would tell, and Alice was, after all, the daughter of a very grand Queen. James bowed: 'Lead on your highness.'

After tucking Riordan in more firmly, Alice led them to the schoolroom. 'We shouldn't go into the corridor,' she explained. 'There's a guard room at the end of it. And though the soldiers spend most of their time mucking about and smoking, they might just see us. All other entrances to the royal nurseries are locked. My father holds the master key.' Ducking behind a Japanese folding screen they found a battered chaise longue, a broken globe and a rocking horse missing one rocker. Hidden by the clutter was a small door. Alice produced a key and opened it.

'Courtesy of Bertie,' she said, looking guilty. 'He was locked in the schoolroom so many times, that he, well, he filched the key from father's dressing table and had a copy made. And one for me, so that I could sneak him a morsel of supper…' The three of them crawled through the small door and into a low narrow corridor, hidden between the inner and outer walls of the Palace. 'It leads to almost every room in the Palace,' Alice told them. 'The workmen used it while they were building the original structure and every-one else seems to have forgotten it. Careful, there's a deep hole coming up, and we'll have to take the ladder down a floor.' They clambered down the ladder and twisted and turned through myriad passages.

James O'Reilly was astonished and impressed. He'd always thought Princess Alice a fairly good sort of girl. Now she went further up in his estimation. 'I've lived in this Palace most of my life, and I never knew any of this existed,' he observed. 'You certainly seem to know your way around.'

'I've had lots of practice,' Alice said. 'Bertie was always in trouble. He once replaced Lehzen's caraway seeds with peppercorns. I do get lost sometimes, though. Now I think this is the door we are looking for. But do keep quiet. The under-housemaids like to meet here in the small hours.' Stooping through the door they were in the grand hallway. 'They've moved everything around on Lehzen's orders,' Alice said. 'But I think that's the sofa, and I believe it's in the same place.' It was high-backed, with straight legs and carved Chinese fretwork. It looked innocuous enough, but the three of them couldn't help approaching it on tiptoe. Suppose it was a magic sofa?

James got down on his hands and knees. 'Here goes,' he said and, closing his eyes, hurled himself underneath the sofa. Instead of being catapulted into another time, his head hit the wall with a loud thud. Katie giggled.

'Shhhh,' Alice warned, but she was smiling too.

They tapped, they prodded, they even looked under the cushions, but the sofa was revealing no secrets. James was so determined to prove his theory that Katie was afraid he might take the sofa apart, piece by piece. 'I knew this wouldn't work,' she grumbled to herself and looked out of the window down into the Palace's inner quadrangle. All was quiet, as well it should be. It was past midnight. As her eyes adjusted to the outer darkness, she noted a slight movement – there was someone or something outside in the quadrangle. Katie blinked, trying to adjust to the darkness. A gust of wind rattled the windows and the moon emerged from a bank of clouds. Yes, there it was, a cluster of figures lurking in the shadows. She could just make out their black cloaks, whipped by the wind.

With a low creak, a door in the north wing opened, and she could see the outline of a man. He stepped across the cobblestones towards the dark figures with a rolling, wheeling walk. Katie could hear nothing and see little, but from what she could see, the group in the courtyard was not getting on very well. After much shaking of heads and gesturing of hands, they seemed to reach an agreement. The man from inside the Palace took a small bulky package from his pocket and handed it to one of the hooded figures. As he hastily retreated within, Katie strained to see his face, but the moon fell back into its bed of clouds. The others melted into the inky night. 'Are the servants allowed outside at this hour?' she asked Alice. 'I just saw a bunch of people in the courtyard.'

'No,' Alice replied, 'Papa would be very angry, but *we* certainly can't report it.' They all looked out of the window, but the courtyard was now empty.

'The sofa,' James prompted, and Katie absently tapped on its wooden frame. There had been something familiar about the man who had come out of the Palace to meet the others – something about his rotund shape, his rolling walk.

'James,' Katie said, 'admit defeat. This is a very ordinary sofa.'

Alice coughed softly. 'Actually, it is a rather good chinoiserie piece. I believe it came from my uncle's pavilion in Brighton. Mama and Papa can't bear the style, but I think it's pretty.'

'You'd definitely be head girl at my school,' Katie replied, 'but whatever style it is, it's not going to get me home, unless we can physically push it into another time.'

James gave Katie a dirty look, but had to agree. 'I don't think it's the sofa on its own. It might be another object in the room – some kind of vacuum or channel – a physical manifestation that creates the time movement. We must use logic. Something will have either expelled you from your own time, or pulled you into our time. We need to know what. And we also need to know why. Is this some accidental freak of the universe – or are you here for a reason?'

'Well, you're finally talking sense,' Katie said. 'At least you believe me now. I mean, why would I fake it? What's in it for me, pretending to be a time traveller? How lame.'

James stopped in his tracks and whirled around, outsmarted by a girl, and not happy about it. 'I did not say I believe you,' he retorted. 'But I have agreed, as requested by the Princess Alice, to play along with this charade and at least try to find some reasonable answer to a frankly absurd…'

Alice interrupted before Katie could flare up. 'I do weary of this bickering. And we've been away from Riordan a very long time. I think we should return to the nursery.'

Coming through the small door back into the school-room, they could hear a noise from Alice's bedroom. Somebody was opening the door.

'It's Baroness Lehzen,' Alice whispered. 'She'll find little Riordan in my bed – and me – up, at midnight, with a boy!'

'You might miss supper for three nights,' retorted James,

'but think if I'm found with you, a Royal Princess. My father will be dismissed for this.'

'And then there's me,' Katie muttered. 'How can you explain me?'

But it wasn't Baroness Lehzen. Two hooded figures moved quickly across Alice's room, their cloaks gliding along the floor. Reaching the bed, they peered down at the indistinct body sleeping below them. 'All alone,' Katie heard one say to the other. His accent showed he was not English. Nor was he German, like so many at Court. It was a strange slippery way of speaking. 'And where are the monarchs, the ministers, the guards and the nurses?' he asked his comrade. 'All asleep in their comfortable beds. Leaving the child to us. How easy? It is a crime, yes?'

He laughed, showing fierce white teeth beneath a dark moustache, and taking the four corners of the blankets, he flipped them easily into a bundle to encase the child and heaved it over his shoulder. As the two men ran from the room, the small figure in the blankets kicked and screamed.

'What a racket for a little girl,' he hissed, 'who would think she would put up such a fight?' But it wasn't a little girl, it wasn't Alice. It was Riordan O'Reilly struggling in the blankets. A small frightened toddler, kidnapped by two unknown men.

'The guard room,' Alice cried. 'They'll catch them in the guard room,' The two men dashed through the schoolroom, in such a hurry they didn't even see the three, standing frozen behind the door. In a moment they were past the Japanese screen and through the secret passage. 'How can they know?' Alice gasped. 'And father has the other key.'

'Somebody other than Bertie must be busy making copies,' James replied. 'Don't panic, let me think, for just a minute, we must be logical,' but his voice was shaking. 'We'll alert the guards – no – that would put Riordan in even more danger – they would kill him on the spot – I must focus, plan.' He rushed up the corridor to the nursemaid's room, and returned with a large pitcher of porter, bread and cheese.

'What are you doing – are you crazy?' Katie shrieked. 'They've just made off with your brother and you're going to eat? At this time?'

'Don't be so stupid,' James snapped. 'Some people can think ahead, you know. They've got to have a coach nearby. So we'll need a horse to follow them. I'll have to placate the stable boy. Alice, we'll chance the corridors, it will be quicker. Unlock that door.' James dragged them down the corridor, past the guard room, and through the courtyard to a cluster of outbuildings. 'Wait here,' James commanded.

James ran as fast as he could into the Royal Mews, darting past the stalls where over one hundred horses were kept behind iron gates. He found the stable provided for the senior household. His father's horses would be there. As he entered the stable lad rose unsteadily. It was a cold windy night and the lad had been hoping to sleep, bedding down in the hay. But here was the doctor's son and he seemed to be in a blazing hurry. James tried to calm himself. He mustn't attract undue attention. They couldn't call the household guard. If the kidnappers knew they were being followed, they'd go into hiding immediately. They'd never be found, and neither would Riordan. The stable lad mustn't suspect anything.

'My father sends his apologies,' James said to the half-awake boy. 'He has an emergency case on the other side of London and must set off immediately. The horse needs to be saddled.'

'I am happy to be of service, Master O'Reilly,' the stable lad replied. 'I will send Gallant around in five minutes.'

'That won't be necessary,' James interjected. 'It is cold and you have settled in for the night.' He handed the stable boy the ale, bread and cheese. 'Take this, with my father's compliments.' James threw the saddle over his father's horse, and led him out of the stable. The stable lad sat back in the hay with more to eat and drink than he'd had in a fortnight put together. For once, a full stomach would not be a dream.

James swung Alice into the saddle, and practically threw Katie on behind her. Springing up himself, he kicked the horse hard.

'Can the horse carry all three of us?' Alice asked.

'We're not exactly enormous,' said James as they galloped out of the Palace gates and on to the road. In the distance they could see a lone carriage, heading through Pimlico and towards the river. 'That has to be them,' James shouted. 'The carriage will be much slower. We'll be able to catch them.'

Katie looked back, and didn't like what she saw. A second rider had galloped out of the Palace gates and was following them. 'James,' she yelled, 'we've got company. There's someone tailing us.' James gritted his teeth and spurred Gallant on. 'Friend or foe, there's nothing we can do about what's behind us – we'll have to concentrate on what's ahead. We can't let the carriage out of our sight. Once they open those blankets and find Riordan instead of the Princess Alice, they will want to dispose of him as soon as possible.'

Katie shuddered and felt sick– dispose of Riordan. 'Dispose' probably meant, well, 'kill'. Would they really kill a baby? James seemed to think so. If they were desperate enough to kidnap the young princess, they'd think nothing of stopping the life of the rosy-cheeked toddler in the bundle of blankets. Who could do a thing like that? She remembered the whispered conversation between Prince Albert and Bernardo DuQuelle, what had DuQuelle said? '…a rabid strain of anti-monarchist… targeting the Royal Family…' A new and dreadful thought occurred to Katie.

What if they 'disposed' of Riordan in the carriage? Before they could reach him? She shook her head and held on to Alice more tightly. 'Get a grip,' she told herself.

The carriage rolled rapidly on and Gallant followed apace, past a changing London. Though it was well after midnight, the grand white-columned residences of the aristocracy were only now going to bed. Through their windows Katie could see imposing footmen in satin breeches and powdered wigs, extinguishing the candles in twinkling chandeliers. The stuccoed mini palaces gave way to row upon row of newly built red-brick houses. These householders had been long in bed. They needed to be up at dawn to earn the money for houses such as these. The brick houses were in turn replaced by the squalid dwellings of factory hands and agricultural workers. Katie pulled her jumper up to cover her nose and mouth. The smell from these hovels was terrible. She could hear drunken shouts, and the occasional cry of a bawling baby soothed with snatches of lullaby by its weary mother. Passing through the market gardens that provided London with its fruit and vegetables, they finally reached the open countryside – the lone rider still behind them, the carriage still in front. At a fierce rolling river, the carriage slowed, and stopped atop a humped bridge.

'That's it,' whispered James, 'they know.' The door to the carriage opened and a man climbed out to speak to the driver. It did not look like a pleasant conversation. This was confirmed when the driver hit the cloaked man, hard, across the face. James sprang from Gallant and pulled Katie after him. 'Alice,' he ordered, 'lead the horse into that stand of trees.' Taking Katie by the hand, he ran dodging through the shadows to the foot of the bridge. Above them the carriage swayed, the horses agitated by the men's argument. The carriage door opened again, James and Katie could hear Riordan crying.

'Thank you,' Katie said to no one in particular, 'he's still alive.'

One of the men suddenly descended from the carriage with Riordan still struggling in the bundle of blankets. He leaned over the stone bridge and swinging the bundle over his head, threw it into the rushing waters below.

James shouted, and Katie found herself running, faster than she ever had before, far outpacing James, heading downstream. The bundle stayed afloat for a few moments, and then caught by an undercurrent, began to sink. Scrambling on to a rock, Katie dived into the icy water, landing within inches of Riordan. She gasped with shock at the cold, and kicking her legs hard against the current, grasped the bundle in her arms and wrenched it above her head. With a splash James was in the river too, but its torrential speed kept pushing him back to the shore.

The water was ice-cold and deep and she hadn't counted on the weight of the wet woollen blankets or the strength of the currents. She began to go under. 'It's not just you who needs to survive this,' Katie said to herself. 'Think of the little boy in your arms.' Her legs were going numb in the freezing water, but with supreme effort she fought to stay afloat.

'James!' she yelled, and with one last burst of energy she heaved the weighty bundle on to the river bank, and sank down under the rushing water, the mud and ice and swirling currents. 'This is it,' she thought, still and leaden, too exhausted to care about death.

But then through the freezing waters Katie could just make out a long dark figure swimming towards her. Katie couldn't move, but the figure flitted effortlessly forward, his hair streaming behind. She felt a sharp jerk, as he caught her under her arms. Was it James? How could he have got there with such ease? James hadn't looked that strong a swimmer. Holding her against his side, he swam strongly against the current and rolled her on to the river bank. James had arrived just in time. She was alive.

As Katie coughed and choked, muddy water came out of her nose and mouth. She sat up, and saw James, just lifting Riordan out of the sodden blankets. Riordan was not crying. This was a bad sign. James bent Riordan over his knee and slapped him on the back. Riordan gasped slightly, coughed up some water, and then lay still again. Why wasn't he breathing? He just couldn't be dead. Katie thought back to her swimming lessons – years and years of swimming lessons. Why hadn't she paid more attention during life-saving demonstrations?

'Remember, you idiot,' she said to herself, 'just get it right.' Katie crawled over to James and took Riordan in her arms. Laying him on the ground, she pinched his nose with her fingers and breathed into his mouth. 'Little lungs,' she remembered, 'little lungs need little breaths.' She counted to three and gently puffed into Riordan's mouth again. Riordan's chest rose and fell. 'One, two, three,' she counted, and breathed into his baby mouth yet again. Riordan coughed up more water, and this time his chest rose and fell on its own, followed by a very loud, very angry cry.

Alice had just struggled up the river bank.

'Thank God,' she cried, running to the wet and shivering group before her.

James turned to Katie. 'You saved his life,' he said.

'Well, you saved mine,' Katie replied.

James looked confused: 'I would have, tried to, but the current was too fast. I couldn't get to you. I was able to catch hold of Riordan, but I thought you were lost.'

Katie remembered the dark figure in the water, the effort-less swimmer with the waving hair. Someone had been there, someone had saved her, but it wasn't James O'Reilly. Whoever it was had no wish to be thanked. They had melted away into the night. Katie scanned the river. The carriage, having disposed of its unwanted cargo, had sped off. In the distance they could hear the gallop of a single horse, its hoofs sharp against the frozen roads.

'The lone rider,' Katie said. 'The one behind us. We'd forgotten.'

'We'll probably never know,' James replied, 'but at least we're still alive, all of us.' As if to underline this point, Riordan renewed his crying.

Alice looked at the three wet and shivering figures before her. 'Having saved Riordan from goodness knows what, we're about to lose him to pneumonia.' Picking Riordan up, she balanced him on her shoulder and taking Katie by the hand, marched them behind a large mulberry bush, where she began to undress quickly. 'Please get Riordan out of those freezing things,' she commanded.

'What are you doing?' Katie asked.

'Sometimes I do think you *are* slow, Katie.' Anxiety had made Alice a bit snippy. 'You are all in sopping wet clothes in the middle of the night. I am wearing dozens of warm comfortable things. Do you really think I wouldn't share at a time like this?' Katie stared at Alice as she stripped away item after item of silk, linen, merino and flannel. She couldn't believe this amount of clothing would fit on to such a small person.

'How many petticoats are you wearing?'

'Only five – the Queen does not believe young girls should follow the height of fashion. Though I love the way the new flounced skirts look – some of them have a dozen petticoats underneath. They say the fashionable women in London can barely get through doorways now, their skirts are so wide.' Alice had the comforting gift of discussing the mundane in moments of crisis.

'I'm surprised a fashionable woman can even stand up,' Katie said, as layer after layer of heavily padded petticoat came off. She thought of Mimi in her signature concert outfit: a Lycra catsuit with a cut-out in the middle to show off her pierced belly button. Alice pulled her gloves over Riordan's feet to keep them warm and her chemise was long enough on the baby to act as a robe. Katie was given an under-bodice and three petticoats.

'Do what you think best with them,' Alice said, 'only do cover up, both for the cold and for modesty's sake.' She then threw her flannel drawers and her short fur-trimmed jacket out to James. An explosion of boyish protest came from the other side of the mulberry bush. Alice wrapped Riordan in her thick cashmere shawl. 'Jamie will come round,' she said. 'It's too cold to protest for long.'

The trip back to Buckingham Palace seemed to take for ever. Katie rode astride Gallant with Riordan in her arms. James led the horse by the reins and Alice walked beside them.

'There isn't a side saddle,' she explained to Katie, 'I can't possibly get on this horse saddled as he is.'

'But you did before.' Katie noticed that both Alice and James were blushing.

'It was an emergency,' she explained, 'I hadn't time to think, but now…'

'You have so many rules that make your life more difficult,' Katie complained. 'I mean, I'm grateful for all the clothes tonight, but it must be a nightmare moving around in them every day. And this riding thing. All women in my time ride western style, like the cowboys. And not just horses. We ride bicycles. Even motorcycles.'

'What is a bicycle?' Alice asked. Katie paused. It was hard to explain something she took for granted.

'Er, it's like a metal frame with two wheels, one in the front and one in the back. There's a seat in the middle, and pedals, and chains. The cyclist balances the bike upright and pushes on the pedals to move the chains and make the wheels go.'

'We have something like that, but it has no chains. How does it work?' James asked. 'Is it similar to a pulley system?' The conversation had become mechanical, so now he was interested.

'Yeah, I think so,' Katie replied. She wasn't really sure what a pulley system was, but she wasn't about to let James know that.

'Then what is a motorcycle?' James asked. 'A bicycle with a motor? How does it move? A motor has to be attached to something that generates steam. A boiler would be far too big to be that mobile.'

Katie sighed. She just wasn't knowledgeable enough to explain the combustion engine. 'It's a different kind of motor – really small and really powerful. The motorcycle can go up to 150 miles an hour.' James had lots more questions, but Alice had grown tired of this type of talk.

'I don't even want to discuss it,' she said primly. 'I am very fond of you, Katie, but I feel this motor circle machine is inappropriate for a girl.'

'You're not alone in that,' Katie conceded. 'Mimi has a Harley Davidson, but Dad thinks it's too dangerous for me to ride.'

'Your father shows good sense. And as for riding astride a horse; it is much better that I should walk.' So Alice stumbled beside them, in her thin, strangely deflated dress, and Katie rode, shivering, her hair crisping with ice and her feet numb.

James felt like an idiot in his flounced drawers and short fluffy embroidered jacket. The relief of having Riordan safe was giving way to grumpiness – and worry. How had Katie got out of the water? Who was the dark figure she described swimming towards her? Could it be the man on horseback, the one behind them? And if so, where was he now? As they rode quietly into the slums of Pimlico, the clocks of Westminster struck four. Putting aside his many worries, James concentrated on the task at hand.

'We'd better pick up the pace. The stable hands and lower housemaids will be up soon.' But when they reached the stable yard, the stable lad was sound asleep in the hay – filled with porter and cheese – warmer and more content than he'd ever been in his ten years.

'It's a pity to wake him,' Alice whispered. 'Poor lad, he'll get a whipping for this in the morning.'

'No need,' said James. 'I'll unharness and rub down Gallant myself. If I know anything about drink, he won't even remember our coming to the stables.' He threw Alice the now empty porter pitcher. 'And speaking of drink, put these back in the Honourable Emma Twisted's room. She certainly won't have woken up, or checked on Riordan if she had.' He pulled off the little fur jacket with great contempt. 'And Katie, do get into bed, your shuddering and juddering is getting on my nerves.' Katie hated being bossed around by this boy who didn't even know what an aspirin was – but her teeth were chattering so hard she couldn't reply.

Alice slipped her through the garden door and skirting the walls of the quadrangle, gave her a leg up through the lower pantry window. 'Better to avoid the servants' hall,' she whispered. 'Mr MacKenzie will roam at night, making certain all his housemaids and scullery girls are abed.'

Katie thought back to earlier in the evening, before the kidnap, when they were fiddling about with the sofa. The dark figures in the courtyard, the creaking door, the heated whispers and exchange of an object she couldn't see. The figure who had stepped from the Palace, he'd had a bloated look, and a distinctive rolling walk. She could see him clearly in her mind's eye, rolling down the corridor in conversation with Baroness Lehzen. MacKenzie! Could it have been Mr MacKenzie?

In her jumbled brain, Katie had a thousand questions, and slowly answers were beginning to come. Could MacKenzie have opened the door and handed something to the kidnappers? Was it a key, to the secret passage? And who were the kidnappers? Were they the anarchists? The ones who wanted to kill the Royal Family? The Prince's Private Secretary Bernardo DuQuelle seemed to know all about them. What else did Bernardo DuQuelle know? She wanted to tell Alice that the danger to her was closer than she thought – was at the very heart of the Palace – but Katie was shaking so hard only a jumble of words came out of her mouth.

'Shhhh, shhhhhh, dear Katie,' Alice soothed, half carrying her friend through the secret passageways and into the nursery. 'Here, give me Riordan, you're about to drop him. Now let me take these things off you, and here's a nice fresh nightgown.' Alice placed Katie into her own bed and pattered down the hall to tuck the sleeping Riordan into his cot and replace the empty tankard.

It was all so confusing for Katie. The images flashed before her eyes – the lone rider and the dark man in the river, the kidnap, the key, and the insider from the Palace with the rolling walk. Was he the one putting them all in danger…? 'Mr MacKenzie!' Katie tried to cry out, but her voice had deserted her, and she sank down.

Chapter Five

Prince Albert

Katie kicked off the blankets and tugged at her night-gown. 'I'm burning up,' she thought, 'why is it so hot?' The heat moved through her, settling in her head. She felt as if there were flames behind her eyes. Through a white haze Katie could see a small figure, coming closer and closer. It was the pretty little urchin girl, the one she'd seen in her own time, in her dreams. Katie needed to feel her cool little hand against her forehead. She knew this would make her better. 'Help me,' Katie mouthed, 'help me.' The little girl nodded timidly.

'I will help you,' the little girl said in a soft French accent. 'There is much bad around us, as I have seen, many times over. But for all that, I believe in the good. I can lead you to what is best in yourself, what is fine…' She bent towards Katie, extending her tiny, sweet little hand.

'Ha!' said a voice behind the girl, and her little hand was swatted away before she could touch Katie. In her place was the smug boy in the velvet suit. He leaned his unpleasant face close to Katie and laughed in a loud flat voice, a laugh with no humour. He locked Katie in a triumphant stare and began to talk in a high nasal pitch. She couldn't understand a word he said. What language was this?

'Doesn't matter,' she thought wearily, 'just from the sound of it I know it's bad. What an awful little boy.' A light shone from his blond curls. It made him look as if his hair was on fire. Katie's eyes felt like they were melting, her head as if it was bound. She tried to turn away but she couldn't move, her body seemed riveted to the bedsprings.

And then she was shivering and shuddering, her teeth clacking together with such violence she was afraid they might fly out of her mouth. She was back in the river, it was so cold… Riordan… the baby… she had to save the baby. And then through the murk of the icy water she was face to face with a man. He was pale in the extreme, with heavily lidded black eyes and a large arched nose. His black hair streamed behind him in the water as he reached out for Katie. Was he going to lift her to safety? Or pull her under? Katie thrashed about, trying to reach the river bank, but found she was in bed, tangled in her blankets. A great heaviness seemed to weigh upon her and then she was too tired to care. 'Whatever,' she mumbled, and fell into a coma-like sleep.

Someone was shaking her by the shoulder, but the light hurt her eyes and she didn't want to open them.

'Katie,' Alice called softly. 'Katie, you need to wake up, you must have something to drink.' Katie rolled over and tried to ignore the voice. But Alice, though gentle, was persistent. 'You've been sleeping for well over two days. Hallucinating too – thrashing about and yelling. We had to move you behind the Japanese screen in the school room, and I bound your head in a muslin cloth to muffle the noise. Even then it was touch and go, whether we'd be discovered. But the fever has passed now, thank goodness. James says in order to make you better, you need to have some fluids. I'll just prop you up on these pillows and we'll have some nice beef broth, it's very strengthening.'

Though the fever was gone, Katie was so weak she could hardly sit up. Alice had to spoon the broth into her mouth.

'Thank, you Alice,' Katie said faintly. 'You'd make a good doctor.'

'You must still be delirious,' Alice replied. 'Girls cannot become doctors, or nurses, though I can still dream. And it's Jamie O'Reilly you have to thank for this broth. He said you must drink something to bring the fever down. He smuggled the broth out of the kitchens himself.' Alice placed a cold compress on Katie's forehead and took her pulse. 'Much more steady,' she commented. 'It was racing away through the night.'

'How long did you say it's been?' Katie asked.

'Two days and two nights,' Alice responded. Katie thought about Mimi. Did time work the same between the two centuries? If it did, they must know she was missing by now. Dolores would be furious. And Mimi? Who knew how Mimi would react? Katie's forehead wrinkled at the thought of Mimi, and Alice reached down to smooth it. 'There's nothing to worry about, dear Katie, though we have been frightfully afraid. You're on the mend now. I'll leave you to rest, and later in the day, if you can stand up, I'll move you behind the screen in the schoolroom. You'll be much more comfortable on the chaise longue, and I can keep a watch on you during my lessons.'

Katie sighed and lay back down, drowsy again. 'Dehydrated... need fluids... beef broth... I guess James O'Reilly does know something about medicine after all... and Alice, you watched over me... all through the night...' Katie, as an only child, had spent most of her childhood alone. This must be what it is like to have a sister, she thought, someone who is close to you, that's what the word *related* must mean... and scrappy and difficult as James was, he had risked much trouble to get her the broth. Maybe that's what a brother was like. Funny, but the wall that separated her from the rest of the world wasn't there with Alice and James.

Time seemed suspended as Katie lay on the chaise longue. The sun moved across the ceiling of the schoolroom, Fräulein Bauer droned through German lessons and chalk squeaked on the blackboard. Alice came and went behind the screen with cordials, gruels and broths. Katie rejected the more modern medicines offered by James. 'Laudanum, barley water, tinctures of alcohol – they're either opiates or palliatives,' she tried to explain to James.

'You know best,' James replied curtly, 'I suppose you have all kinds of really effective treatments – medicines you think we're too stupid to discover.'

'It's not that,' Katie protested, 'yes, we have antibiotics and chemotherapy, and we can give people a mechanical heart and a liver from a pig. But everything we know is based on the discoveries your time has made. Come on, James, you live in a time that believes in progress. We've just progressed, from you.'

James struggled between hurt pride and burning curiosity. 'Can you really make a mechanical heart?' he finally asked. 'How do you do it?'

'I haven't the slightest idea.'

'And a pig's liver? I'm not very religious, but that seems... well... ungodly.'

'Really, James, I'm not a moral judge of these things. I don't do the transplants myself, I mean...' They argued back and forth until Katie's temperature shot up again and Alice had to intervene.

'Katie needs her sleep,' she remonstrated. 'And when she's rested I believe there's something a bit more urgent than a pig's liver that we need to discuss.'

In Katie's waking moments, they went over and over the kidnap attempt. It was obviously directed at Princess Alice. Whoever was behind it knew the layout of the Palace, had access to the most private quarters, and had not been detected by the numerous guards stationed throughout the building. More worrying still, they knew about the secret passage.

'It's got to be an inside job,' Katie said. 'How else could they come and go undetected? I'm almost certain MacKenzie is involved, and he has access to everything.'

Alice looked more grave than usual. 'Though they've failed once, they are certain to try again. We will have to act immediately,' she decided. 'The seriousness of the situation is beyond us. We'll need to involve the adults. I will have to tell my father.' Katie thought about Prince Albert, the stooped and tired man in the nursery. He wouldn't have been her first choice of confidante, but then she'd never really had a father around.

James looked sceptical too. 'Are you certain, Princess Alice, that it is wise to involve your father, even if he is the illustrious…'

Katie cut across him. 'Illustrious or not, he's still a grown-up, and from my experience they always make everything worse.'

Alice went to her writing desk and dipped her pen in ink. 'I thank you for your concerns about my judgement, but I am comfortable with my decision. I will send a note, explaining briefly and ask Papa to come to me. If the foot-man delivers it this afternoon, he will be with me by tea time. He will know what to do. Now Katie, back to sleep for you – you're still too weak for such sustained effort.'

Leaving Alice to her writing, Katie lay back down – she was tired, and the worry made it more acute. Her anxiety was greater than Alice or James knew. On top of every-thing else, there were those strange visions. Katie decided to keep them to herself for the moment. It was all so confusing, too exhausting.

The noise that roused Katie was a most annoying guttural screech. It was the Baroness Lehzen, and she was hissing with anger.

'So I find the footman with the note. And what do I find in the note? A silly, silly story from the Princess Alice – hooded intruders! This is what one does get when the silly child does get the newsprint sheets from the footmen. So – you think your father would want ever to hear a silly tale that you might write? No, you are to be cured of the lies. We will change your lessons. There will be no more of the poetry, the science and the history – they are for the clever *Kinder*. You will learn only the needlework and the scripture. And there will be no outings, no treats. Only the needlework, the darning, the prayer book.'

Katie peeked over the screen. Baroness Lehzen was strid-ing back and forth, waving her arms in jerky fury. Clenched in her fist was an unfolded piece of paper – the letter to Prince Albert. Princess Alice stood very straight in front of Lehzen, looking at the floor, but at Lehzen's ban on her few favourite studies, her lips trembled and she reached involuntarily for Woolie Baa Lamb. In a rage, Lehzen grabbed the toy from her, pulling so hard one of its ears tore off, and it bounced across the floor.

Just then, the door to the corridor opened. Prince Albert and half a dozen members of the Royal Household ap-peared. Woolie Baa Lamb hit him in the foot. 'He's got to have heard at least some of this,' Katie thought, 'Lehzen has a voice that could wake the dead.' The Baroness curt-sied deeply, stuffing Alice's letter into the pocket of her skirt. The Prince, barely acknowledging her, picked up the soft toy.

'Ah, a game of catch with the toy between your studies,' he said, handing it to Alice, 'a good idea, yes, to clear the brain.' Taking Alice's hand he turned to the Baroness Lehzen. 'I have been thinking about the Princess Alice's academic progress. She has lost her schooling companions as the Princess Royal and the Prince of Wales prepare for the wider world. The Queen and I feel strongly that she must be allowed to study what she likes, at least for a few months, to adjust to this change.' He fixed the Baroness

Lehzen in his gaze. 'We particularly wish her to concentrate on history and science. And of course poetry – so nourishing for a young person's imagination, don't you agree?'

Baroness Lehzen curtsied her assent, but Katie could see a muscle in her cheek twitching angrily.

Princess Alice kissed his hand, her eyes glowing. He was her dear Papa, her guide in everything. 'It is bold to ask for more,' she said, 'but I have one more favour. I would so love to study medicine – well, nursing at least. Would that be possible?'

Dr O'Reilly was standing behind the Prince. 'The study of medicine is not to be attempted by the female, even from the highest pinnacle of society,' he interrupted, smoothing his glossy side whiskers. 'Nursing would not be appropriate for a Princess of the royal blood. Princess Alice will be busy enough soon, as a leading ornament of our society, and perhaps the blushing bride of some fine foreign Prince – though I don't believe there's a man in the world fine enough to wed any of the English princesses.' He bowed to Prince Albert and the assembled courtiers, very pleased with his speech.

Prince Albert sighed. The Queen liked Dr O'Reilly with his good looks, flourishes and flattery. For himself, he would have preferred a doctor in the Royal Household who was more interested in medicine and less interested in society. His reply to the doctor was stiff and cold.

'Everyone is in agreement that women cannot and should not be doctors,' he replied. 'But nursing, if privately undertaken, is a fine accomplishment – of far greater value than glittering in society. What more could a woman want than to tenderly care for the health and well-being of her family? It is what God has made them for. Perhaps Dr O'Reilly will not find it beneath himself to teach the simpler elements of his trade to a princess?'

Dr O'Reilly bristled at the word 'trade' but bowed grudgingly to Prince Albert. This was not the outcome he had anticipated from his grand speech.

Alice was overjoyed, but at this moment there was something far more crucial she had to discuss with her father. She had to get her father alone, to tell him about the intruders and the kidnap attempt. 'Father,' she blurted out, 'I cannot thank you enough for all you have given me today, but there is one more thing of great importance – if we could talk in private for but one moment.'

Bernardo DuQuelle was once again at the Prince's elbow, a paper in his hands. Katie noticed, again, how DuQuelle seemed to drink in the words. 'I do apologize for interrupting,' he murmured. 'But I have had a report from the O'Reilly nursemaid, the Honourable Emma Twisted…' DuQuelle's lip curled slightly as he pronounced her name. A twitter was heard amongst the courtiers. Dr O'Reilly turned bright red.

'Does it need to be discussed now?' Prince Albert

enquired. He didn't think much of Emma Twisted, but he particularly disliked the cattiness of the courtiers.

'I am afraid so. She has reported a break-in. Someone has entered the O'Reilly baby's room by night and they have, well, drunk all her porter and eaten her supper.' DuQuelle held a handkerchief to his mouth, stifling a laugh. The courtiers sniggered and giggled.

Prince Albert wheeled around. 'Silence,' he admonished. Even the gentlest of princes could be galled. 'DuQuelle, I suggest we discuss this another time.'

DuQuelle, following him from the room had the grace to look apologetic. 'Sir, on face value I know it looks like a trifle,' he whispered to Prince Albert. 'But with the threat of the anarchists all Palace security must be rigorously reviewed. If the Black Tide...'

'Father,' Alice interrupted. 'Please, one more thing.'

Prince Albert had had enough. The courtiers, the governesses, and the ever-present irritant of Bernardo DuQuelle; even his young daughter could not stop pressing him for more.

'My dear Alice, will there always be "one more thing"? To importune like this is not an attractive trait.' Stopping at the door, he had one more decree. 'Baroness Lehzen, please do mend the Princess Alice's little toy. I know the lamb is a favourite of hers, and the ears seem to have fallen off.'

Katie had been utterly absorbed by the scene before her. But she was still very weak, and standing on tiptoe behind the screen had made her dizzy. 'I don't know what to make of him,' Katie thought, staggering back to the chaise longue. 'How can Prince Albert say women can't be doctors – but then agree that Alice can study medicine? And he is maddened by the flattery and falseness of the courtiers, but he doesn't do anything about it. Why? And one minute he's a really good and loving father, and the next he snaps, cold and withdrawn, like he barely knows her. But one thing's clear, Alice thinks the sun shines out of his moustache – so I'd better keep my thoughts to myself… and he did really stick it to the Baroness. She must be totally hacked off…' Katie smiled and sighed. But she was still far from well. Alice was right, she needed sleep.

It was hunger that finally awoke Katie – the kind of hunger that yells inside of you 'hamburgers, doughnuts, cookies!'

'Fat chance,' Katie told her churning insides. Not a lot of eating goes on here, at least not in the nursery. We'll be lucky to get a cucumber sandwich. She could hear the rain beating against the schoolroom windows. Peeking over the screen, she was surprised to see Alice asleep at her desk, one cheek resting on a map of India. The room was cold and dark, the fire was out and Alice was in her rumpled day-dress. Katie padded across the room and gently shook her shoulder.

'Wha? Oh dear. What time is it?' Alice asked, rubbing her eyes and shivering.

'I'm having enough trouble with the century, so don't ask me about the hours,' Katie replied. 'What are you doing here? Why aren't you in bed?'

'Punishment, Baroness Lehzen. She intercepted my note to Papa and then…'

'I know, I saw the whole thing this afternoon. How can she punish you after your father's visit, though? He won the day, hands down.'

Alice smiled. Her father, he had been wonderful. But then he'd left. And the moment he was gone, Baroness Lehzen was back in charge. 'She returned, and quite rightfully found fault with my needlework. So now I'm being punished – I fear with doubled harshness due to the incidents of this afternoon. No food or water and no fire in the hearth until I have correctly filled in all the territorial lines of the sub-continent.'

Katie looked at the map, strewn with rulers, slides and compasses. 'Double yuk. I'd starve or freeze before I could do that, but then we're doing both already. Alice – can we get to the kitchens without anyone seeing us? I've just got to eat – real food – not gruel food.'

Alice looked at the tiny watch hanging from her waist. 'We can certainly get to the kitchens without being detected. Bertie scavenged ninety per cent of his meals that way. I'll just let Jamie O'Reilly know you're awake and hungry – a definite sign of returning health.' She shot Katie a sly look. 'He has been terribly worried about your illness.'

As Alice stepped towards the door, Leopold called out from the next room. He was still in bed – cross, bored and hungry too.

'Alice, what are you doing up?' he asked fretfully, 'and who were you talking to? I know you're being punished, I heard it all.'

Alice went to her brother's bedside and stroked his hot forehead. 'Don't worry yourself, dear, I'm just talking to my dolls to keep myself company. Poor Leo – you haven't done anything wrong, yet it's as if you are being punished too. Are you in pain?'

'Mostly just hungry, and so tired of lying here alone, thinking and thinking of what I don't want to think about. The Reverend Duckworth is here all day, but I can't bear his put-on cheer. He's a dreadful tutor, paid to be nice to me, all servants are. Father's been to visit me every day since my bleeding attack, and Mama came once too. But they both looked so grave that I became even more frightened. Alice, am I going to die?'

Alice ruffled his dark hair and managed a bright false smile. 'Now that is nonsense. Dr O'Reilly has everything under control. I'll tell you what, suppose I sneak down to the kitchen and get us both a bun and some fruit?'

Leopold smiled back, but then looked anxious. 'I am absolutely famished, but O'Reilly says too much food will thicken my blood and bring on the bleeding. He says only strong tea and beef broth for five days.'

'Maybe just a bit of fruit then,' Alice reassured him. 'And some wine. That will thin your blood down and give your stomach something to hold on to.'

'Alice, you will come back soon?'

'Quick as a flash. And then why don't we read some stories together – yes?'

'Yes,' Leopold answered, tossing his head on his pillow. 'But don't let them catch you. All the shouting when you get into trouble hurts my head. And don't read anything too frightening or adventurous to me – that will certainly quicken the blood and you know how bad that is for my recovery. And you shouldn't be talking to your dolls – you're too old for that, and besides you're being punished, and…'

Alice sighed and, plumping Leopold's pillow, crept out of the room. Katie turned to her in exasperation. 'A lowering diet? Wine? And do you really think Dr O'Reilly has everything under control?'

Alice had tears in her eyes. 'I can only follow Dr O'Reilly's instructions. If you really understand this disease, Katie, then tell me what to do, and I'll do it.'

'I'm not a doctor,' Katie replied. 'I've barely started studying biology, much less medicine. But I do know what *not* to do. *Don't* bring him any wine, and *do* give him something solid to eat. It won't hurt him, I promise.'

They both jumped when the door opened, but it was only James. 'I came to see how Katie was getting on. I can see she's back to her old self: not only up, but already arguing.'

'Alice and I were not arguing.'

'Of course not – Princess Alice is far too well mannered to argue, even with a know-it-all like you. Now that you're on your feet we can try and send you back to your own time, *if* you really do come from…'

'That's enough,' Alice ordered. 'Katie, you've been so ill you could barely speak for several days. Jamie, you've been worried beyond all recognition, popping in every hour or so with a possible new cure. But the moment you two are together it's bicker, bicker, bicker. I'm too hungry for all this. I'm going to find something to eat – if you wish to join me, fine.'

With muttered apologies, the two followed Alice behind the screen and into the secret passage between the Palace walls.

Chapter Six

MacKenzie's Cupboard

They twisted and turned, went down stairs and up ladders. 'I don't remember the kitchens being such a long way from the nursery,' Katie thought.

'I sense that we've walked in a circle,' James ventured after quite some time.

Finally Alice had to admit: 'I'm so dreadfully sorry, but I'm afraid we're slightly lost.'

'There's a door,' said James, 'just opposite that niche in the wall. We can nip out for a moment to see what room it leads to and catch our bearings.'

Opening the low door, they ducked into a large room, which would have been comfortable if it hadn't been so crammed full of things. In the centre of the room, two large mahogany desks were placed flank to flank, each piled with red leather boxes. They were surrounded by a battalion of upholstered chairs and sofas – all tasselled, braided and fringed. Little tables scattered about held an endless number of objects: miniature bronze statues, porcelain vases, dried flowers, framed photographs, carved ivory. Katie picked up a curious item and immediately put it down. It seemed to be some kind of animal's hoof.

'We're in Papa's private study,' Alice explained. 'He and the Queen sit side by side at those desks – often late into the night – there's so much work to be done. And he keeps the books and reference materials he most needs in here.' One wall was crammed with books – floor to ceiling – with a little brass rail halfway up, supporting a ladder on wheels. Katie could just imagine clambering up the ladder to find the book she wanted. With a pang she remembered her own library, but it was under the bed, in New York City, trapped in another century. They really must be looking for her by now.

The other walls were covered with paintings: men in Roman tunics, women in Grecian draperies, children, dogs, the odd cow, landscapes, seascapes, Highland idylls, still lifes of fruit, fish and artfully broken crockery. Hanging behind a plump sofa was a large pastel of the baby Alice, dimpling and dancing in a Spanish shawl. Above the fire-place, in a place of honour, was a vivid oil painting of a much younger Prince Albert – his close-fitting hunting jacket and tight leggings leaving little to the imagination. He looked dreamily into the middle distance, one suede booted foot resting on an enormous dead stag.

'The last of Bambi,' Katie thought, 'of all the stupid paintings...' But then she remembered the one in her mother's bedroom: Mimi, stark naked, except for some flowers in the wrong places. Maybe it was just parents... Her attention was diverted by something that looked like a large doll's house. On closer inspection, she could see it was an architect's model. The child-sized building wasn't stone, or brick or wood, but was made up, almost entirely, of iron arches filled with glass. Each storey was shorter and narrower than the one below, so that the building resembled nothing more than a greenhouse in the shape of a gigantic wedding cake. It was very pretty.

'This is Papa's grand project,' Alice told her. 'It's the model for a great exhibition hall that is being built in Hyde Park. It will show everyone the outstanding design and quality of our manufactured goods – all under one roof. It will celebrate our country's achievements in modern times. Father has worked so hard, putting all his time and effort into this wonderful plan to better the nation. But the newspapers have, well, they've been more than cruel, calling the project a "white elephant", an albatross, and begrudging Papa the funds for this building, even the land it is being built upon.'

James looked at Katie. 'You say you know the future. So

what is the outcome? Will the exhibition be the failure they're all predicting?'

But of course – Katie recognized the building now. She'd seen pictures of it in history books – so it must be a big deal – though the pictures somehow looked different from this model. For once her knowledge of the future brought good news. 'The Prince's project, it's still called the Great Exhibition – and there have been like zillions of exhibitions since then. Everyone, all over the country, and from other countries too, will rush to see just what Britain can do. It's a really big deal – it changes the way the world sees you. It kind of makes you into a super power.'

'And Father?' Alice asked. 'Does it finally make the country value Father?' Katie looked at the portrait of the man standing on the dead stag.

'Yes, it helps people to understand that he is much more than Mr Queen.'

'And the press will admit that they've been wrong about him?' Alice asked.

James laughed. 'I don't need Katie to tell you *that* future. The newspapers will pretend they always knew the exhibition was a brilliant idea and probably suggest that they thought it up in the first place. Then they will find some other grievance against the Prince. Don't look so shocked, Alice. Do you think the press actually wants to tell the truth?'

Katie had to agree. 'Look at Mimi,' she explained. 'She

has a personal stylist, a PR agent and a media manager, but ninety per cent of what they write about poor old Mimi is total rubbish. Just made-up stuff.'

Alice looked so downcast by this worldly wisdom that Katie decided to change the subject. 'Can we get back to looking for the kitchens? I'm sick with hunger.'

'You think more about your stomach than anyone I've ever met,' James retorted. 'And girls aren't supposed to talk about their appetites. It's unseemly.'

'So you starve girls then, do you? Is that how you keep them in their place?'

Even Princess Alice had to laugh. They re-entered the secret passageway, giggling and scuffling, when a sound at the far end of the low dark corridor froze them in their tracks.

'Shhhh,' said Alice, 'someone else is in this passage.'

James blew out their candle. 'It must be the kidnappers. We knew they had access. How else did they get to Alice's room the other night?' The sound of footsteps was coming closer, and they could see a faint light appearing some distance behind them. 'Quick,' he hissed, 'a door, any door.'

'But some of them lead into bedrooms or servants' quarters,' Alice cautioned, 'we might be caught.'

'Well, we're going to get caught here, and by someone we know to be brutal. Now hurry! Go!' The sounds were coming closer.

Katie spied a particularly squat wooden door, different

from the others. 'This might be a storage cupboard.'

'You're probably tumbling us down a coal shoot,' James grumbled. But crouching down, he pushed Katie and Alice through the low door, shutting it firmly behind him. Within minutes they could hear the footsteps in the secret corridor passing by. Everything around them was dark and there was no sound of human life. 'Now, where are we?' James asked, relighting their candle.

The room was surprisingly large, and filled from bottom to top with boxes, crates and baskets. Katie opened one after the other – there were jams, smoked meats, cordials, wines, pickled vegetables and rounds of cheese in their waxy rinds. On other shelves she found candles, boot polish, beeswax, string, pillows, linens and cutlery. 'Is this some kind of housekeeping station?' she asked. 'Like in a hotel?'

Alice looked puzzled. 'I don't believe it is. Just look around you. It's a terrible mess. And most of the things have been ever so slightly used. The candles lit and quickly extinguished, a single spoonful taken from a jar of jam.' Her eyes widened. 'It looks as if someone has been taking these things from the Palace and hiding them here. But why?'

'I think someone is hording all this stuff, then moving it out of the Palace and selling it on,' James said. 'This is someone's private little kingdom, and it's earning them a pretty penny.'

Alice looked appalled. 'I remember now. There's a household rule that the Queen must be served with new things at all times. If a candle is lit once, it is inadmissible to light it again. No wonder we never have enough supplies in the storerooms and pantries. Father is always complaining to Baroness Lehzen and Mr MacKenzie. He's written many a memorandum on the subject. They're always saying they will look into it thoroughly, but…'

Voices from the next room stopped her mid-sentence. James blew out the candle again and the three moved cautiously through the clutter towards the sounds. There were several voices, but one of them made Katie clutch Alice's arm in horror. She could distinguish a voice they all knew well – the Scottish burr of Mr MacKenzie.

'How many trips will it take?' he was asking. 'We'll need to clear out the perishables tonight. The meats will spoil and then they'll be of no worth to us.'

'We'll try to take the meats and cheeses, but it's too dangerous to go back and forth all through the night. There's too much of a chance that someone will see us. We need more frequent access to the Palace and we need to come and go as we please.' Alice let out a gasp. James put a finger to his lips but he too was unnerved. It had been startling enough, hearing MacKenzie blatantly swindle the Royal Family – but the other voice held even more terror. All three recognized its sliding cadences; they'd heard it before, at the foot of Alice's bed, on the night of the kidnap. 'Our leader is unhappy with the progress we are making.'

MacKenzie gestured impatiently. 'Tell that overseer of yours that he can save his breath to cool his porridge. He's a slippery character enough. I can see your point, though,' he conceded. 'It would be easier for me if you could let yourself in. It's a risk to meet you each time with the key. Plus I have my own duties to attend to, and these sleepless nights are affecting me badly... and then there is that other matter... I will look into obtaining a separate key for you.'

'That is a wise idea, Mr MacKenzie,' the foreigner replied. 'It's our job to make the things as easy as can be for you, right, comrades? But a word of advice, sir: our leader is no matter for the jokes. He has powers and connections of which you know naught. We take our profit from him, but keep the respectful distance. I suggest you do the same. Now we must work. Morning is almost upon us, and I believe you will need to preside over breakfast in the servants' hall.'

'The upper servants' hall,' Mr MacKenzie corrected him. 'I'll help you shift some of this stuff, for which I will want payment, in advance. I have some debts of honour to settle.' The door to the storage room began to swing open. James grabbed some things from the nearest shelf and shoved Alice and Katie back through the low door, into the not-so-secret passageway.

'Honour,' gasped Alice. 'How can he speak of honour?'

'Come on. Let's go,' James tugged at her arm.

Alice seemed both hurt and angry. 'Mr MacKenzie? How could he? Really! Oh, that puffed-up, red-faced, stealing – he's as bloated and rotten on the inside as he is on the outside. I've half a mind to confront him this very moment.'

James pushed her down the passage and kept pushing her until she was up the ladder and into the relative safety of the nursery. 'That's right; you go on back there and have your say. I'm sure the nice gentlemen with him will welcome such a visitor with great gallantry.'

When Alice flared up, it was a sight worth seeing. She turned on James, cheeks flushed, eyes emitting sparks. 'You have pushed and shoved me through doors, up ladders and down corridors all night, Jamie O'Reilly. I am tired of the pushing and shoving – but I am even more tired of your sarcasm. You really do seem to have forgotten to whom you are speaking. I suggest you—'

Katie cut across her friend, for once she would have to be the peace-maker. 'Come on, guys. Even I know this isn't the time or place for a scene. James, it's not like you to be sarky with Alice, this MacKenzie stuff has been a shock to her system. And Alice – isn't Leopold waiting for you?'

At the sound of her brother's name, all of Alice's anger was replaced by remorse. 'Oh, poor Leo – he's probably building up to a tantrum waiting for me. Did we get any of the food in that storeroom? And I need to find some nice, calming book.'

James handed her a jar of jam and she ran through the door into Leopold's sickroom.

Katie had been famished – but sitting behind the screen in the schoolroom, sharing a strange meal of cheese and candied ginger with James, she didn't have quite the appetite.

'I know it's a strange combination,' said James, 'but I had to grab what was at hand.'

'It's not that,' Katie replied, 'it's MacKenzie. Is he up to what I think he is?'

'Isn't it obvious? He's skimming the Palace provisions and passing them on to a middle man.'

'I know he's doing that,' said Katie. 'But is he also involved in the kidnap attempt on Princess Alice? I'm really sure that I saw him in the courtyard the night of the kidnap, handing over the keys to the Palace. The two men with him – they had to be the kidnappers. I recognized their voices. And then, tonight, MacKenzie made that strange comment: *and there is that other thing* – what other thing? Is he trying to harm, even kill the Royal Family? And what about Baroness Lehzen? Is she involved? She loves the Queen, but her hatred of Prince Albert, and the children…'

Katie pushed the cheese away and walked over to the

window. She could see the faint glow of dawn, struggling through another rain-soaked sky. So much evil seemed so close. 'It's kind of frightening,' she admitted. 'I'm here in the wrong time and I don't know how to get out. I know what the future should be, but things don't seem to happen the way I think they will. And James, I've been having these visions. I began seeing them in my own time, in New York City. It's like, I'm not just travelling through time. There's something stranger going on.'

James snorted. 'Even stranger?'

'Yeah, I know. It sounds stupid. But there's something else underneath it all. Something even weirder. I've seen Alice and DuQuelle and these two children in my own time – and now I'm seeing them here. I don't know if they're the good guys or the bad guys, except, that is, for you and Alice. It's like there's you, me and Alice on one side, and the rest of the world on the other.' She stared out of the window for a long time. 'But at least it's the three of us now,' she added. 'I used to feel like it was just me – that everyone else was living this fun happy life, and I was all alone, like in a bubble, just watching. Then Alice came along, and it's like she popped the bubble. I think that's how you're supposed to feel about a sister, or brother – that they're on your side, always.'

Families and relationships. James hated this kind of talk. He carefully moved the conversation back to his comfort zone – science. 'That's an interesting point about the visions,' he observed. 'So you were seeing the visions in your own time, New York, did you say? And now you are seeing the very same visions in a different time dimension, 1851 to be exact. Perhaps they are the channel, the road back – you might need to confront each of the visions, as in a quest or a medieval trial.'

Katie was tired. Too much excitement had exhausted her. 'Oh, James,' she practically wailed, 'I couldn't confront Alice, she's the best thing that ever happened to me. I feel…'

James O'Reilly was growing desperately uncomfortable. Katie was talking about her feelings. Luckily it was her feelings for Princess Alice, but any moment it might be her feelings for *him*. At the thought of this terrible possibility, he began to sweat profusely. 'It must be morning,' he mumbled in a panic, 'I have to go…' and then an answering bustle from the corridor saved him.

'Another day begins,' James said, weak with relief. 'I wonder if the Princess got back to her desk in time.' Peeking over the screen they saw Alice bolt back into her seat, pulling the map and compass towards her. At the same time, the Baroness Lehzen finally managed to get the door open. With a bang she entered the room, trailed by Fräulein Bauer.

'Look at you,' said the Baroness, cracking a caraway seed between her teeth, 'a disgrace to the blessed Queen. She was a tidy und obedient child, *das Lammfromm.*' She turned to Fräulein Bauer. 'Well, don't just stand there, brush her hair and get the Princess into the clothing that does suit for the occasion.'

Seeing the questioning look on Alice's face, she took the ruler from the desk and rapped her knuckles. 'You never will understand. The Prince Albert has recommended you to come to the presentation of the exhibition building that is being made for the Queen, the courtiers and the government. Why they would want you, I do not know, but what the Prince does request we must bow to.'

Fräulein Bauer had been giving the Baroness quick, timid glances. She finally rallied the nerve to speak. 'Forgive me, Baroness, but the Princess has had no breakfast, and no supper the night before. Perhaps now, shall I…' Baroness Lehzen whipped around, the lace of her sleeve striking Fräulein Bauer in the face. For a moment Katie thought she would knock the other woman down.

'This girl does not deserve the breakfast. She tells the falsehood, and the needlework, it is slattern. Now, brush the hair, harder! I will return for her in the ten minutes to come.' Baroness Lehzen leaned towards Fräulein Bauer, and practically spat in her ear. 'Fräulein you know your duty. When you are done here you must watch Mr MacKenzie.'

The door slammed shut. 'That woman really knows how to make an entrance and an exit,' Katie thought. 'Mimi could learn some stage presence from her.' Forgetting her exhaustion, she turned to James and caught his hand. 'This is going to be so cool. We'll get to see the beginnings of the Great Exhibition first-hand. Let's go.'

'Oh yes,' James replied, shaking her off, 'absolutely. We'll march down the hall together; all the guards at the end of the corridor will look the other way. The Queen herself will be fascinated to learn about your experiences with time travel – and you are certain to enjoy the rest of your life in a lunatic asylum.'

Katie gave him a sharp shove. 'We're going to have to hide me,' she said. 'Come on, James, you're supposed to be the brainy one – so find a way.'

Chapter Seven

The Crystal Palace

Ten minutes later, Katie was in the Throne Room, crouching in a large lacquered Chinese chest along with the wood for the marble and gilt fireplace. 'Let's just hope some footman doesn't decide to throw another log on to the fire,' she whispered to James who was standing stiffly beside the chest.

'Needs must,' muttered James, 'but they won't put more wood on the fire. The Queen believes that cold is good for the health, and all the chimneys in Buckingham Palace smoke horribly, so they always keep the fires banked down. That's why everyone shivers all the time.'

Katie lifted the lid and had a peek around. The room was more than sixty feet long. The walls were hung in striped crimson satin with a white marble frieze running across the top. The ceiling was gilded with arms and armaments. At the far end of the room was an oversized arch, supported by two winged figures bearing garlands. Beneath it stood the thrones of the Queen and Prince Albert. 'So homey and cosy,' Katie remarked, 'perfect for a family get-together.'

'Oh, do pipe down,' James snapped, 'and get back in that box. You can see through the holes in the side. Shhhhhh, they're coming.'

The enormous double doors to the room opened and in walked the Queen, followed by Prince Albert and a mass of people. 'Why, she's pretty,' thought Katie. 'She isn't the fat old black bombast of a Queen Victoria we see in old photographs – but young and pretty.' Not that Mimi would have rated her. The Queen was very tiny and plump, with a round body, round arms and a round face. But her blue eyes were truly lovely, if slightly protruding. Her hair was soft and bright. 'What makes her attractive… it must be that she's so happy,' Katie decided, watching the Queen take her husband's arm and look up into his face. She wished she could get a better view of the Queen. Katie had a feeling she'd seen her before. Was she part of her visions too? Everything was so jumbled together, between the past and present. Katie couldn't quite figure it out.

Though the holes in the side of the Chinese chest were quite large, it still wasn't a very good vantage point.

People's legs kept blocking her view. Finally she saw Alice coming through the doors, Baroness Lehzen holding her firmly by the elbow. Lehzen's frown turned to smiles as she bobbed the ridiculous cap atop her high hairdo at the Queen. MacKenzie was there too, looking more like an overripe plum than ever. Katie noticed Fräulein Bauer close by MacKenzie, acting as Lehzen's spy. Then Leopold was wheeled in, his chair pushed by his tutor, the Reverend Robinson Duckworth. Dr O'Reilly entered with other senior members of the household to stand at the back. Bernardo DuQuelle darted and wove his way through the crowd until he was standing close to Prince Albert. As the Queen and Prince Albert took their places on their thrones, a cluster of dark-coated men came into the room – 'the representatives of the Royal Commission for the Exhibition of Manufacturing, Art, Design and Commerce…' the announcement boomed through the room. 'Lord John Russell… The Duke of Buccleuch… William Cubitt Esquire… The Rt Honourable Richard Cobden… The Rt Honourable Benjamin Disraeli…'

Katie could do nothing but crouch in her hiding place. Each man came forward and bowed: deeply to the Queen, with a less rigorous bend to Prince Albert. Between the courtiers, the Royal Household and the Royal Commission the room became crowded. The doors opened again, and four footmen in powdered wigs and silk stockings entered, carrying the model of the exhibition hall. They were followed by a mild-featured man in a plain broadcloth frock coat; a sheaf of papers tucked under one arm. With his long stride and weatherbeaten face, he looked more like a farmer than an aristocrat. Some of the courtiers twittered at his abrupt bow. 'Joseph Paxton Esq.' rang out as he walked towards the royal couple. Prince Albert sprang forward and clasped his hand.

'Ah Paxton, the man of the hour,' he exclaimed, presenting him to the Queen. 'This, my dear, is the man I told you about, the architect of this extraordinary building. Over two hundred drawings were submitted for the exhibition hall, none of which served the purpose. Until Paxton arrived with a doodle on a bit of blotting paper, and there it was, the perfect building to house our Great Exhibition.'

'You have broken ground on the project, I believe.' The Queen looked kindly at Paxton. If Albert admired this man, so would she. 'And do you really think the project will be ready by May?' She had a lovely voice.

'More than ready Ma'am,' Paxton replied. 'We've completed many of the building parts away from the exhibition site, and now they're ready to be erected in Hyde Park. When the exhibition is over, the building can be taken down with the same ease.'

'It is the most cunning plan,' Prince Albert added, 'it is – how do you say – pre-fabricated – of very little expense and so easy to put up and take down.'

'We have 2,000 men and 100 horses working on the

project Ma'am,' Paxton continued. 'It will be done within these four months.'

The Queen stood up and reached out her hand to Albert. Together they circled the model of the building. Katie couldn't quite hear what they were saying, and couldn't see much through the gaps in legs and frockcoats – but she did hear Paxton – his voice was decidedly rougher and louder – answering question after question from the Queen. 'I estimate we will use almost 300,000 panes of glass in the end,' he was saying, 'reinforced by 4,500 tons of cast iron.'

'It will collapse in the first windstorm of the season,' Katie heard one courtier mutter to another. 'It will end in catastrophe.'

The Prime Minister moved forward and bowed to the Queen. Katie almost laughed aloud. Lord John Russell had to be the smallest grown man she had ever seen. He looked more like a doll than a prime minister, but this was countered by his great self-importance.

'Ahem, please excuse my intrusion on this otherwise jubilant occasion, but there is one problem I wish to present to the Commission today, before the building may proceed. In Parliament there is great consternation about the elm trees.'

'Elm trees?'

'Yes, elm trees. Three of them. It seems that the site chosen for the exhibition hall in Hyde Park is also home to some of the most ancient and magnificent elm trees in the British Isles. They are the works of God, created over hundreds of years. To destroy them for the sake of a warehouse that will be taken down again within the year…'

'It is not a warehouse,' Paxton interrupted. Prime Minister or no Prime Minister, his beautiful glass building was not a warehouse.

Prince Albert looked perplexed, but then his brow cleared and he nodded vigorously. 'We will simply have to build around the elm trees,' he decided. 'If Mr Paxton can come up with his grand design in hours, he can most certainly redesign in minutes.' Joseph Paxton caught the Prince's enthusiasm. Taking the papers from under his arm, he smoothed them out on the table beside the model. Scanning them briefly, he too had a plan.

'Yes, I know the trees, very large, three of them, but aligned quite tidily. If we move the axis of the building by 30 degrees and create a vaulted glass ceiling through the central transept, the building will encase the trees…'

'There, Prime Minister, your problem is solved.' Prince Albert and the Queen beamed with delight.

Alice had managed to get away from Baroness Lehzen and was standing near James O'Reilly. Prince Albert turned in her direction. 'And what does our baby think of this miracle building?' Alice blushed, knowing that the entire court – and Jamie and Katie – had just heard her called 'baby', but she curtsied to her father and answered respectfully. 'I think it looks like a palace out of a fairy tale – a glittering palace of crystal.'

A murmur of approval ran through the room. The Prince clapped his hands. Even the Queen turned her gaze from Albert to smile fondly at her daughter.

'You have caught it exactly, *liebchen*,' he responded. 'We will call it the Crystal Palace – as christened by the Princess Alice.'

Looking around the room, Katie saw rows of smiling faces, with a few exceptions. Lehzen was decidedly nettled at the *Dummkopf* Alice's cleverness. And Dr O'Reilly in the back of the room was less than pleased to see his son – supposedly hard at his lessons – standing coolly next to the Princess Alice. But the figure who most fascinated Katie was Bernardo DuQuelle. The red damask of the room turned his skin to ivory and his inky black hair fell in artful disarray. He was obviously not spellbound by the building of glass. Throwing his head back, he peered around the room and repeated his irritating gesture of sniffing the air. For a brief moment his gaze landed on Katie's lacquered chest, but then he turned back towards Paxton. There was something about the way he stood, the hook of his nose in profile. Katie wondered. He was in her visions, and in the Palace, but also somewhere else. Suddenly she could see him swimming towards her, the dark figure in the river. She felt sure that it was Bernardo DuQuelle who had been her saviour the night of the kidnap.

'James!' Katie hissed, 'Jamie!' James was trying to listen to Paxton's description of how a building of glass could be totally supported by slender iron arches. It was amazing. But Katie, as usual, had to interrupt. He could hear her clearly from inside the Chinese chest. If she didn't stop, someone else might hear her too. 'Jamie, I need to speak to Bernardo DuQuelle, he's standing by the painting of the fat red guy,' she said.

'Don't call me Jamie. And the fat red guy is George IV. Now be quiet.'

'Whatever, Jamie, I mean James, this is important. I really have to talk to Bernardo DuQuelle.'

James bent down, and taking up a pair of tongs, prodded the fire, while muttering to Katie through the hole in the Chinese chest. He prayed no one would look at him. 'The last person you should be talking to is Bernardo DuQuelle. He's one of the great survivors at court. No one remembers a time when he didn't have an eminent position. He's the Prince's Private Secretary, the Keeper of the Royal Archives, and the Curator of the Queen's Collections. But he's also a gossip, a meddler and a man who would do anything to stay on top. You'd be out of the Palace and into a straitjacket before he could finish kissing your hand.'

'James, I think he's key in all of this,' Katie said. 'Not only is he in your time, and in my visions, but also – James – he's the guy who saved me, in the river, when you blew it.'

'I didn't blow it, as you so charmingly say,' James grumbled. 'I tried to get to you. Maybe DuQuelle is key, but this isn't the time. You'll have lots of opportunities. It's not as if he's going anywhere. DuQuelle just loves being at court.'

Joseph Paxton had finished answering questions and was bowing to the Queen and Prince Albert. 'We are ready to show the Prince the building site at his convenience.' Turning, he bowed to the tiny Prime Minister, 'And we extend the invitation to our Members of Parliament who have shown such interest and generosity towards this project, the newly named – what was it – the Crystal Palace?'

Katie poked James through a hole in the lacquer box. 'We need to go too. I've got to see the Crystal Palace – and maybe DuQuelle will be there.'

Why would she need to go to the Crystal Palace? James had no idea, but several courtiers had turned to stare at him as he talked to the Chinese chest. Best to placate her until everyone else had left. With a final 'be quiet, Katie!' he stepped forward and muttered something into the back of Princess Alice's neck. Alice neither looked at him, nor seemed to hear him. She didn't move a muscle. 'She could be the Queen herself,' thought Katie, catching Alice's still face in profile, 'such cool.' At that moment, Alice moved forward and curtsied to her father. 'Please forgive the forwardness of my request. But I would like ever so much to see the construction of the building too. May I go on the excursion?'

The Queen gave Alice a stern look. For such a young girl to speak out like this in public – it was not acceptable. She turned to Albert to see his response – and as Albert began to smile, she smiled too. She would always trust dear Albert on the children, as on everything. Prince Albert pinched Alice's cheek. 'As you have just named the Crystal Palace, you must definitely see it. You may go, and Prince Leopold too, if he is well enough. Baroness Lehzen will attend you and the Reverend Robinson Duckworth and Dr O'Reilly will travel with us for Leopold's health.'

The Prince, seeing James O'Reilly standing behind Alice, added, 'So the young master O'Reilly has an interest in Crystal Palaces too. He shall come as well. We will pack a hamper full of goodies and make it a day of instruction and play for the children.'

The Prince was not by nature a spontaneous man, but the Crystal Palace had fired his imagination. 'In fact, we will go tomorrow,' he suddenly announced. 'We shall meet Mr Paxton along with the Royal Commission and the parliamentary delegates at Hyde Park. I suggest three o'clock tomorrow afternoon to be an excellent time.'

The Queen now beamed from ear to ear. 'My husband is right,' she said, 'a bit of learning and a bit of fun for the children. I wish I could go myself, but the red boxes of state are filled with government decisions I need to make. They will keep me at my desk when I would rather be in the open air, enjoying the success of my husband's great project.'

The royal couple glowed with satisfaction, but Katie noted the rest of the room looked fairly glum. Paxton, though a supremely confident man, was worried. A royal visit, at this short notice – they'd want to see something fairly spectacular, an arch going up or a roof being raised. Plus, he needed to redesign the central transept. The site itself was a sea of mud – totally unsuitable for a party containing the Royal Family. He and the builders would be up all night preparing. The Members of Parliament were vexed. A government Bill was going through the House of Commons tomorrow, and now they would have to spend another day kowtowing to this foreign prince and a parcel of children. All this for a project that was sure to be a costly failure. The Reverend Robinson Duckworth was worried that Leopold was still in his wheelchair and not well enough so soon after a bleeding attack, and Dr O'Reilly wondered what the devil his son James was doing, putting himself forward like that. Social climbing was well and good, but one mustn't try to aim too high. Baroness Lehzen simply hated the idea of the children having any type of treat.

Only Bernardo DuQuelle seemed truly happy. Katie had seen him looking keenly at Alice throughout her conversation with Prince Albert. DuQuelle now stepped forward and doubled into a theatrical bow. 'On behalf of the Royal Household, may I say we are delighted that such a large number of the Royal Family will be in attendance.' Bowing again, he added, 'And so many of the Royal Family's friends as well.' Katie could have sworn that DuQuelle's second bow was aimed directly at her Chinese lacquered box.

Later that evening, Alice sat in a muslin nightdress and flannel wrapper – far from the silks and bows of a royal presentation – sharing her nursery supper with Katie. James ambled into the room, looked flustered, and began to back out. 'What,' said Katie, 'what now? Oh yes,' she added clicking at the sight of Alice hastily throwing another shawl around her shoulders, 'I can't believe you two. Alice is wearing more clothes than an Eskimo in a blizzard. And I'm drowning in this cloak of hers. Get over it.'

'Grumpy,' said James as Alice wrapped the shawl more tightly around herself and passed Katie another spoonful of shepherd's pie. 'Why is Katie always so grumpy? Doesn't she like our century?'

'I'm making the best of your century that I can,' Katie said. 'And since I'm here, I'd like to see one of the great wonders of your time – the Crystal Palace. Now you two get to go and I have to stay cooped up behind a screen in the schoolroom or shoved under Alice's bed. Bernardo DuQuelle will be there. I just know he has the answers we're looking for. It's the perfect opportunity to question him.'

'You're not just grumpy, you're rather stupid,' said James. 'Can't you even see that the Princess has worked things out perfectly; isn't that right, Alice?'

'I just thought if I could get there myself, I could get you there too,' Alice replied. 'James didn't give me a lot of time, hissing into my neck, and I'm not that quick on my feet, or that clever.'

James grinned. 'But you thought of the picnic hampers?'

Alice laughed. 'I hadn't, but of course, you are right. Dear Katie, we will pack you with the game pies and fruit-cakes – or bundle you in with the picnic blankets. They'll travel in a carriage with the junior household staff. The servants will be too busy enjoying a day out to notice much.'

'I'm awfully heavy,' Katie commented, thinking about her big bones. 'Won't they notice such a heavy hamper?'

'You've obviously never had a palace fruitcake,' James said. 'They weigh a ton.'

The idea of the day out and the great building excited them all. Katie felt her anxiety lessen. 'Baskets, boxes and chests,' she joked, 'I'm beginning to think I live in a basket – a regular basket case.'

Chapter Eight

Amongst the Girders

The next afternoon Katie was rolled in several blankets and lashed to the back end of a carriage. The wooden wheels hardly guaranteed a smooth ride, particularly when pitted against cobblestones. Lying on her back, almost crushed by the heavy wrappings, Katie was being shaken about like one of Mimi's favourite martinis. As she jolted along half suffocated by the blanket and choking on the dust raised by galloping horses, Katie thought she'd like to be back home, in New York, hailing a taxi and sitting comfortably in the back seat. This was so bad, she'd even have settled for the subway.

They'd spent most of the morning finding something for Katie to wear on her first public outing. Nothing Alice had would fit, so in the end Alice sent James to filch some things from the Honourable Emma Twisted's wardrobe. 'I know they are too grown up for a girl your age, but they are your size, Katie.'

'Yes,' said Katie, 'I'm definitely built on a more robust twenty-first century model. Oh, Jamie,' she added, just to be mean, 'don't forget to bring me a complete set of girl's underwear.'

So there she was, dressed appropriately for a governess in serviceable dove-grey cashmere with a touch of good lace at the neck and wrists. She even had a little mesh reticule with a few sovereign coins inside. Her waist had been cinched in so that she could hardly breathe. 'Otherwise,' Alice explained, 'there won't be a dress in the Palace you will fit into.' She'd been lucky to get away with four petticoats.

'All this effort to look like "a lady" and it's being rumpled beyond saving by heavy wool blankets,' she grumbled to herself. 'I'm sweating like a pig. And Alice pulled the stays so tight, I can barely breathe. How do women eat in these corset things? One slice of pizza and I'd burst all the lacings.'

Hyde Park was only a ten-minute walk from Buckingham Palace, but based on the supplies and carriages provided for the excursion, it might have been a trip to the North Pole. Prince Albert and Bernardo DuQuelle shivered in an open landau. The Prince would have preferred a closed carriage, but the Queen was fanatical about fresh air, and tenderly entreated he get as much as possible. Alice and Baroness Lehzen travelled in the next. Prince Leopold followed in a third closed carriage with the Reverend Duckworth, Dr O'Reilly and James. Behind the carriages were five additional brake carts carrying hampers, blankets, chairs, tables, awnings, wind breaks, plates, cutlery, linen napkins and two complete tea sets. At least a dozen servants bounced along on the wooden benches or clung to the running boards. Someone had to serve the picnic.

As the entourage turned into Hyde Park, Katie's blankets lurched and swayed. Was she lashed on tightly enough? Trying to readjust her weight, she wiggled her head free of the blanket folds. A burst of sharp air hit her and she looked up to see a cold, bright sky, big billowing clouds chasing across it. She could hear the building site before she could see it: a clamorous din of both man and machine. The royal carriages drove through the hoardings and directly into the centre of the construction itself. Katie just had time to burrow back into her blankets before two footmen picked her up and dumped her unceremoniously behind a pile of timber. Scrambling out of her wrappings she navigated the mud and, balancing on a joist, took in the scene before her. She'd never seen anything like this before, and neither had anyone else from her own time. They could not have imagined this epic Victorian building site.

The columns and girders of the construction interwove

a hundred feet above her like a huge iron web. Hundreds of workmen clambered up ladders and hung from high beams, like so many tiny spiders spinning away. On the ground, even more men worked in groups, their foremen shouting orders through speaking trumpets. They rolled huge timber planks on wheels along the ground and hammered columns into iron pipes dug deep into the mud. A scalding white vapour poured from the steam engines used to power drills and saws, and the enormous boilers that generated steam for the engines were red-hot. Interspersed between the wood and iron, glass and machines were the elm trees the Prime Minister had intervened to save. They looked out of place in the midst of this modern industry, but would probably outlive the whole project by hundreds of years.

Amongst the grime-streaked workers were pedestrians – ordinary Londoners who had come to see the building of glass. As Katie watched, a well-dressed man in black frock coat and top hat leaned forward to observe the work of a mechanical saw. It bit into a piece of iron, covering the man in thick metallic dust. A boiler then doused him in hot steam. 'This is a health and safety nightmare,' Katie thought, 'I've never seen a lawsuit more ready to happen.' But the man just wiped his face with a handkerchief and walked away through the mud. 'I'm safer here than any time since I arrived at Buckingham Palace,' Katie thought, strolling about to have a good look. 'With all these people and all this activity, no one will notice me.'

As Prince Albert descended from his carriage, Joseph Paxton came forward, motioning to his supervisors. The foremen barked through their speaking trumpets and a silence fell, as tremendous as the noise had been a moment before. Only the horses continued to whinny and snort. Prince Albert turned and turned again, then bent backwards to the sky. His shoulders squared, his stoop was gone and his tired eyes were wide awake. 'He's never even seen a skyscraper,' Katie realized. 'This must be even more awesome for him than it is for me.'

Albert bowed his head and clasped Paxton's shoulder. 'This is an accomplishment that will reverberate throughout the world. I am proud to know a man who can create such a thing.'

Paxton bowed in return. He'd have to write to the wife about this. Paxton was a man of simple origins. His father was a farmer and he himself had been an ordinary gardener's boy. 'What a time we live in,' he thought, 'when a man like me has the opportunity to create such a building, and is honoured by a Prince.' He cleared his throat and pointed to the far end of the construction. 'We are raising the trusses, the ribs of the central roof,' he said. 'The workmen have waited until you arrived. Does your Royal Highness have time to watch?'

'I wouldn't miss it for the world,' Albert replied. He clapped his hands together. 'Children, come – you must see this.'

The workmen laid down planks for Leopold's wheelchair to roll along. Prince Albert watched with Leopold on one side and Alice on the other as a team of six horses was harnessed to a series of pulleys and ropes. These in turn were fed across a high mast and attached in three places to a long iron truss. The foreman gave the order, and the workman urged the horses forward – straining and pawing the ground under the great weight. Slowly the huge iron truss rose, swaying back and forth. Then one of the horses bucked and the onlookers held their breath as the truss tilted dangerously. 'Steady now,' Paxton muttered as the horse was brought back into line. Up, up, up went the truss, until it was almost parallel with the top of the mast. The workmen clinging to the side columns quickly hoisted it into position. A cheer went up from the ground.

'We have two teams of horses working from either end of the building,' Paxton commented. 'I estimate we'll be able to get eight roof trusses up per day. This most difficult part of the project will be accomplished in a week.'

'It is a miracle of modern construction,' Prince Albert reflected.

To Katie's eyes, it was the most curious mixture of ancient and modern. The workmen in smocks with their harnessed horses could have been building a medieval cathedral. Yet the steam-powered machines were just one step from those used by workmen in her own time. Alice, standing next to her father, was stiff with excitement.

Prince Leopold's mouth was slightly open as he stared and stared. 'To them it's like the first rocket launch,' Katie thought. 'And I have to agree, it is amazing.'

For James O'Reilly it was a life-changing experience. Now he knew; this was how knowledge should be used. For him the Crystal Palace wasn't just a sea of mud with shouting men and horses and pulleys and planks. It wasn't even a great building of inspirational design made with new materials. This was science, technology and industry: all working together. This was the vision of modern man. This was the future.

A temporary platform had been built and curtained off, and the royal party now ascended to take tea. The servants bustled about, laying cloths and plates and emptying hampers of their delicious cargo. They had even packed Indian carpets to cover the wooden flooring. Katie couldn't help noticing what a hindrance this was to the construction going on around them, but Paxton now seemed delighted with the visit, and the workmen were excited to get a peek at royalty.

As Katie wasn't officially a member of the royal party she had to stand back and watch as Alice and James sat down to a large selection of sandwiches, pies, scones and cakes. As usual, she was hungry. And as usual, she wasn't going to get fed. Alice caught her eye, and tried to signal some kind of plan, but Leopold was demanding her attention. His blankets were askew and he wanted a toasted crumpet instead of the carefully measured glass of port Dr O'Reilly was trying to give him – for medicinal purposes, of course. James was being treated to a mini-sermon from the Reverend Duckworth on 'how the might of God could be seen in the works of man'. While James shifted from foot to foot, impatient to see more of the building site, the Reverend ate and talked and waved his hands, using the Crystal Palace as his example, and scattering fruitcake all over James. It did look heavy.

The sight of all that steaming tea and lovely food was too much for Katie. She had turned away to examine some of the machinery when she spotted Bernardo DuQuelle. He looked unreal, even sepulchral in the bright cold sunlight. While he had seemed theatrical at Buckingham Palace, his artifice was both menacing and absurd on a construction site. Walking casually over to the royal carriages, he looked around to see if anyone was watching. The servants left to oversee the various boxes and baskets had abandoned their posts, too. They too wanted to take in the wonders before them. DuQuelle had the field to himself. He began to open hampers, unroll blankets and peek into ice chests. His hooked nose was everywhere, and it was sniffing. 'He's up to something,' Katie thought, 'but is it good or bad? He's obviously looking for something. What could it be?' She remembered the river, the arms reaching out to save her, and realized with dread – he was looking for her. She screwed up her courage to approach him.

Two footmen, seeing this distinguished member of the household amongst the litter of the picnic, dashed back to their duties. 'May we help with anything Monsieur DuQuelle? A cup of tea? Or perhaps something stronger?'

DuQuelle smiled very slightly and continued to look around him, as if for a lost object. 'I thank you kindly, but no, I am nourished by this bright winter day and the astounding project before me.' He wandered away, leaving the footmen to roll their eyes at his eccentric behaviour.

'He really would be ridiculous,' thought Katie, 'if he wasn't so frightening.'

James had finally escaped the Reverend Duckworth. He was looking for Katie – he had a buttered scone for her and a clutch of questions on modern construction techniques. But as he approached, James was waylaid by Bernardo DuQuelle. Katie could hear everything as she crouched behind one of the newly rescued elm trees.

'It is young Master O'Reilly, I believe,' DuQuelle began, trying to look friendly. 'Your father takes supremely good care of the Prince Leopold. It is, how would one say, a tragedy for the Royal Family, do you not think? A terrible illness, and so strange that the taint would appear – out of the blue – in the royal blood. But then the dear Prince Leopold is not the heir to the throne, thank heavens, and he's been placed in such competent hands.'

James bowed slightly; he had no intention of gossiping about the Royal Family or betraying any kind of medical confidence, particularly to one as powerful and puzzling as Bernardo DuQuelle.

DuQuelle continued. 'You are, I believe, a great help to your father in his duties at the Palace. And of course you are invaluable in looking after that little brother of yours – is it Riordan? He does have a tendency to take the odd midnight stroll, not really suitable to one of his age. Ah, the escapades of childhood – they can lead to danger, you know. What a pity your father hasn't found a better protector for that little chap. The Honourable Emma Twisted, really…but then, for some, breeding is all.' James tried not to scowl, tried to be polite to this important man, to cover the revulsion he felt for DuQuelle. 'And your sister?' DuQuelle asked, 'is she not also a favourite in the Palace?'

'My older sister Grace is away at school, sir,' James replied.

'I meant your younger sister.'

'I have no younger sister. My brother Jack is at the military academy. My older sister has not lived with us for several years. She was sent abroad to relations after my mother died. Her health has been poor this winter, and she is convalescing in Florence. There is only myself, my father and Riordan within the Palace.'

DuQuelle lifted his walking stick, and knocked a block of wood off a pile nearby. He seemed hugely amused. 'How curious. I am certain I have seen you with a young girl – and at strange hours too. The relationship must be familiar – a cousin perhaps?'

James became taller and stiffer, but he answered evenly. 'Sir, I am privileged to live in the Palace and respectful of my position in relation to the Royal Family. I will endeavour to control the movements of my little brother. He is but a baby, and needs the mother he does not have. As to a little sister or cousin – there is none. There is only my older sister and, as I said, she is convalescing abroad – in Florence to be exact. You have perhaps mistaken my identity with that of another.'

The more uncomfortable James looked, the more relaxed DuQuelle became. 'Ah, but I have angered you. Forgive my words, yes? Sometimes I do not find quite the right ones,' DuQuelle said cheerfully. 'It must all be a mistake.' Doffing his top hat DuQuelle bowed slightly and moved away.

Katie was not taken in by DuQuelle's buffoonery. His sudden and unexplained appearance in the river, the way he'd looked at the Chinese chest where she'd hidden in the Throne Room, and now the conversation with James today. 'It's obvious, he knows,' Katie concluded. 'DuQuelle knows I am here. But he doesn't know everything – otherwise he wouldn't be questioning James like that. But does he know who I am, and more importantly, how I can get home?'

Bernardo DuQuelle passed the raised platform where the Royal Family was still absorbed in their tea. Alice had managed to filch a toasted crumpet for Leopold, which he ate eagerly. Prince Albert, cheeks flushed, was talking non-stop to Joseph Paxton, pausing only to point out a particular arch or angle in the project. 'We can reuse the wooden hoarding to make the floorboards of the edifice,' the Prince was heard to say. Nothing escaped his detailed brain. Paxton nodded repeatedly, all the while taking notes in a little book. The workmen continued raising columns, and were adding girders to support the roof. Katie watched the workers sway industriously above her. It was dangerous work, as they had no real support above nor a net below.

With a flourish of his walking stick and an exaggerated bow, DuQuelle directed an elegant little speech towards Prince Albert. 'We see before us the elements that are still but wood, steel and mortar, but the magic of our time will create an enchanted pile...' Both Alice and Leopold looked as if they wanted to laugh. Prince Albert sighed, and rolled his eyes upwards, where a single workman now swung along the roof girders. DuQuelle continued. 'This castle of industry, built through the sagacious taste and prescient philanthropy of an accomplished and enlightened prince will be raised for the glory of the world...' The children began to giggle. Dr O'Reilly looked annoyed, after all, he was the one with the flowery speeches. Only the Reverend Duckworth seemed to take DuQuelle seriously.

'Hear! Hear!' Duckworth cried. Prince Albert glared at him. Katie noticed the lone workman swinging from girder to girder, ever closer to the platform where the Royal

Family sat. He was lugging a large vat of something with him. It must have been even more difficult and dangerous to move about with such a burden.

'This Palace of Crystal,' DuQuelle droned on, 'will be the envy of the continents…' He broke off suddenly, his attention also caught by the workman above, now pouring something from the vat he carried. DuQuelle sprinted forward. With one leap he was on the platform, pushing Alice to one side and hurling Prince Leopold from his bath chair.

'Good God, man,' Dr O'Reilly roared. 'Are you insane? Don't you know his condition? You could kill the boy with that kind of rough treatment!'

'Move aside!' DuQuelle bellowed back, 'for your own safety, move aside!' With a long and menacing hiss, a stream of molten liquid poured down from the heights above them, burning a hole right through the bath chair and the wooden platform below as well. The bath chair careened off the platform. Prince Leopold began to cry.

Alice ran to Prince Leopold and, whipping off her cloak, wrapped her brother in it. Dr O'Reilly bent down on the other side, taking the child's pulse. The Reverend Duckworth paced beside them, muttering something that might be a prayer, or perhaps a curse. Prince Albert was white with rage. The object of his fury was Joseph Paxton. He turned to his former favourite and addressed him with a cold, biting formality. 'We have heard much of speed on this project. And yes, it is commendable, and admirable, but not with the sacrifice of efficiency and basic safety. There isn't a person here today that might not have been killed by that accident.'

Poor Joseph Paxton looked twenty years older. He bent down and examined the steaming liquid, now congealing on the platform. 'I can't understand,' he said. 'I gave specific orders to secure the safety of the royal party – I banned dangerous substances such as this.' He lifted some of the now cooling substance on to his finger, looked at it closely, and then licked it. 'This liquid is a molten compound that will be used to glaze the windows. It shouldn't be on site for weeks yet. Who could possibly be using it today? Against my very orders? And how could he be so careless as to spill it?'

A crowd of workmen had gathered around the platform, Paxton's senior foreman pushed through them. Bowing to the Royal Family he turned and addressed Paxton. 'We cannot find the man responsible for this careless accident. He has fled the construction site.' An angry protest rose amongst the workmen – this was despicable, cowardly behaviour from one of their own rank. 'It might have been one of those foreigners, brought in to work on the overseas exhibitions,' one was heard to mutter. 'There was a swarthy fellow hanging around the edges,' another volunteered, 'might be a Turk or summat.' The jubilant day had gone decidedly sour, and the ever-growing crowd had the air of a lynch mob, looking for a scapegoat.

Bernardo DuQuelle sized up the situation. At any moment this crowd might spill over into riot. The masses had to be quelled. He strode over to Joseph Paxton and, placing a hand on his shoulder, spoke loudly, so that all could hear. 'It was the Royal Family's choice to come today,' he cried into the crowd. 'We wanted to see the wonders of this Crystal Palace, even at such a precarious time in its construction. A building site is always dangerous. Accidents may happen. We must take the consequences for our own enthusiasm.'

Turning to Prince Albert, he spoke in a much lower voice. 'We must, by all means, keep this incident out of the newspapers. The British press hasn't exactly warmed to the Crystal Palace, and reports of a mishap like this could scupper the project for good. The papers would sink Joseph Paxton's reputation, and the Crystal Palace would go down with him. There would be no great glass building, no exhibition, no celebration of Britain's superior industry. And this, Your Highness, will not reflect well on you.'

Prince Albert acknowledged DuQuelle's reasoning. He didn't like the man, but his cunning was supreme. Sighing, he moved to the front of the platform. The crowd grew quiet, anxious to hear Prince Albert speak.

'Our esteemed courtier, Bernardo DuQuelle, is right,' he said through gritted teeth. 'My apologies to Joseph Paxton for my hasty speech – it was spoken in anxiety for my son, and I am happy to report, he is unhurt in the incident. This is a great building, the home of an exhibition that will change the history of Britain for ever. I salute Mr Paxton for the genius of his design and the ingenuity of his construction.'

Again the mood changed, and cheers rang out through the building site. As Prince Albert turned from the waving, heaving crowd, his face took on a sullen cast. 'My thanks, DuQuelle,' he remarked curtly. 'You were right, as usual. It was an unfortunate accident and the blame cannot be placed on Paxton. I take full responsibility. Now I must get Prince Leopold home. There is no need for you to return to the Palace.'

The Prince quickly bundled Leopold and Alice into a carriage while the footmen cleared the crowd to make a path for them. Baroness Lehzen followed behind. 'The Crystal Palace,' she spat through a stream of caraway seeds, 'more of The Crystal Pig Sty.'

The carriage lurched its way through the mud, splattering DuQuelle in its wake. Katie looked into his face. He was an enigma, wrapped in a mystery. He had saved Prince Leopold's life and, when the mood of the crowd grew ugly, defused the anger. His quick thinking had probably saved the entire Crystal Palace project. Yet Prince Albert had not been generous in his thanks. It was obvious – the Prince loathed DuQuelle. Then why was DuQuelle standing there, humming an aria from *Rigoletto*, while wiping the mud from his well-tailored trousers? 'Accident,' Katie heard him say. 'Accident, hah! Accident my boots. An assassin is more likely. An assassin bearing all the marks of the Black Tide. Ah… The Black Tide… is rising…'

Finishing his aria, DuQuelle moved towards an empty carriage. Katie followed. She had been right. DuQuelle was the key to everything. She must confront him, on her own. Squeezing herself under the groom's jump seat she prepared for another bumpy ride, a muddy face and a lung-ful of dust. As they trotted past the construction site, she waved to a startled and furious James O'Reilly.

Chapter Nine

Lucia and Belzen

The carriage bumped along past the Serpentine Lake and up through the dormant gardens of Hyde Park. As it hit the cobbled streets, Katie's head banged against the bottom of the groom's seat. From her position she had a close look at all the rubbish and waste found on a busy thoroughfare. The hundreds of horses on the move had been particularly prolific. Something spattered her face – she didn't want to think what. From this far down, the smell was horrendous. 'Some day I'm going to sit properly in one of these carriages,' she thought. It was a weak joke, but Mimi had always told her, 'If you're frightened, crack a joke,' and she was frightened – very jostled, sick to her stomach, and frightened. She was alone, in a different time, with someone who might be her protector or her betrayer. And they were about to meet, face to face.

The carriage turned from the wide thoroughfare of Piccadilly to the darker regions of Mayfair. Twisting through the narrow lanes, they came to a stop on Half Moon Street. DuQuelle's house was old to the point of decrepit. No brilliant white stucco and marble columns here, but a half-timbered structure, its small windows divided into diamonds by lead strips. The upper floors bulged out over the street, leaving the pavement in shadow. Katie shivered. This house wasn't exactly welcoming. She could see DuQuelle's square-toed boots tripping down the carriage steps. 'I'm half dead from the cold,' he complained to the footman opening the door. 'Don't just stand there gawping, man, take my hat and gloves, and bring me a warm shawl. There had better be a fire in my private study. And tell cook…'

In the ensuing bustle of coats and canes, Katie slipped past the iron gates and below stairs. Wedging a basement window open, she found herself in a pantry off the kitchen. Katie now knew it was possible to be very frightened and very hungry at the same time. Baking smells were coming from the kitchen, gingery, sugary baking smells. She could see the backside of a very wide cook, stooping down to take something from the oven. The cook put the tray hastily on the counter as the footman came in with her orders.

'A bit of pottage!' she wailed. 'Hot water and lemon!

Steamed fish! The things that man eats, you'd think he was on his deathbed, day in and day out. No wonder he looks like nothing more than a cadaver. And what does this do for my reputation? No cook wants a master who won't fatten up with her good food. Well, the servants will just have to eat the nice things I've made for his supper, and they can bless him and bless him twice for making their lives so plush. I'll have his invalid's victuals up within this half hour.'

'Lucky servants. I'd eat anything,' Katie thought ruefully, eyeing the sugar buns just out of the oven, and the steaming soup cook was now stirring. But the kitchen wasn't the place for her. She needed to get to DuQuelle. Creeping out of the room, she started up the back stairs. Looking out of the stairwell windows, she could see the final light of day disappearing over the park. Within, it was darker still. The rooms were small and low, the wooden floors worn and uneven. DuQuelle's staff had neither lit a lamp nor kindled a fire. Ancient furniture loomed black in the fading light and strange aged faces peered down at her from portraits. As she ascended, each floor grew gloomier than the last. Yet she must find him. Floor by floor Katie searched for DuQuelle.

On the fourth floor she could see a flickering light underneath a door. She had been seeking DuQuelle, and here he was. But she couldn't bring herself to confront him. 'Best check things out first,' she said to herself, knowing she was a coward. She pushed the door open softly; it didn't creak, thank God. DuQuelle was seated with his back to the door, leafing hungrily through a dog-eared book. He was huddled before a smoking fire, which sent light and shadows flickering across the dark wooden panels of the curious furniture. The chests and wardrobes were deeply carved with leering gargoyles and grotesque hybrid animals: griffins, dragons and snakes seemed to jump from the walls as the light from the fire randomly hit them. They stared down upon stack after stack of books, lining the walls and rising in columns from the floor. 'He has a thing for books,' Katie thought. 'You'd think he was devouring the one on his knee.' They had something in common. This should have been comforting, but it was not.

She screwed up her courage, and stepped towards DuQuelle. 'Bang!' The door swung behind her with a blast. Air whipped through the room, pushing Katie into a corner. A bright flash of light filled the entire space. It was like being caught in a cyclone. Katie's hair slapped across her face and she clung to the side of a wardrobe as the tapestries rattled against the walls. The books flew through the air, pelting down like cannon balls. A dresser skidded across the room, fencing her in. She crouched down. She was trapped, but at least she couldn't be seen. And then the wind and light died down, ever so slightly, and she heard DuQuelle speak.

'So you have come, Lucia. And for all your sense, you

make a sensational first impression. Did you cause a commotion downstairs?'

'They always think it's a lightning storm,' a breathy whistling female voice answered. 'Humans can be so simple.'

'Do sit down. And please help yourself to a book.'

'Not now, DuQuelle, we have no time for pleasantries.' But she glanced greedily at the books, now scattered across the floor.

Katie peered over the dresser, trying to see the woman by the fire, but she couldn't get a good look at her. It was so bright, and the strange woman seemed to be the source of the light. Everything in the room shimmered and shook. Only DuQuelle remained still. 'I would invite you to take a seat,' he said, 'but I know you prefer to keep moving. If you will excuse me, I will remain by the fire. Blue skies, yes, but a bitterly chill day to spend in Hyde Park. One would think the Royal Family had better things to do than poke around a timber yard in the mud and ice.'

Despite his conversational air, Katie could hear the strain is DuQuelle's voice. The light magnified everything in the room, throwing him into sharp definition. Katie could see every detail of his face. The heavy lids over his eyes twitched slightly and deep crevices lined his face from nose to chin. Despite the talk of the cold, slight beads of perspiration dotted his temples. He continued to stare at the fire, as the shining figure flitted before him.

The woman spoke again, but in such a rushing torrent of words, Katie couldn't make them out. DuQuelle had no such trouble understanding his visitor – though Katie noticed he looked less louche and amused than was usual.

'It is good news and bad news,' DuQuelle said. 'Like it or not, the experiment proceeds apace. The children have entered the century. All three have arrived in this time. I have made contact with one of them.'

The tapestries began to bang again, as the woman responded with a sweep of excitement, but DuQuelle put out a hand to stop her. 'I have made contact with one of the children, but I do not know which one. It could be the child who brings peace, the child who brings war and peace or the child who brings the war to end the world. One of these three definitely – the question is, which one? I would have known last week, but for the interference of others. And that is the bad news: the child has become involved with the British Royal Family.' DuQuelle paused, took a scented handkerchief from his pocket and delicately patted the beads of perspiration that had spread from temple to brow.

The windows rattled in their frames as the visitor's excitement turned to displeasure. The tables lifted from the floor and the curtains flew high into the air. The room grew static with angry electricity and the books thudded against the dresser. Katie ducked down further. DuQuelle stood up, and the two figures, one light, one dark, circled the room. Katie was thankful they only had eyes for each other. This was not the moment to be discovered. The figure of light spoke again. 'Bring me the child,' she demanded.

'That I cannot do,' DuQuelle replied. 'I will not tamper with the Royal Family. It is their destiny to intermarry with half the crowned heads of Europe. To disrupt that would lead to political instability, international tension, paranoia.'

'Bring me the child,' the woman repeated with growing insistency.

DuQuelle dropped his gallantry. His nerves had turned to anger. His green eyes gleamed and his skin glowed white. He was hardly recognizable as human. 'I will need time,' he thundered. 'It will take some delicacy to disentangle the child. Lucia, you are playing into the hands of Mr Belzen, and all that is evil. I know what is at stake. You think the Verus will save the world, but you are marching down the wrong path, towards the war you so wish to stop, the destruction of the world you need to save. And isn't that exactly what Mr Belzen wants? I weary of the Verus, your dogma, your lack of imagination. You will annihilate this world and our own with your pig-headed, narrow-minded concepts of good and right. Now, Mr Belzen would under-stand. Evil can be so creative – The Malum can see things from different angles. Perhaps I am engaging with the wrong side after all.'

Each time DuQuelle said 'Mr Belzen', the woman's light flared and then dimmed. Even hearing his name seemed to lower her energy. When DuQuelle used the term 'Malum' she had to sit down. Picking up a book, she opened it and inhaled. The pages flipped rapidly, from beginning to end. The words flew up, on a trail of light, and were absorbed into the woman's eyes. This steadied her, refreshed her. 'You may choose to reject the Verus's beliefs, DuQuelle, but I cannot believe you would truly embrace evil, really work with evil. And there's no point in threatening me. Mr Belzen would suck the life from you before you could finish bowing and smiling. You say you need time. Will Mr Belzen give you time? Should the Malum find these children first, this world you've grown so fond of will be destroyed in a flash.'

She snapped her fingers and light shot from them, bouncing across the walls. 'I am not interested in time, or delicacy. We must save ourselves, and in order to do so, must save this world. The Verus relies on reason, not mercy. Now listen, DuQuelle: you must find these children, you must protect and nurture the child who brings peace. The other two – they must be killed. So far each one has slipped through your fingers. Do not think they will escape Mr Belzen.'

'You do not understand.'

'I do understand,' the woman interrupted. 'I understand that you are the worst possible choice for this most important of missions. But you are the only one of us who can remain in this atmosphere for any length of time. How long have you been here?'

Bernardo DuQuelle suddenly looked smaller and older, his anger gone. 'Since the Chasm,' he replied in a low voice. 'You should remember, Lucia. It was the end of our, how shall we say, intimacy? And that was over 300 years ago.'

Lucia shook her curls, rattling the windows in her wake. 'Please don't be sentimental, DuQuelle. Sentiment is the most useless of the human emotions. Passion or anger might give one energy, but sentiment simply wastes time. And please address me in the correct form. No one has called me Lucia in over 300 years, and I wouldn't say we were on a first name basis at this point.'

DuQuelle shrugged, regaining some of his usual jaunty composure. 'To me you will always be Lucia. And you will always be dependent on my abilities. I have adapted to this atmosphere and I know this century – I am the only one with the authority and access to carry out this mission. So do try to relax for once, my dear – I said I needed time, I didn't say I would fail. Child or no child – I will be ruthless in my pursuit. I know the other two are here – and the one I have spied is well within my grasp, I will find out which child she is, and take the appropriate steps. May I get you anything before you leave? Another book? Or something more regional? I must admit, I have developed a great affection for some of the English customs. Gone native, so to speak. A cup of tea?'

The offer of tea irritated the woman no end. Her light

flared up and the room again filled with brightness and air. The door banged repeatedly as she swept through it, leaving twisted rugs and upturned books in her wake. DuQuelle surveyed the wreckage, then sank back into his chair and stared into the fire. 'I will act,' he said to the flames, 'and soon.'

'He will be ruthless,' Katie thought, her breath catching in her chest. 'Ruthless with me, and I am ten feet away, crouched behind a dresser. That's not much protection.' As she had suspected, DuQuelle was key to her appearance in this time. But to confront him might mean death. The door opened and the footman entered with DuQuelle's sparse supper, crying out at the chaos he found in the room. As DuQuelle continued to stare into the fire, Katie climbed over the dresser, as silently as possible, and slipped out of the door. With shaking legs she crept down the stairs and into the outer darkness.

After the terror of DuQuelle's townhouse, the London streets seemed very normal. Yes, it was a street in a different century; but at least it was a street filled with people – not book-eating, light-flashing supernatural beings. The lamplighters were going about their work, their long torch poles swung jauntily over their shoulders. She skirted away from the house, thinking it wise to stay out of view of DuQuelle's bulging bow windows, and crossed Piccadilly, heading towards what she hoped was Buckingham Palace. Following the sound of carriages, Katie turned into a busy shopping thoroughfare. The shops' shutters were still up and pyramids of fruits and vegetables tempted passers-by. Fresh fish lay on wet marble slabs, their scales gleaming in the lamp light. Old ladies wrapped in shawls had set their pitches on street corners and dozed by small fires as they roasted chestnuts and apples, the smell of smoke and cooking covering the less appetizing odours of old fish, rotting vegetables and horse manure. Of a more active nature were the coster-girls, hawking their wares from their pitches on the street. 'Walnuts, Miss, walnuts a penny a dozen! Wouldn't give you a bad one for the world, which is a great thing for a poor 'oman to offer to do,' one called to Katie as she walked by.

From the other side of the street, a girl called out 'Apples! An 'apenny a lot, apples!' Her voice was hoarse from the call and she had a large wooden tray loaded with apples harnessed around her neck. Her shoulders stooped from the weight – it must have been at least 30 pounds of apples.

Crossing the street, Katie fumbled in her little reticule and found a penny. 'I'd like some apples, please.'

'Two lots, yes Miss?'

'No, just one,' Katie replied, 'but keep the change, OK?' Katie had grown up in New York and was hardened to street life: beggars, drug addicts, even prostitutes invaded her privileged uptown world. But she still felt very sorry for this girl. Katie could guess that she'd been standing on the street since early that morning, trying to sell a batch of apples that frankly didn't look that great. She deserved a break.

The girl looked suspicious. The lady in the fine grey dress had a funny accent and strange ways. 'You'd be pay'n' me twice what I'm askin'. Take the two lots of apples or take the change, Miss.'

'But I really only wanted one apple,' Katie protested. 'Please take the money. I have more, and you could use it.' The girl thought of what awaited her at home. Four little brothers and sisters depended on her wages for all their needs; mother couldn't earn nought, with all the children at home, and father was long gone. She handed Katie the apples.

'Two lots, Miss,' she said stiffly. 'Wot you paid for. I am a poor girl, but I am no beggar.'

'Thanks, great, that's cool. Don't work too hard,' Katie mumbled and retreated with haste.

Turning the corner, she deposited most of the apples in a neat pile on the sidewalk. She bit into one. It was withered and pitted with worm holes and the tight corset made it hard for her to keep any food down. She wiggled a bit and felt the corset strings loosen. What an idiot she'd just been – 'don't work too hard!' – of course the apple girl had to work too hard, how else was she going to live? She could imagine James laughing in that unpleasant superior way of his.

Katie remembered DuQuelle's words to his strange visitor: '*the Royal Family must not be interfered with*'. 'I'll be safe with Alice,' Katie thought, 'DuQuelle won't attack me if she's there. But will she be safe with me?' Katie's knees buckled again. She hadn't eaten for two days and the apple was making her nauseous. 'I've got to find something more substantial to eat, and then I've got to get back to Buckingham Palace, and we've got to find a way to get me out of here. We are all in more danger than we'd ever imagined.'

The noise and bustle of the street increased. The calls of the street vendors and the rattle of the carriages were joined by the jingle of a tambourine and the blare of a trumpet. Across the thoroughfare a troupe of street performers were giving a sample of their arts and handing out leaflets. They were a jolly, swarthy, robust lot and Katie watched them with pleasure.

'Feats of daring and strength,' cried a large woman, crammed into a greasy green shooting jacket. 'Orso of Segovia will lift over 300 pounds, and Signor Salamander, the great fire-king, will dine on flames with a knife and fork! And I, the Countess Fidelia, will look into the future and reveal your heart's desires.' The Countess Fidelia had seen better days. Her hair resembled a sagging haystack, and her jacket was fastened together by one button in front, all the other buttonholes having been burst through. Protruding from her bosom, a corner of the Pandean pipes were just visible. She took them out and played a merry tune to liven up the crowd. 'Acrobats and musicians,' she cried. 'And top of the bill – straight from her success at the Eel-pie-house, Peckham, ready to give us her heart-breaking rendition of 'Only a Cabin Boy' – we bring you the Little Angel!'

The large woman pushed forward a tiny girl, very different from the rest of the performers. She could only have been five or six years of age and was slender, with fine features and a sensitive manner. Her skin was so white, it was translucent. Her dark enormous eyes were ringed by lashes. They looked like pansies set in her face. Katie blinked as the tiny girl caught her gaze and seemed almost to glow.

'The visions,' Katie cried. She'd seen this child in her visions. Here was another piece of the puzzle. She moved forward to take a leaflet from the child, but a man stepping out of an ornate phaeton blocked her way.

'Lord Twisted,' Katie heard the crowd murmur, and she instinctively reared back from him. The pretty little girl darted behind the Countess Fidelia's voluminous skirts.

Lord Twisted laughed, and observed the child through his pince-nez. 'I do fancy her, you know,' he addressed the large woman in the green shooting jacket. 'A little angel indeed. She would make a lovely little mascot in the manner of my Jamaican servant boys. How well they'd work together. So light with the dark. Quite the effect. Today is your lucky day. I will pay you fifteen pounds for her services.'

The woman swelled with rage, looking as if she would burst the last button of her jacket. 'The child is not for sale, my lord,' she said stiffly, trying to contain her temper in front of this grand man, 'the child is my daughter.'

Lord Twisted laughed again. 'Oh come now, I have eyes in my head. This is not your daughter. You've obviously come by her the same way I wish to – through a few pieces of silver. I suggest you hand her over now. I will double the amount of money I've offered. Thirty pounds, that's two years' wages for a footman, I believe. What do you think of that?'

The crowd had grown, and a rebellious mutter ran through it. 'This is my daughter,' the woman insisted. 'Who I 'ave loved and tended since she was a wee babe in arms. She is not for sale. As for what I think – I think you should be gone, quick as ever, if you want to live to see another day.' A man pushed through the crowd and stood shoulder to shoulder with the woman. It was the strongman, Orso of Segovia, and his hands were the size of ham hocks.

Lord Twisted shrugged. 'Threats and temper from such people,' he admonished. 'Losing the opportunity to make good money. Well, you shall end your days in the work-house, that I can guarantee. Pity. This child – the Little Angel you call her – would have made a delightful tableau.' Sighing, he stepped into his carriage and tapped the roof with his cane. 'Hanover Square,' he cried, and the carriage whipped down the street, leaving a wave of mud behind.

Katie stepped forward again, and the little girl, seeing her, stepped forward too. But the child's rough protectors would have none of it. 'No more of the streets for you today,' her mother admonished, and, taking the Little Angel brusquely by the shoulders, she bundled her down the street and out of sight.

First DuQuelle, then Lucia, and now she'd come face to face with her vision, the Little Angel. Katie was shocked to her core. 'It is like a really bad dream, I don't get what's happening at all.' She mumbled to herself, walking blindly ahead, bumping into the passers-by. Eventually the curious looks directed at her brought Katie down to earth. 'They might clap me in prison as a drunkard,' she thought, her sense of humour returning briefly. Turning the corner she came across a store, much grander than the rest and shining with new paint, its large glass front lit up like a Christmas tree. 'Belzen & Mackie' the sign above the door read, 'Purveyors to the Gentry of Jellies, Wines, Cheeses, Aspics, etc.' An excited hum came from within the busy shop. Katie was still ravenous, and she felt she'd be less conspicuous in such a crowded place. Her good – though not grand – clothes and the coins Alice had insisted on putting in Katie's purse made her look like any other upper servant sent out by their lady to make a final purchase before the shops closed.

The store was filled with just such servants, as well as the ladies themselves. They were trailed by male clerks in striped trousers and tail coats. These clerks carried the customers' baskets for them, leading them down aisle after aisle of goods, helping them with their choices along the way. 'I suggest you sample this marmalade m'lady,' Katie heard one say. 'I've been told it is remarkably similar to that the Queen takes on her own toast.' Katie looked closely at the orange marmalade and saw more than a passing similarity in the jar and labelling to the Queen's. Looking around her she saw candles, cheeses and bottles of wine – all identical to what she had seen in MacKenzie's secret storeroom.

'So this is what MacKenzie is doing with his stashed provisions – setting up his own shop, selling the Queen's jams and soaps to the great British public.' Katie couldn't believe his boldness, or his greed. The store was doing a booming business; at least a dozen people were waiting to be served. 'MacKenzie, what a jerk,' Katie said aloud. Several of the tail-coated clerks look around at her in surprise. Down the aisle, a familiar figure caught Katie's eye. A small elderly woman in a prim black dress, her grey hair braided and wound around her ears. It was Fräulein Bauer. Who could forget the Danish pastry hairdo?

'She hasn't seen me,' Katie reminded herself. 'I'm in no danger, and might as well follow her. She could be my ride back to the Palace.' Fräulein Bauer was definitely looking for something or someone. She nipped around the aisle and down a staircase to the basement, Katie following behind her at a discreet distance. The basement was filled with enough pickled and preserved foods to feed the entire royal household, as well as cask after cask of the Queen's wine, her coat of arms blacked out on the side. Katie helped herself to some provisions. She didn't like stealing, even when the goods were stolen in the first place, but she was so hungry. Fräulein Bauer too had figured out exactly what was in the basement, and who it all really belonged to. Katie could hear her clucking and scolding under her breath.

'Tech, tech. The shame of it. Mr MacKenzie is stealing from our Queen. I must go back to the Baroness at once. He will be clapped in irons; he will be hanged.'

The Fräulein came to a sudden halt at the doorway of a smaller room. Inside was Mr MacKenzie, splayed across a chair, his shirt buttons popping under the pressure of his bloated stomach. The table in front of him was piled with pies and sweetmeats, as well as several bottles, already uncorked. 'Well, we certainly have enough wine to sell, so a drink on the side won't do any harm,' he laughed to himself. 'Princey wincey will never notice it's gone. *Dear Albert* doesn't approve of taking to the drink.' Clearing his throat and spitting on to the floor, he began to mimic the measured foreign tones of Prince Albert: 'What can one accomplish with the senses blurred from drink?' MacKenzie laughed until he coughed and then uncorked yet another bottle. His senses, it seemed, were already blurred.

A sound from the stairs made both Fräulein Bauer and

Katie start. The Fräulein spun around, jumping at the sight of Katie, but there wasn't time for explanations. 'Hide,' Katie mouthed, diving into an empty wine cask. Fräulein Bauer was less agile. She shrank behind the door, barely escaping the notice of the three men entering MacKenzie's room.

MacKenzie made a clumsy attempt to hide the bottles under his coat, but the three men didn't seem very interested. Two of them were dressed exactly like the figures in the courtyard of Buckingham Palace – the men who took the key from MacKenzie and tried to kidnap Princess Alice. This time Katie could see their faces. With their bristling black moustaches and fierce dark eyes, they had the look of men who would murder you rather than smile. And when they did smile, their sharp white teeth looked ready to tear you apart.

The third man was new to Katie, and seemed to be their leader. At first sight, he was an attractive man, well dressed, in a blue velvet waistcoat and a long hooded silk cloak. But there was something about him… The closer Katie looked, the less attractive he became, until he was a source of revulsion. He was of medium height, with a slender frame, fair hair and pale blue eyes. His nose was rather large and beak-shaped, starting high in his forehead. It was oddly blunted, as if it had been moulded from wax and then left in the sun. His head met his neck at an awkward angle, and waved ever so slightly with a will of its own. His small close-set eyes glittered with wetness. He glanced at MacKenzie in sheer contempt but remained silent. One of his henchmen spoke up.

'Yes, MacKenzie, you've seen the books, and yes, soon you will be a man of riches. But your presence here is as irritating as that corruption of your name over the shop door. We have a business that works, and we don't want you bringing it down with your drunken babbling. Now try to sober up and be gone – we've called a hackney cab, you'll find it through the back courtyard.' MacKenzie was far gone, but not so far as to miss the scorn in the other man's voice.

'How dare you,' he spluttered. 'How dare you speak to a man of my position, my importance… you thugs, you…'

The two henchmen moved forward, arms raised, but their leader stopped them. 'If you care about the Black Tide, you will restrain yourselves.' He murmured under his breath. 'Mr MacKenzie is still of use, still providing the money that will bring you arms and ammunition, the very backbone of your revolutionary plot. Leave the room. I will take care of this.'

Shaking their heads and grumbling, the two men went out of the back door, to the waiting hackney cab in the courtyard. Once they were out of sight, the fair-haired man approached MacKenzie, taking him by the arm. MacKenzie seemed to find his touch repugnant. He pulled away with a little shudder.

'You do understand, MacKenzie, the store's lease is in my name and the business contract as well,' the fair gentleman softly explained. 'Despite this, you take the lion's share of the profit. Now the two gentlemen in the next room have a calling to change the world, revolutionary new ideas that need money to back them. That is why they do business with you.'

'I don't understand their plans, Belzen. Don't want to know nothing.' MacKenzie mumbled in the sullen tones of a drunkard.

The other man sighed, and tried again, in his low soft voice. 'Fair enough, Mr MacKenzie. But my dealings with you are far more reasonable – it will be easy for you to help me. I am no revolutionary, but a simple citizen, looking for something. Three children, not of royal blood – one, at least, I believe to be secreted within Buckingham Palace. All I ask of you is to keep an eye out, perhaps search a bit, and report back to me if you spy any strange child within the Palace walls.'

MacKenzie's dislike of the man increased. 'I don't know who you think you are, Belzen, but I am the Master of the Royal Household. I make my own decisions, go my own way.' He picked up a bottle of wine by the neck, and throwing back his head, drank deeply. 'You wouldn't be in the Palace but for me. I'm not going to spy for the likes of you.' Katie could only see Mr Belzen from the back, but that looked bad enough. The movement of his head became more exaggerated, writhing on his neck.

'Careful, MacKenzie,' he said, 'you don't want to make me angry.' His voice had altered strangely; it had a moist and fleshy texture to it, like water sucked down a blocked drain. The room darkened and the air became dense and humid.

There was a loud clank, and a cry, as a bottle rolled into the room. Fräulein Bauer had stumbled into the doorway. MacKenzie lurched from the table. 'You little German witch,' he roared. 'What are you doing here?'

The poor woman trembled and gibbered. 'I do as the Baroness Lehzen does ask. She is worried. She does say "keep an eye on that man". So I do follow you. To this place. I am not to know…'

'MacKenzie,' hissed Mr Belzen. 'Have you been so stupid as to be followed? You are a bigger fool than I suspected.' His voice sounded feral, inhuman. He pulled the hood of his cloak over his head.

'I do only as my orders say, I…' Fräulein Bauer turned to Mr Belzen, her voice trailing off, her eyes growing wide with terror. She could see what Katie could not.

'My sweet Lord,' she gasped. 'What is this? What evil is before me? It is the snake in paradise. Jesus, Mary, Joseph, have pity on me. Have mercy…' This was too much for Mr Belzen.

'You do not like what you see?' he spat in his wet, thick voice, encasing himself in his cloak. 'Then I will make sure you see no more. Now watch, MacKenzie, watch the fate of those who thwart me.' His body writhed like an angry eel caught in a net. His hooded head seemed to duck down and snap at Fräulein Bauer. A strange tendril-like limb – it couldn't possibly be an arm – whipped out from beneath his cloak, wrapping around Fräulein Bauer's neck.

MacKenzie fell to his knees, covering his face. 'Oh terror!' he moaned, 'such terror!' The room went dark, rain pelted down from the ceiling and all Katie could hear was the woman's shrieks, followed by a hissing, and a truly horrible slurping and glugging.

And then a silence that seemed to go on for ever. The rain stopped. The room began to lighten. She could hear Mr Belzen gagging and breathing heavily. 'Comrades,' he called hoarsely to the courtyard. 'I am bringing you MacKenzie. He has passed out – too much drink, I assume. No, do not come back into the room. Send him back to the Palace. I must have some air. I will return.' Pulling his cloak close over his face, he heaved the unconscious MacKenzie through the back door and dumping him in the courtyard disappeared into the dark of the night.

'Belzen might be gone, but he will be back,' Katie thought, sweating profusely. She quickly climbed out of the cask and spied the hackney cab waiting outside. There was a space under the driver's seat. Perfect for luggage – or a girl. With her back against the wall, she slid across the room, glancing briefly towards the limp pile of black cloth and grey braids in the corner. Fräulein Bauer, she knew, was beyond help. There was nothing she could do for her and Katie knew she couldn't be there when Belzen returned. She did not intend to be his next victim.

The bumping of the carriage was nothing to the shaking of Katie's limbs. She was frightened in a way she had never been before. She was in terrible danger, and she was certain her friends were too. 'I need to talk to Alice and James. We'll have to stop MacKenzie and those men.' But this was the tangible part. The human part. The rest was an unknown country. While she had set out, on purpose, to confront DuQuelle and discover why she was here, never in a million years had she expected to hear what she'd heard. Things had got decidedly worse, and she had no idea how to escape. No, this wasn't a dream, but it was becoming a nightmare. She could hear MacKenzie's inert body rolling in the carriage. The driver's horse whip, dangling at his side, snapped back to give her a stinging slap. A drop of icy rain splashed against her cheek, and then another. Soon it was pouring down from the skies and splashing up from the streets. 'Perfect,' she thought, and was sick on the cobblestones.

Chapter Ten

The Three Time Travellers

It must have been three a.m. Katie sat opposite Alice and watched her feed little Riordan, out on night patrol again, and wrapped in the royal shawl. 'I just don't think pork pie and port wine are the correct diet for a toddler,' she commented, watching Riordan clutch a glass of ruby liquid in his two podgy hands and down it in big gulps.

'He's become so thin, though,' said Alice, holding out a leg that looked humorously plump to Katie. 'I don't believe the Honourable Emma Twisted ever feeds this child.'

'The Princess watered down the wine, Katie,' said James impatiently. 'Riordan isn't going to stagger down the street, singing beer house songs. Now try to pay attention, both of you. Katie, you should never have gone off on your own like that – ever.' He put out his hand to stop the tirade he knew was coming. 'But at least you've come back with lots of information. Terrible information, but lots of it.'

'Was there nothing you could do for Fräulein Bauer?' Alice asked.

A wave of remorse swept over Katie. 'I should have tried to do something. But I was hiding, it all happened so fast.'

James interrupted. 'There wasn't anything you could have done, Katie. If you'd tried, you wouldn't be sitting here tonight.'

'Poor Fräulein Bauer,' Alice said. 'She was a good woman, and would have been kind, but for her great love and fear of Baroness Lehzen.'

'And this loyalty has killed her in the end,' James added. All three were silent.

Alice hugged Katie. 'It sounds so horrible,' she said. 'I still think you should go right to bed, Katie. Such a terrible shock.'

'I am still in shock,' Katie replied. 'My hair must have turned white with fright. I'd look in a mirror, but I never like what I see.'

'No,' James commented absently, 'you wouldn't like it very much. You're a mess, Katie. Now, please let's concentrate on the problems at hand. We just need to piece everything together logically, scientifically.'

Striding over to the schoolroom blackboard, James took up a piece of chalk and began to write rapidly. 'We'll lay out the facts in diagram form, that way we can see the prob-lems and solutions more clearly.'

As the chalk dust flew, Katie muttered, 'Solutions, good luck.'

But James ignored her, covering the blackboard with names, interlocking circles and arrows.

'I begin to see the connections now,' he said, moving his index finger rapidly across the board. 'Lucia belongs to this group, the Verus. She uses Bernardo DuQuelle as some kind of agent. She also knows, and fears, Mr Belzen. Now Belzen is using the Black Tide to gain whatever he is after. The Black Tide in turn is using Mr MacKenzie, who is the connection to the Royal Family. And then there's DuQuelle to the Royal Family, Katie to Alice…'

Alice strained with concentration. This was worse than the royal progenitors. Henry I through William Rufus was nothing to this.

But James O'Reilly was excited. For some people, there's nothing that clears the mind like a good diagram. 'Lucia, that female who visited Bernardo DuQuelle, and the repel-lent man, Mr Belzen – they are both here on a mission, to capture Katie. That is one unifying feature,' he explained.

'Well, that's just great,' Katie said, biting off a piece of pork pie. 'Glad I can be of help.'

'The other common denominator is DuQuelle. He is working with Lucia – that we know – but he might be working with Mr Belzen as well, you can never tell with someone of DuQuelle's dubious character,' James said, writing rapidly on the blackboard. 'They all want something. What is it?'

'DuQuelle's visitor, Lucia – doesn't she want to save the world?' Alice supplied helpfully.

'Kind of,' Katie said. 'But only for her own good. I think we have something they need. And we'll destroy this if we go to war. So they have to protect us. It might have something to do with books. Maybe paper, or ink, or print. I don't know, but they are really weird about books.'

'Books,' James wrote on the black board. 'Whatever it is they need,' he said, 'the three children they keep talking of are the key to success or failure. They are the ones who can save, or destroy this world, the three time travellers.'

Alice wrapped Riordan's feet more firmly in her shawl. 'Three time travellers,' she murmured in his baby ear, 'the child who brings peace, the child who brings war and peace, and the child who brings the war to end the world.' She repeated it again, rocking Riordan in her arms, like a strange lullaby. Somehow Alice's innocent sing-song made it sound even more terrible. A child who brings peace would be a wonderful thing, a child who brings war and peace they could understand – it's what had happened throughout all of history. But a child who brings the war that ends the world… all three shuddered and stared at the candle they'd placed between themselves. The rain thudded against the nursery window.

Trying to speak casually, even affectionately, James looked to Katie. 'You are obviously one of the three time travellers. So which one *are* you, Katie?'

She looked at her friends and saw the doubt flicker across their faces. They were suddenly just that little bit afraid of her, and she was afraid of herself. 'I don't know,' she stuttered. 'I'm not sure. I think I might...' Alice interrupted her.

'Katie, you just *can't* be the bad one. You're not a bad person. I believe you are good, and will bring good. You were sent here as the child of peace. But whether Bernardo DuQuelle has enough goodness in himself to see this, I don't know.' The look of doubt was gone from Alice's face, replaced by a radiant certainty.

James's face was still dark with doubt. 'I think you are too quick to decide, Alice. We have to look at the facts. There is no way of knowing which of the children Katie is. She is in danger, which puts you in danger, and your safety must come first. I think if we could... erm... isolate Katie... keep her away from you... just until we can gather more facts...'

As Alice interrupted, she lost her normal grave and gentle manner and began to resemble her mother, to throw the cloak of royalty around her small frame. 'I have made our decision,' she told James O'Reilly. 'We must do everything we can to protect Katie. And being with me is the surest way to succeed in this. You heard what DuQuelle said. They *dare* not interfere with the Royal Family.' Riordan, innocent of the crisis at hand, had fallen asleep. Cradling him in one arm, Alice put the other around Katie's shoulders. 'You will be safe here with me.'

James was silent for a moment. Alice was not being logical. One couldn't simply assume Katie was the child who brings peace. But to see her as anything else would be a betrayal of someone who had become… become… He blushed deep red as he realized: Katie had become his friend, a good one, an important one. And then there was Princess Alice. She had given her orders, and obedience to Queen and country ran deep in him.

After a moment's struggle he bowed his head to Alice. 'Yes,' he said, 'you have made our decision, and I will abide by it. But in order to protect Katie, we must protect ourselves too. There is only a one in three chance that you are the child DuQuelle will save. It's best to keep him guessing. The key to which child you are lies in your own history – the inventions, medical discoveries, famines, plagues, revolutions and wars that happened in your own time. These will reveal which child you are. DuQuelle is canny. He probably knows something of the future. Anything you say could be a clue. And if you tell us, then we are vulnerable, and could give you away. You mustn't tell us anything else about your time'

'But I know so much,' Katie protested. 'There are so many ways I can help.' She thought about the simple way to prevent typhoid – clean water – and the thousands of lives she could save. She could warn Alice about her nephew, the Kaiser – not even born yet, but not to be trusted when he arrived. There were messages for future generations. 'Don't sail on the *Titanic*, I know a blimp looks fun but don't fly on the *Hindenburg*, and whatever you do, stay out of San Francisco on 18th April 1906.'

'Couldn't I pass on information if it would make things better, save lives, change things?'

'That's just what you can't do, Katie,' James said firmly. 'I'm desperate to learn these things from you, but you can't change our time, or give your own time away. I think the Princess's faith in you is a gamble. But I will take this gamble and do all I can to protect you. You in turn must be careful to protect yourself.'

'And in protecting yourself you protect the future of the world,' Alice added brightly. 'This one in three notion is nonsense. You are going to bring us all peace…'

Katie thought for a moment, listening to the rain. 'James can draw and connect, diagram and dissect all he wants,' she said, 'but he can't solve the real problem. This isn't science. What's going on is beyond reason. Lucia, Bernardo Du-Quelle and – God help us – Mr Belzen, they do not belong to the natural world. They belong to the supernatural.'

James put his chalk down quietly, and Alice held Riordan closer. The room suddenly seemed very cold, the light of the candle very small. James spoke up stubbornly,

'I still think that science can be applied to the situation.'

'Needs must,' Alice added. 'It's all we have, along with our faith and our belief in each other.'

Katie squeezed her friend's hand. 'That doesn't really arm us against all the hocus-pocus I saw tonight. But there is something we can do, something where we are on equal footing. We can concentrate on the danger at hand; and that's MacKenzie and his nasty little bunch of so-called shopkeepers. It's pretty rotten, selling off the Queen's teas, but I think that dark-eyed moustachioed duo are up to something a lot worse. DuQuelle talked of the Black Tide. Since I can't tell you what I know, why don't you tell me what you know?'

'They are the most dangerous underground movement in existence,' James explained. 'The Black Tide's mission is to create a world where all men are equal, where each man has the same rights as his brother. So far so good. But to achieve this, the Black Tide believes the world as it stands must be destroyed. Their credo is a system of total anarchy.' He glanced nervously at Alice. 'A class system, with an aristocracy, is repugnant to them. Social inequality must be annihilated, from the top down. Their primary target is the most important monarchy in existence today, the British Royal Family.'

Katie looked at Alice, still rocking Riordan in her arms. 'We knew those men were brutal, and now we know why. The attempt to kidnap Alice was not a one-off. I'm certain that "accident" at the Crystal Palace was no accident – that man shouldn't have been up in the girders, and he shouldn't have had that vat of molten stuff. DuQuelle thinks it was a murder attempt by the Black Tide – I pretty much heard him say so. They're not just thieves trying to make a buck or kidnappers hoping to score a big ransom. They have a cause, something they believe in more than life itself, and they are willing to die for it… or kill for it. And think – they've got a hold on MacKenzie. They have complete access to the Palace – and their prey. But there's one bright spot. They're not serpents, or cyclones. They're people, just like us. We can try to fight the Black Tide. We can try to protect Princess Alice, but we'll have to be doubly vigilant.'

The rain was heavier now and a deep gloom settled over the trio. There were, after all, only three of them. And it was a heavy burden for small shoulders. Alice was the first to shake it off. 'Sleep,' she said, 'is what we need. Look at little Riordan, sleeping like an angel. I'll go and tuck him in. Couldn't you drop your father a hint about the Honourable Emma Twisted, Jamie?'

'Oh yeah,' Katie added, 'I think I ran into Emma's father yesterday. What a family. He tried to buy, yes buy, a little girl – who, by the way, might be mixed up in this stuff too. Boy, was he a creep.'

James still didn't say anything, so Alice spoke up again. 'Jamie O'Reilly, you'll definitely need some sleep. Isn't tomorrow the first day of practice for the big cricket match?'

This punctured James's gloom, he was mad on cricket, and even Katie looked interested. 'It's the Royal Military College cadets versus the Queen's household,' Alice explained. 'Jamie is one of our top batsmen and a devious spin bowler. And Jamies's older brother Jack is one of the cadets. A fine young man and a fast bowler, up to seventy miles an hour they say. We never win, but Jamies's game has improved so much this year. I hope the ground dries out in time… all this rain… And Katie, you forget who is protecting whom. There are servants and soldiers all over the Palace with express orders to keep me safe. But you are alone, except for me and James. I'm afraid you're sleeping under my bed again. The schoolroom isn't safe enough. I know it's not very comfortable, but I'll loan you Woolie Baa Lamb.'

As she left the room with Riordan in her arms James commented: 'She's very bossy, and she is a girl, but at least she's brave.'

Katie lay under Alice's bed. She could tell by the bustle barely audible from the floor below that the chambermaids were lighting fires in each of the rooms. Though it was still dark, it must be near morning. As she turned over, Woolie Baa Lamb let out a low 'Baa'. Katie hadn't slept a wink. She was utterly miserable. Everything, just everything was a mess. She still didn't know how she had arrived in this time, and she certainly didn't know how to depart. And which child was she? Her life was in jeopardy – and worse, so were those of her friends. Even without Bernardo DuQuelle and his cast of grotesques, this was no place for Katie. She made a very bad Victorian girl, just couldn't stomach the decorum, modesty and obedience and she was an unlikely Victorian child, in total rebellion against all that hero-worship of parents. If Alice and James could get through the present dangers, they had a future, in this time. They would grow up to do whatever history had in store for them. 'What about me?' Katie wondered. 'How can I have a future in a time where I don't exist?'

Katie found herself thinking about her mother. Mimi wasn't exactly dependable, and yes, she was shallow and selfish and lived in a pop culture vacuum. But Mimi wasn't a complete waste of space. Her toughness and street smarts had propelled her into a successful music career. Katie needed some of that toughness now. Plus, Mimi was the future. 'I want to go home,' Katie thought. 'I want to go home, have a laugh with Mimi. Hail a taxi, go out to brunch and eat normal food – bagels and lox and cream cheese. If Mimi could see me now, she'd be thrilled with my weight loss.'

And that was the problem. Mimi would probably never see her again. She was trapped in the wrong time and no one knew how to set her free. If she had to stay in the nineteenth century, she had hoped, at least, to protect Alice. But from what DuQuelle had said, she would only do harm. Alice's words kept ringing in her head: *'You are going to bring us all peace.'* 'Peace,' thought Katie, 'with what's going on in my time!'

Mimi wasn't exactly a reader of newspapers or a follower of events. For this indifference Katie was grateful, it kept a scary world at bay. But what she learned in her current affairs class in school – what she inadvertently picked up as Dolores switched between soap operas – all that was the opposite of peace. Israel and Palestine, India and Pakistan, America and Iran, North and South Korea, the nations of the world seemed to hate each other.

Katie groaned as an even worse thought hit her. Alice didn't know about the great wars: the 58,000 casualties in one day at the Battle of the Somme, the 13,000 men and women killed during the London Blitz, the 6 million Jews gassed or shot or starved to death just because of their religion. These are the things that lay in the future, the future Katie was bringing. 'Alice is wrong to have such faith in me,' Katie decided, 'and James's suspicions are probably right. Whatever my time brings, it is the opposite of peace. But is it the war to end the world?' Katie shook her head, trying to think more clearly. 'No,' she said aloud, 'I am not the prettiest, smartest person around – and I'm a disappointment to Mimi – but I'm just not the worst. You'd think I'd *know* if I was going to destroy the world.'

She could still see Bernardo DuQuelle in his townhouse, speaking into the fire. '*I will be ruthless…*' and still hear the terrible hissing and gagging of Mr Belzen. The one thing Katie knew for certain was that they were all in jeopardy. The night dragged on forever, and a part of her hoped the sun would never rise.

Chapter Eleven

The Cricket Match

It was the day of the cricket match, and a strikingly beautiful one at that. The sun was strong for early spring and the sky was achingly blue – the kind of day England delivers every six months or so.

After three sleepless nights, Katie was willing to miss it, but Alice had other plans for her. 'Come on lazy head, up you go,' she said, 'it's almost too late to get you to the cricket match.'

Katie struggled to understand 'What cricket? What match?'

'You can't have forgotten! It's the Royal Military College Cadets. They're playing us, the Royal Household, today. It's an annual event. My whole family will be there. Vicky's back from her tour of the North, and even Bertie's been let off his duties. The cadets always win, but this year the household team has a good chance. They've been practising every hour they have off-duty. Everyone says Mr Drummond can't bowl but to take a wicket and that James's leg spin delivery is unplayable.'

Katie rubbed her eyes. This was gibberish, and she was tired. 'I think I'll take a nap instead,' she said, burrowing back under the blankets. Alice began to get her steely regal look.

'Well, I have to go, Mama's orders, and I can't leave you here.'

When Alice was in this mood, 'yes' was the only answer. 'OK,' Katie said, 'I'll come. I don't know anything about cricket, but I do play softball for the school team.'

'Softball?'

'It's like baseball, only the ball's bigger and you can throw underhand.'

'Baseball?'

Katie sighed. 'I think it's kind of like cricket. Anyway, it's what we play, and I'm really good at it. I'm the best fielder on the team. Coach says I can catch anything.'

'How interesting.' Alice looked at Katie, puzzled but admiring. 'These are games that girls play?'

'Well, girls and boys both. In my time they're really keen for girls to play sports. But on real professional teams, men are still paid a lot more money.'

Alice was getting more and more confused. 'Katie, are you paid to play this bast ball?'

'Hardly,' Katie replied. 'I'm good for my age but no pro.'

Alice passed Katie a bundle of clothes far plainer than what she had been wearing. 'I borrowed these from Mabel Evans, one of the kitchen maids. I gave her my rabbit muff in exchange. She thinks I want to play pretend as a servant girl.'

'So the plan is that I'll play pretend instead,' Katie said. 'OK, I'll go, but why the demotion? Last time I went out I got to be a minor part of the aristocracy. Now I'm a scullery maid.'

'I know it's not as nice,' Alice said. 'Though Mabel is an awfully nice girl; and she's not a scullery maid, she's a kitchen maid. She was ever so helpful when I had to smuggle food to Bertie. But you couldn't wear the grey cashmere. The entire Royal Household will be at the cricket and that includes the Honourable Emma Twisted. She might be a bit of a tippler, but she'd be certain to recognize her own gown, and *that* would be a scene. If you dress like a servant, everyone will think you are a child from the household, the daughter of a cook or a maid or a gardener.'

Katie looked at the bundle of sturdy calicoes and coarse cottons. 'But what about the cooks and maids and gardeners themselves?' she asked. 'I might be invisible to your class in these clothes, but they're sure to sniff me out as a phoney. I'll be hauled in front of MacKenzie and then we'll really have that scene you're talking about.'

Alice paused at this, but wouldn't be deterred from her plan. 'They probably will know you're not one of them, and will gossip amongst themselves,' she admitted. 'But they wouldn't dare bring it to anyone's attention above stairs, and certainly won't tell MacKenzie. I've spent enough time in the servants' hall to know they hate MacKenzie – who wouldn't? And please don't say *"your class"*, it makes me feel horrible, and besides, the Royal Family is supposed to be above class.'

From outside the nursery they could hear Baroness Lehzen calling Alice. Katie looked more closely at the little bits of cotton with buttons and laces. 'How am I supposed to get these things on?' she asked crossly. 'Even a servant has to wear 800 layers of clothing.'

'Katie, I can't stop to help,' Alice replied. 'I'm late, my dress has yet to be changed and Baroness Lehzen is already cross. Sometimes I think you've never seen clothing before, but then you were half naked when I found you. When you've got the things on, take the secret passageway to the kitchens and line up with the other servants. There's a seating area for the household staff near the pavilion they've set up for us.' Alice was enjoying herself, making plans without the usual interference from James. 'If you get into any trouble, yell something – a code word. I know, shout "Crystal Palace" as loud as you can and I'll come to help.'

With an unusually self-satisfied nod, Alice ran from the room, leaving Katie to struggle with the little heaps of clothing. A good hour later, having wrestled with baggy cotton stockings, a chemise, drawstring drawers and the inevitable innumerable petticoats, she looked presentable. Yet despite her best efforts, there were still three or four items of clothing left. She'd pulled them over her head, tied them around her waist and even wrapped them around her ankles, but she couldn't figure out where they might go on her body. Picking up the straw bonnet that topped her outfit, she stuffed the extra bits of cotton and calico into the deep crown. 'Next time I travel through time I'm going to do it as a boy' she told no one in particular, as she slipped behind the schoolroom screen and into the secret passageway.

Katie had missed the line-up of servants and had to make her own way through the grounds of Buckingham Palace to the match. Play was about to begin when she arrived. The gentlemen cadets were immaculate, almost gleaming in their uniform white caps, shirts and trousers. The Royal Household had made the utmost effort to look smart, but didn't quite carry it off. It was the contrast of quasi professional and decidedly amateur. Katie could see James in the field, warming up. She caught his eye and braved a little wave. James scowled and looked away. 'He wants to concentrate on the match at hand,' Katie realized. 'He doesn't want to think about MacKenzie or Belzen or me.' She thought about going back inside and sliding under Alice's bed again, but the day was so bright and the sky so deep. She put aside her own questions and doubts, and decided to try and enjoy her first ever cricket match.

Underneath an elaborate canopy, the Royal Family were chatting with the most senior members of the Royal Household. Katie noted that Baroness Lehzen was particularly hideous in a grey, mustard and olive green paisley print, a small straw hat perched coquettishly forward over her wrinkled brow. Her snaggle teeth were braced in a broad smile as she bent over double to hear what the Queen was saying. The Honourable Emma Twisted moped near the punch bowl: sour and sad and old beyond her years.

At the back of the royal grouping Mr MacKenzie was sweating profusely, looking over his shoulder and starting at the slightest sound. He'd come to after the night with Mr Belzen and assumed it had been a drunken hallucination. But still, Fräulein Bauer had never returned to the Palace. There was much talk of this below stairs. Baroness Lehzen viewed him with more suspicion than ever and had suggested alerting the Queen to Fräulein Bauer's absence. Her suspicions about MacKenzie grew. Even on a mild spring day the heat was too much for MacKenzie. His face was so pink, his collar so tight – Katie thought he might burst, and hated to think what would come oozing out. Katie wasn't the only one watching MacKenzie. Bernardo

DuQuelle gazed at him intensely then scanned the crowd for another face. Katie drew back, and pulled her straw bonnet down.

Alice's sisters were there for the day and all the girls were dressed in identical plaid taffetas of rust, green and blue, their hair tied back in matching tartan ribbons bunched at the side. The eldest of the royal children, Princess Victoria, was seated on a gilt chair next to her father. She chatted away, making many points and interrupting others when they tried to add their own views. Vicky was unusually tiny and looked a great deal like her mother. 'Why is it the smaller they are, the more overbearing they become?' Katie wondered. Prince Albert held Vicky's hand and nodded approval at the observations and theories streaming from his young daughter. Vicky was his first born, he had tutored her himself, and all of his beliefs and ideals had gone into her education. She was his masterpiece. He rather missed the fact that, while Vicky was certainly knowledgeable, she wasn't exactly likeable.

There was another reason for tiny Princess Victoria's self-importance that day. Though still in her teens, Vicky was newly engaged to Prince Frederick William of Prussia. The two of them had just finished touring northern Britain. It was a way to get to know each other, and an intimate introduction to Britain for Prince Frederick William – with just thirty British and Prussian courtiers in attendance. Vicky was filled with enthusiasm for the trip. 'I cannot express the cunning of the northern factories,' she explained to those around her. 'The workers are used in a "relay system", so that machinery is manned for the longest possible hours. Of course, the Factory Acts have done so much to help the workers. Particularly the factory children – they now cannot be employed until the age of eight – so much more humane. And the new systems give them much leisure time – only seven-hour shifts. Before that the little mites toiled from five in the morning until eight in the evening!' She had inherited her father's talent for facts, and his tedious way of relating them. Several courtiers stifled yawns.

Prince Frederick beamed, holding a sunshade over his fiancée's head and adjusting her shawl. 'The smoke,' she continued, 'was abhorrent. The coal stacks puffed away day and night. Sometimes it looked like midnight at high noon. I am convinced the smoke was the cause of young Felix's illness. As soon as we sent him from Manchester, he made a complete recovery.' Vicky turned to smile and pat a little boy with blond curls.

Katie almost leaped from her skin. It was the small, smug boy in the shorts, jacket and ruffles. She'd seen him in New York, and she hadn't liked him then. He spoke as in her dreams – that same flat, high nasal voice. She couldn't understand him.

'German,' she suddenly realized. 'He's speaking German. And what is he doing here? I read about him, in those letters Alice wrote to Vicky – during this same tour of the North. Prince Frederick's nephew, young Felix – he dies – of scarlet fever – and yet here he is.' The child, briefly, caught Katie's eye – he too looked startled. And Katie could have sworn that he began to glow in the bright sunlight.

Standing behind Vicky was a rather lumpen teenage boy with a round face, bulging eyes and unkempt hair. It was Bertie, Alice's older brother, the heir to the British throne. He looked to the field with great earnestness, waving his arms and talking hard. In his enthusiasm he spilled punch in every direction. 'We can expect a maiden over from James O'Reilly,' Bertie was telling the Reverend Duckworth. 'He's first rate, that boy. But dash it, they can't open the bowling with him. We'll need a fast bowler, what with the new ball, and it had better be Drummond. He's the damnedest…'

The Queen turned around, her face like thunder. 'Bertie! I will not have that kind of profanity in this family, or in any persons surrounding this family. I demand an apology now and insist you retire from the event should any such language cross your lips again.' There was silence in the gay little pavilion and Prince Albert's usual burdened and exhausted expression returned to his face.

Bertie turned bright red. He'd been speaking quickly and easily, but now began to stutter.

'Pardon me, Mother, it is un, un, unfff-forgivable, but it came out all, all, all wrong, but, but, but…'

Seeing Bertie flounder, Alice spoke up. 'Please do excuse Bertie, dear Mama,' she said. 'The language is terrible, of course, but his heart is in the right place. He simply wants the household team to perform as well as possible. And we should remember that he has used his own personal allowance to purchase lovely new willow bats for our team. I do believe Bertie wishes he were on the field himself.'

The Queen looked to Prince Albert for his response. Standing up, he put one hand on Alice's shoulder and the other on Bertie's. 'The language is unacceptable, Bertie.'

'Yes Father. I am s-sorry, Father.'

'And now that is settled. Alice, you are right about one thing. What young man would not want to play cricket on a glorious day like this? If I were a few years younger, I would be on the field myself.'

Everyone laughed and the Queen smiled thinly. Vicky just looked annoyed as she blotted a punch stain on her silk shawl. What a trial this bumbling brother was.

Seating herself on a velvet cushion next to Leopold's bath chair, Alice smoothed the shiny material of her skirt carefully over her knees. Katie admired Alice for her spirited defence of her brother, and she didn't want to make fun of her friend, but the outfit – it really was laughable. 'She thinks this is a good look for her – as Mimi would say. But anyone standing within fifty yards of Alice and her sisters would need sunglasses. Who chooses those girls' clothes?

It's a shopping mall meltdown.' Katie was talking to herself again, a sure sign that she was nervous. She felt vulnerable outside – and alone – in a foreign country and a century that wasn't her own.

Just then Alice caught Katie's eye and nodded her head to the left, towards the area cordoned off for the household. Here were scullery maids, kitchen maids, laundry maids, under housemaids, upper housemaids, chambermaids, between maids, nursemaids, lady's maids, stable boys, pages, grooms, coachmen, footmen, gardeners, butlers, valets and stewards. It took a lot of people to look after the Royal Family. They were all dressed in their very best. The men and boys had scrubbed their faces and spat upon their hair to slick it back. The women and girls were in their finest bonnets, newly trimmed for the occasion.

The cadets had won the toss and elected to bat. They were playing on a large field of flat grass, about a hundred yards across. In the middle of the field was a long rectangle of groomed lawn, clipped and rolled to create a much harder surface. At either end of this rectangle were three small wooden stakes hammered into the earth close together. The Royal Household's captain, a broad-shouldered footman Katie had seen from the nursery window, was having a final discussion on field placement with his team-mates. Katie was surprised to see that James was not going to bowl. Instead, he was taking a position behind one of the sets of wooden stakes. She didn't understand this game, and strolling up to either James or Alice for an explanation was out of the question. So she perched on the edge of the back bench, positioning herself near an eager-looking coachman. He was explaining the game to a pretty chambermaid. Katie noted with relief that the young girl looked as confused as she felt.

'There are two teams,' he was telling her, 'each with eleven players. The cadets are going to bat first and we're fielding. What they want to do is hit the ball and score runs. What we want to do is get them out so that we can bat and score our own runs. We each have an innings, and then the team with the most runs wins.'

'What are those little wooden bits stuck in the lawn?' the girl asked. The coachman laughed. It seemed a perfectly intelligent question to Katie, but he thought it was hilarious.

'Why, those are the wickets,' he said. 'They're made of three stumps topped by a pair of bails. You use them to get the batsman out.'

The chambermaid wasn't quite getting this, but the coachman *was* very handsome, so she ventured another question. 'And how do you get the batsman out?'

'Actually, there are two batsmen in at a time. Each batsman stands in front of a wicket: one is the striker, he tries to hit the ball, the other is the non-striker, and he simply runs. The two go back and forth between the wickets scoring points.'

The chambermaid was struggling to understand. 'Can they run whenever they want?'

'No, they have to wait until the ball is bowled and can only run when the striker has hit the ball. But the striker is out if he hits the ball and a fielder catches it, or if he misses the ball and it hits the wicket, or if…' The chambermaid was smiling, making 'umm, hmm' noises and twisting the curls under her bonnet. Katie suspected she had lost track of the match altogether and was merely admiring the young man's profile. Anyway, Katie had grasped enough to know that cricket *was* a bit like baseball, only more complicated, with more people running, and more poncey uniforms.

Despite his language, Bertie had been right. Drummond opened the bowling. A fast bowler with a new ball is a deadly combination, but the cadets were still managing to make contact with the ball. By the time James O'Reilly replaced Drummond, the household team had taken only two wickets and the cadets had 106 runs. At first Katie didn't think James was as good as Drummond at bowling the ball. He spent a lot of time examining the ball, and polishing it against his trouser leg. His run up and delivery were much slower. The ball itself looked slower too. But then she noticed he was using his wrist and fingers to spin the ball as he threw it, and this was making it much harder for the batsman to hit. The batsman snicked the ball and a fielder behind the stumps caught it. The umpire raised his finger, the batsman was out. Then the next batsman missed the ball completely and it went crashing into the wicket.

'Crikey,' the coachman muttered to the chambermaid. 'His bowling was top-notch there. But look, Jack O'Reilly is next in, he's certain to give his little brother a rough ride.'

Katie turned to examine the young man swinging the willow bat in preparation. Jack O'Reilly was taller than James and broader in the shoulders, but they both had the same strong nose and thick straight hair. As he walked on to the pitch he shot James a challenging look. While James's eyes were dark, almost black and often angry; Jack's blue eyes were full of laughter. His challenge to his brother was more impish than defiant. 'Jack must have his mother's eyes,' Katie thought. 'Kind eyes. Fun eyes. Those boys must miss her very much.'

Jack lived up to his billing. As James bowled his first ball, Katie heard the distinct 'thwack' of leather hitting willow. The ball sped past James, then bounced through the legs of a despairing fielder. The two men at the wickets were running up and down the pitch, scoring runs for the cadets. Jack knew James as well as any brother could. They'd lost their mother as young boys, and their sister had been sent abroad. Their father was always more interested in his own career than in his little boys. Jack and James had brought each other up as best they could. Jack could guess what James was thinking, feeling and how he would act. He knew in advance what type of ball James was going to bowl. Who else could have this advantage on the pitch? Jack batted superbly, blocking the good balls, and driving and cutting the bad. James finally ran Jack out, but the damage had been done. The score was now 172 for five. The cadets shouted themselves hoarse. With a cheery wave Jack loped off the pitch.

Katie turned her eyes from James's sullen, disappointed face to the player coming up to bat, a powerful thickset man. The batsman was good, and James was struggling with him. It was early afternoon. The sun was hot for so early in the year, and Katie gave up trying to follow the match. Baseball made much more sense: first base, second base, third base, home. One, two, three strikes and you're out. Plus there was the wide screen at the stadium showing instant replay, the organ music, the ice cream and the hotdogs. Mimi had once sung the American national anthem before a big baseball game… mimed it actually… but just when she hit 'and the rocket's red glare, the bombs bursting in air,' she'd had a 'wardrobe malfunction'. Something snapped, something else popped out, and two million fans saw more of Mimi than was necessary. Katie smiled to herself. Mimi was a total pain, but at least she wasn't boring. Not like cricket. The score was 826 for six… or was it 127 for three… 'Bizarre,' she thought, and started to fall asleep.

James was running towards the wicket, ready to bowl

again. As the ball left his hand, the rough-looking batsman stepped forward, stumbling slightly. 'Thwack!' He made strong contact with the ball, but at an awkward angle. It was travelling – at high speed – directly towards the royal tent. Now Katie was awake, adrenalin pounding through her veins. A ball at that speed could knock someone unconscious. Everyone in the royal party was at risk. But if it hit Leopold – a blow like that would surely kill him. He'd bleed to death.

It all happened in a flash. Katie might not understand cricket, but she did know how to catch a ball. She grabbed the crown of her straw bonnet like a catcher's mitt and ran backwards, leaping over the cordon separating the Royal Family from the household. Without ever taking her eye off the ball, she scrambled through the gilt chairs and taffeta-clad princesses to get to it. With a final effort, she leaped into the air, arm outstretched, directly in front of Leopold, and 'thud!' She caught the ball in her straw bonnet. Katie thanked the fates that the straw bonnet was stuffed with her excess underwear. Even with that, her wrist snapped painfully, and the force knocked her backwards into the Reverend Robinson Duckworth's lap.

Looking across the field, Katie could see the batsman sink to his knees in despair. The Queen and Prince Albert were beside Prince Leopold. Dr O'Reilly was taking his pulse. 'Very rapid,' he said, 'the closeness of the accident has disturbed his nerves.'

'Please,' Leopold said weakly, 'no ice baths, no purges. I'm fine.'

'Perhaps just a rest in his rooms,' the doctor conceded.

The Reverend Duckworth was trying to push Katie from his lap. 'If you will excuse me your Royal Highness, I will remove Prince Leopold now. If only this young girl would please…'

Katie, too, was trying to untangle herself, to get away from the hundreds of eyes focused on her. Staggering to her feet, she looked up to a most unwelcome sight. It was Bernardo DuQuelle. 'I believe we have much to thank this young girl for,' he commented, lifting her hand still clutching the bonnet and cricket ball. 'Without her quick actions the ball would most certainly have hit Prince Leopold, with disastrous consequences.' DuQuelle bowed – he seemed to adore bowing – 'That was quite the catch,' he said to Katie. 'Might I have your name, young lady? I am certain the Royal Family would like to thank you properly.'

Katie stood frozen. The entire court was staring curiously. Leopold was open-mouthed and Vicky – for once – had shut hers. The Queen and Prince Albert, having ascertained that Leopold was fine, had turned their attention to his saviour. Alice looked relieved and alarmed in equal measures. Katie suddenly saw the flaw in Alice's plan. She couldn't shout 'Crystal Palace!' any more than she could reply to DuQuelle's question: 'I am Katie Berger-Jones-Burg if you please, sir'. Not with her broad American accent. The questions would never stop. She'd be placed in an orphanage or deported to Australia.

The silence became heavy and DuQuelle spoke again. 'The child is shy, uncomfortable with the attention.' Turning to the Queen and Prince Albert, he bowed. 'I believe she must be the child of one of the Palace servants. If you would permit me, I will take her back to the Palace myself and seek out her family.' DuQuelle took Katie by the arm and began to lead her away. Katie could see Alice trying to reach her, but Leopold was clutching his sister's arm and had begun to whimper.

'Well, this is it,' Katie thought. 'He's got me now.'

Then James pushed through the crowd around DuQuelle and Katie. 'Excuse me sir,' he said politely, 'but I know this girl. She is the niece of one of the kitchen maids – here for the day to enjoy the cricket match.'

DuQuelle looked peeved. 'Ah – young master O'Reilly yet again. Always on the spot with an explanation, I've noticed. Your young friend is certainly silent,' he added. 'I believe the Royal Family would like to thank her and her silence is beginning to border on the insolent.'

'She is a mute,' James replied, with more stubbornness and less politeness. 'It would be a great thing indeed to get a mute to speak.' One of Alice's sisters giggled at this.

Beneath DuQuelle's pallor, Katie could see a fury raging. For one moment she thought he would strike James with his cane; and then he regained control. 'Well, that does answer all of our questions, doesn't it?' he replied softly. 'It would be best, perhaps, if now I took her…'

Alice had managed to break free of Leopold and was at Katie's side. 'I am returning to the Palace with Prince Leopold,' she said. 'I will take this girl with me and make certain she is returned to the kitchens.' Alice did not look at Katie. She stared at DuQuelle, her usually mild grave eyes turning steel grey with determination. Even the brazen DuQuelle had to look down.

Alice's glance flickered briefly towards James. 'Your spin delivery is excellent, but its direction is quite predictable,' she commented. 'If the household is going to make any kind of show in this match I suggest you produce a few good top spinners, or even a flipper – if you are capable of bowling such a tricky ball.'

James could do nothing but bow deeply. Bertie was roaring with laughter, the princesses were giggling into their handkerchiefs and the cadets were heckling James without mercy. Alice had managed to divert everyone's attention away from Katie. 'Come along now, this way, girl,' she fairly barked. DuQuelle could do nothing but let go of Katie and watch her disappear – out of his grasp yet again.

The little procession wended its way across the lawn; Alice stalking regally over the grass, followed by Prince Leopold, his chair pushed by a perspiring Reverend Duckworth. Last (and least she thought) came Katie, frog-marched between two footmen – her coarse clothing in great contrast to their silk stockings and brightly buckled shoes. 'A miniature Queen parading with her miniature court,' thought Katie. It would have been funny, if Alice hadn't carried it off with such dignity. 'There must be something to DNA after all,' Katie reflected. 'Alice's blood is truly blue.' As they went down the field the various onlookers involuntarily bent their heads or bobbed a curtsy. Alice had that effect on people – when she wanted to – and right now she was in need of her dignity.

Once they were in the Palace, the Reverend Duckworth tried to take control, but Alice was determined to stay in command. 'Leopold looks exhausted. I suggest we return him to his rooms immediately,' she ordered. At Leopold's feeble protest she adopted a gentler voice. 'We can see the cricket pitch from your window,' she coaxed. 'And I'll tell you what's happening while they tidy you up and make you more comfortable.' Turning to the footmen, Alice added, 'I will take the girl below stairs to her aunt myself.'

The footmen didn't dare say a word, but Leopold had no such qualms. 'Why would you become involved with a servant girl?' he asked peevishly. 'She looks like a rag-bag, and I'm not certain she's washed. Even being near her I might catch something dreadful.'

'Do hush up, Leopold!' Alice interrupted. 'She might not be able to speak, but this girl can certainly hear. How dim, how insensitive can you be? That cricket ball was heading directly for you. You would probably be bleeding to death this very moment if it weren't for this "rag-bag" as you call her. I am going to thank the girl's aunt and give her some form of reward for her good deed. Invalid or no invalid, sometimes Leopold you are a spoilt and selfish child.'

Leopold began to cry and Alice softened. 'There, there,' she said, smoothing his dark hair from his pale forehead. 'You're tired and this has made you cross. Now let the Reverend Duckworth settle you and we'll see who wins the cricket match.'

'It's always the cadets,' said Leopold – but he stopped crying and let the Reverend Duckworth push him into his cool, darkened room.

'You are dismissed,' Alice told the footmen. As they hesitated, she continued with a smile. 'The cricket match is at an exciting moment. I'm certain you do not want to miss it.' With this, they bowed quickly and beat a hasty retreat. As they disappeared around the corner Katie saw all the royalty melt from Alice. In its place was a small tired girl.

Katie understood. She could feel the energy leaking from her own body. Her wrist ached from the difficult catch she'd made, and her head was swimming. 'That was a narrow escape,' she said, as she and Alice slipped into the secret passage and headed towards the schoolroom. 'I'm all jitters now, and tired, and starving… Things just seem to get worse and worse.'

'What you need is a short nap. Lie down on the chaise longue behind the screen in the schoolroom. I need to check on Leopold, and then I'll nip down to the kitchen …'

'You think a nap solves everything,' Katie complained. But as she eased herself on to the sofa, the world did seem a better place. She could hear Alice next door, talking to Leopold. Her voice drifted further and further away.

Chapter Twelve

What's To Be Done?

Alice sat on a footstool by Katie's feet, absently nibbling a sticky bun. 'I've been thinking about today,' Alice said. 'I was so stupid; I almost exposed you. Why did I ever believe I could come up with a plan all by myself? That's for more intelligent people like you, or James or Vicky. I should stick to sitting quietly with my hands folded in my lap from now on.'

'You always put yourself down,' Katie said. 'The plan wasn't that bad – and, as you said yourself, Leopold might be dead right now if I hadn't been there. Can I have some of whatever you're eating?'

Alice passed her the rest of the sticky bun. 'Where did you learn to catch a ball like that?'

'It's called baseball. The game I told you about before. The one that girls play as well as boys.'

'Well, boy or girl, I'm not certain even James could have caught that ball,' Alice said admiringly. 'Though you did look about as ladylike as a chimpanzee when you leaped for it – and landing on the Reverend Duckworth! I don't know how I kept my countenance.'

They both laughed. 'To yell "Crystal Palace" was not your best idea,' Katie conceded, 'but the rest of your plan was really good. And though James is sure to hog all the credit for "sav-ing me" you were the one who came up with my escape route. If it weren't for you I'd be with DuQuelle right now.' Alice shuddered.

'I can't even begin to think about that – would he really hurt you?'

'He'd kill her,' James said, coming around the corner. 'If he decides Katie is the wrong child in time, he will kill her. We must never forget that.' James was trying to look stern, but kept breaking out in a grin.

Alice clapped her hands. 'You won!' she exclaimed. 'The household won the cricket match!'

'Yes,' said James. 'The cadets were decidedly unnerved when one of their own team-mates almost killed a member of the Royal Family. They fell like rabbits after that. And once we came to bat, they couldn't bowl to save their lives.'

'How did your brother take the loss?' Alice asked. James's grin doubled in size.

'Jack? He had to take it. He laughed and clapped me on the back. But Jack's a gentleman through and through. He told me he'd leave the bats to me and stick to his horses from now on. You should see him on horseback – the finest equestrian of his class. The military academy is grooming him for the cavalry. He's hoping for the 17th Lancers – the Light Brigade.'

The Light Brigade. Katie didn't like the sound of that. Was the Light Brigade a bad thing? Somehow she thought so. Was it a war? Or a song? Or a scandal? Again, she just didn't know enough. All those books under her bed, and she still didn't know enough. 'Damn,' she said to herself.

Alice shot her a look of disapproval. 'If Bertie can't get away with that, neither can you. Please do watch your language, Katie.' But Alice could never be harsh for long. 'Of course you are a bit anxious. I put you in such jeopardy today. I am sorry. And Jamie, you will wonder at my half-baked plan...'

'It is not my place to question the actions of a princess,' James replied stiffly. 'Nor is it necessary for a princess to apologize to me. And besides, Katie is quite capable of getting into trouble without your help.'

Katie butted in. 'Admit it, James, I was a star today, and so were you. The mute story was great – saved the day – but it has put you on a collision course with DuQuelle. He might seem like a total bozo, but he's powerful and danger-ous; I wish you would stay out of his way. Do be careful,

James.' James turned bright red, and Katie realized he thought she was flirting with him. 'Alice says you could never have caught that ball,' she added, desperate to change the tone of the conversation.

'Of course I could have caught that ball – and not in a poky straw bonnet either. As for DuQuelle, we're all in his sights.'

'I know my last plan rather backfired,' Alice said, 'but I've been thinking, we don't have our priorities right. There are an awful lot of people we need to avoid right now: MacKenzie and the Black Tide, DuQuelle and his strange visitors… We need to understand what's going on – to resolve the mysteries – but doing so puts us all in danger. We can only really tackle one thing at a time, and the most important is to get Katie home. The future of the world might depend on that.'

Katie and James protested vigorously. This wasn't the answer. First and foremost they must foil the Black Tide. Look at the kidnap attempt they argued, and the 'accident' at the Crystal Palace. But Alice could be stubborn when she chose. 'My family can and must take care of themselves,' she maintained. 'Being Royal is not just about privilege. We all know that, even a girl like me. And if fate has a shock in store for my family, we must face it with fortitude. I cannot continue to endanger the two of you.' She took Katie's hand. 'My affection for you is great,' she said and, turning to James, added, 'and I have grown to admire you. It is my duty as a princess to protect my people – and there have never been two people I wanted to protect more.'

Katie began to object again, but James's training as a loyal subject kicked in. Moved by the princess's words, he bowed his head. 'Yes,' he said. 'I understand. We will object no further.'

'Katie will have to stay in the nursery,' said Alice, 'guarded by one of us at all times. We will arrange regular outings and experiment at night with ways to send her home.'

'There's no way to send me home,' Katie protested. 'Our one and only idea was the "magic sofa" and that was a total flop.'

James looked annoyed. The 'magic sofa' had been his idea. 'You claim to be a great reader, but you never think of books,' he countered. 'I suggest extensive reading and research. There are rules that regulate everything. We will find those rules.'

'I could be a lot more help to you if you'd let me talk about the future. I do take physics at school, you know, and that's all about time and space and…'

Alice, as usual, made peace between the two of them. 'You can both help,' she said. 'My father's excellent library is stocked with scientific and philosophical works. Jamie – I'll pass them on to you and Katie – I can slip them under the bed. At least you'll have something to do all day while you're hiding.' Alice hugged her friend. 'I'm so sorry,' she said. 'I don't want to part with you – ever – but your welfare must be foremost.'

'I thought you were done making plans,' Katie grumbled. But she hugged Alice back. 'Don't worry, Alice, I've spent most of my life under a bed, reading a book. This isn't going to be, like, that hard.'

'Katie, we'd both like you to stay,' James added awkwardly. 'You're unreasonable and obstinate, but no one can say you are not interesting to have around. Alice is right, though, you're in the wrong time and it has become dangerous for you. Don't worry about us. We'll solve our own problems, all by ourselves, without help from another time; but first we have to send you home.'

Home. Katie had never understood that word. Her home had often appeared in magazines: 'Modern & Marvellous: Madcap Mimi's Manhattan Bolt Hole' or 'Mimi's New York Apartment: It Rocks'. The best interior designers in Europe had created it as a showcase for Mimi's celebrity, but it wasn't much of a home. It was depressing to think about the slick chrome and white interior. And then there was the water feature. Nothing was more irritating than a tinkling fountain in a tranquillity pool. 'Look on the bright side,' Katie said to herself, 'James has called me interesting. INTERESTING!' She thought of herself as a fairly average person and knew Mimi found her downright boring. Yet here was this boy, someone who didn't suffer fools gladly, and he found her interesting. 'Thanks, Jamie,' was all she said.

'Don't call me Jamie.'

'But Alice calls you Jamie.'

James wanted to push her over. Why could girls never leave well enough alone? 'Alice is the daughter of the Queen. She can call me whatever she wishes. Unless you can prove your own royal standing, which from the looks of you would be impossible, I suggest you stick with James.' His fleeting moment of affection for Katie seemed to be over.

Leopold began to call from the next room. 'Alice, who are you talking to, you promised to keep me amused. I'm so hot and bored.'

'Poor chap,' said James.

'I must go to him,' said Alice, 'but we'll meet again tonight and map out a plan of action.' Tonight, they all agreed, and went their separate ways.

Chapter Thirteen

To Open Time

The bright day had clouded over. Moon and stars made no impression on the thick, close clouds. Katie's curly black hair formed a net of frizz about her head, while damp tendrils circled Alice's neck. 'Even when it's dry here,' Katie thought, 'it's wet.' Things were as Katie had feared. Sending her home was proving near impossible.

The first stop was the corridor where Alice had found Katie, but the furniture had been moved yet again, and six nearly identical chinoiserie sofas now flanked the long hall. 'They really liked matching things when my great uncle commissioned these,' Alice explained sheepishly. 'I suppose they look nice in a very large room…' Sportingly Katie climbed under each sofa, and attempted to push herself through time. How had she got here in the first place? She remembered being tired, and then it was as if she were flying through time. Flying or falling. She tried to imagine home, but for some reason New York and the twenty-first century seemed very far away. She couldn't even see her home inside her own head, much less travel to it through time.

The next night they were back in the nursery and back to square one. 'There must be some kind of key that will open time for us,' James thought aloud. 'There must be something that will connect Katie to her own time. Was there anything else under your bed, Katie, that might have travelled with you?'

'What about the book I was reading right before I arrived here – the letters from Alice and her sisters? When I was reading, I could see Alice, and then suddenly, I was here. But the book's back in New York.'

'No, I believe it's here,' Alice exclaimed. 'There was a book under the sofa. I took it with us on the first day and hid it in the schoolroom.' Alice fished it out of a chest filled with her old dolls. 'Do you think it's safe to read it?' she asked. 'I believe it contains letters I haven't written yet, letters from the future.'

'I'll look first,' Katie decided. 'Since I'm the only one the future cannot harm.' But when she flipped through the pages, half the book was blank.

'This must be it,' said James excitedly. 'The book is the key to the future. Look where it stops.' It was a letter from Alice.

Dearest Vicky,

I have prayed for the recovery of Frederick William's nephew, young Felix, so your last letter was received with much joy. We are all thankful that young boy's life has been spared. It is wonderful news that you are returning for the household cricket match. We are to have the prettiest matching dresses and ribbons for the outing. The colours chosen are most perfect for your complexion – though I look a bit green in them. The Baroness Lehzen has punished me over my neglect of my lessons, but I suppose she is used to a more apt pupil in you. I do try though…

'I wrote that letter six days ago,' Alice gasped. 'But why does it stop there?'

'I can't figure it out,' Katie added. 'Here's young Felix, alive and well, when I swear he died in the letter I first read.'

'Died!' Alice recoiled.

'I think this letter shows that there is some form of active energy working between the centuries,' James said. He'd been reading prodigiously – they all had. Michael Faraday, James Clerk Maxwell, T. H. Huxley, Herbert Spencer – anything they could get their hands on that discussed science, time and progress. 'If the book is still writing, the opening between times must still be active. We have to find the opening and move Katie through it.'

Katie could feel the gears in her mind, turning slowly, trying to figure things out. 'When did Vicky leave Buckingham Palace?' she asked Alice.

'The day after the cricket match she left for the Isle of Wight.'

'Would she have received this letter yet?'

'Oh yes, definitely. And I've had a reply.'

'Have you written again?'

'Yes, two days ago,' Alice answered. 'But she won't have received that letter yet. Where are your thoughts going, Katie?'

Katie frowned with concentration. 'I don't really know. I'm trying to figure it out. Somehow the letters don't exist until your sister's read them – and then 150 years later they appear in a book. But this letter isn't right. Look at the part about young Felix: I remember this letter. It's like I keep saying. In the book I read young Felix dies. I'm sorry, Alice, but he dies of scarlet fever. Yet here he is, recovered and well.'

Alice look worried, and James looked grim. 'The sooner you are out of here, Katie, the less change there will be. So rather than chatter away and distress everyone, I suggest we return to those sofas, and you try reading that book under each and every one – and concentrate!'

Back in the corridor, Katie crawled meekly under the first sofa. 'I'm so sorry, Alice,' she said. 'It must be so creepy – me coming from the future.'

Alice got down on her hands and knees and watched Katie open the book. 'Perhaps,' she said, 'the reason we can't make you leave is because we don't want you to go.'

'James is desperate for me to go.'

'Jamie O'Reilly doesn't know what he wants,' Alice replied. 'He finds you quick and funny. In addition you are able to catch a cricket ball at 300 paces. But you are an attractive girl – that is the part that so confuses Jamie.'

'You don't confuse him – and I'm not attractive, I have a huge nose.'

'I'm a Princess, otherwise he'd be just as rude to me. Royalty has its perks. And you do not have a huge nose, you have what's termed a Roman nose, and it's a sign of good breeding. Now let's try again. Read the last ten pages leading up to the current letters.'

'You lead an exciting life, but you write really boring letters,' Katie said.

Alice pinched her. 'What's that expression you use? Is it slam up?'

'Shut up.'

'Well, shut up then.'

Day after day Katie, James and Alice absorbed everything they could read on space and time. Alice used her access to the extensive royal library to keep them provided with reading materials. Cramped under Alice's bed, even Katie began to tire of books. What she really wanted was TV – a silly comedy show with pre-recorded laughter. A gameshow where people jumped up and down and won lots of money. Instead she was cooped up with John Stuart Mill's *A System of Logic*.

James, on the other hand, was in seventh heaven. Every book, pamphlet and tract available on the modern sciences was at his disposal. At almost any hour of the day he could be found in the linen cupboard across from the nursery, shirking his apprenticeship to his father and scanning academic journals until the words blurred on the page.

'Your eyes will give out if you keep reading at this pace,' Katie warned him.

'Nonsense,' said James. 'There's an interesting treatise on electric velocity that Professor Thondike Verber-Brun read at the Royal Academy of Sciences. Do you think Prince Albert has a copy in his library?'

Katie shook her head. 'Sometimes James, you are such a geek.' James looked confused.

While the three spent most of the day reading, the night was reserved for carrying out their experiments. Alice was certain the answer lay in phrenology. 'The shape of one's skull tells a great deal about one's character,' she explained. 'By studying the individual's skull shape – all the different curves and indentations – we can learn what kind of person they are. Papa is a great believer. Last year he had a specialist come to the Palace to examine Bertie. The specialist consulted his charts and using Bertie as his specimen was able to diagnose his learning and behavioural difficulties. See – the specialist left a chart behind for us to use. The skull has been divided into forty-three separate areas. This little bit here, above the right eye, represents willpower. Bertie's skull has a slight indent there, his willpower is low. But if you look at Katie's head, you'll see that her skull protrudes in the same area.'

James smirked. 'So your chart shows us that Katie has great willpower; in other words, she's impossible and bossy. I don't think we needed a chart to show us that.'

Alice ignored James. Boys. They always wanted to pick a fight. 'The ability to time travel must lie within Katie herself,' she continued. 'We need to stimulate her brain so that she can remember how to do it. If we simply massaged the cranium this could activate…' So for two nights running Alice kneaded Katie's temples, pushed forcefully on the back of her head and even tapped it with a small hammer.

James enjoyed the spectacle, but did finally protest. 'It would be a wonderful thing if you knocked some sense into Katie, but frankly, I don't think the key lies in the lumps and bumps on her head.'

'Quite a few new lumps and bumps since we started,' Katie said ruefully, rubbing her head. 'Boy, do I have a headache.'

They tried James's pet theory next. He was absolutely certain the solution lay in electromagnetic theory. 'It's called mesmerism,' he explained to Alice and Katie. 'The universe is filled with an electromagnetic fluid that can move through space and time. If only we could hook Katie up to this fluid, she could travel with it.'

'And how are you going to hook me up to this fluid thing?' Katie asked sceptically.

'Through a process called animal magnetism. We put you in a type of trance and get control of your mind. Through auto-suggestion we can move you forward in time.'

'I wouldn't get your hopes up, James,' Katie said.

'There have been great successes with mesmerism,' James argued. 'Legs have been amputated with no pain, the deaf can hear again.'

Katie knew perfectly well that mesmerism was as big a hoax as phrenology. 'We might as well pull out Mimi's New Age crystals and perform a vision quest ceremony,' she thought. But she'd promised not to reveal anything from her own time, so she donned midnight blue silk robes and listened to James chant and chant and chant at her.

'You don't have enough sensitivity to connect to the universe,' he accused her.

'Maybe you don't have enough animal magnetism,' she countered. The experiment was a failure.

They tried to run her through time – literally – but Katie

was so out of shape from her life under the bed that she passed out in the rose garden at two in the morning and had to be carried back inside. Another idea James read in a book was to starve her to bare bones, put her in a long box, filled with ice, and slide her under the sofa. 'If we lessen the importance of the actual flesh and blood,' James conjectured, 'Katie's soul will be able to travel more easily.'

Both Alice and Katie shook their heads vehemently. 'Sending me into hypothermic shock is your worst idea yet,' Katie said.

Alice agreed. 'It would be too dangerous.'

James thought for a moment. 'You're right. If we killed Katie it might cause a great deal of damage. If she is the child who brings peace, removing her from the world might lead to its destruction. I do like my shock idea, though. I've been reading about electric shock treatments and…'

Katie sighed. James's enthusiasm for science was turning to obsession – and a painful one as far as Katie was concerned. To him Katie had stopped being a person and had become a human test tube; his very own walking, talk-ing experiment.

After two weeks of bumps, jolts and shocks Katie threw in the towel, and they all had to admit defeat. One night, as they sat eating jam and biscuits from MacKenzie's secret larder, Katie spoke up. 'There is, of course, one person who can probably get me home: DuQuelle.'

Alice looked at James. 'We know,' she said. 'We've talked it over and decided it is too much of a risk. He might send you back, or he might kill you.'

'Maybe we should take that gamble,' Katie said.

James shook his head. 'You underestimate the duplicity of DuQuelle. You've seen him at work. You know what lurks beneath the smiles and the exaggerated courtesy. And we don't even think he's human now. Steer clear of DuQuelle. We'll find another way.'

A noise from the hallway ended the discussion. James blew out the candle. Their night-time movements were becoming restricted – as other activity increased through-out the Palace. MacKenzie's London shop had become a success and, because of greed, he'd patched things up with his business partners. More and more provisions were being moved out of the Palace and on to the shelves of Belzen & Mackie. They noted with increasing anxiety that the Black Tide were in the Palace two to three nights a week. Katie was beginning to notice a pattern. They'd come in, take the goods for the shop and give MacKenzie several bottles of fine wine. Once he'd settled into a blurred stupor, they'd roam the Palace. MacKenzie had showed them hidden passages to reach the stolen goods. Now they used these passages for more sinister purposes.

Sacks of papers, plans and blueprints were leaving the Palace with them. This was worrying Katie, but she had promised Alice to stay put, stay safe. She lay awake at night and listened to skittering and creaking in the walls around her, until one night she simply couldn't take it any more. 'They've spread everywhere,' she thought. 'Like a cancer in the Palace. And by protecting me, Alice is endangering others. I have to find out what they are up to.'

Slipping out from under the bed, she tiptoed into the schoolroom and ducked into the secret passage. The stone was cold beneath her feet, the walls damp around her. Following the noises, she wondered, 'What will I do when I find them?' She turned the corner; there – directly in front of her – was a dark figure, hunched in the passage. She had the answer to her question. She panicked and, turning tail, fled back towards the schoolroom. Footsteps pounded behind her, the figure was too close. She darted down a side passage, heading for a ladder and an escape to the outdoors, but the dark figure gained on her; a hand grabbed her nightdress, her shoulder, and pushed her against the wall. She squeezed her eyes shut, thinking, 'If they'd try to kill a baby like Riordan, they won't hesitate to murder me.' She forced herself to open her eyes, to look directly at – James O'Reilly.

'Blast you, girl,' James hissed, 'what are you doing here? You promised the Princess.'

'I know,' Katie gasped, 'but I can't lie under a bed while those cloaked devils invade the Palace. Something very bad is going to happen. I've got to stop it.'

'Well, you needn't worry,' James snapped. 'Every night

after we're done trying to transport you out of here I've been following them.'

'Why didn't you say something?'

James shook his head. 'It's not good news – and I didn't want to further alarm the Princess until I had a plan of action. I've been eavesdropping and they've confirmed everything we've ever thought. They are a violent and fanatical branch of the Black Tide. They want to change everything, let the people rule themselves. To do this, they need to wipe the slate clean. They attempted to kidnap Princess Alice and were hoping to kill Prince Albert at the Crystal Palace. They won't stop until they've succeeded in murdering one of their targets.'

'What about MacKenzie?' Katie asked. 'He can't possibly be their ringleader?'

James laughed. 'MacKenzie has never recovered from his encounter with Mr Belzen. He's so drunk these days he couldn't lead himself out of his own rooms and into the courtyard. No, they've used MacKenzie – terrified him and played on his greed and gluttony. Even now he's closed his eyes to their true ambitions and given them the keys to secret rooms and knowledge of secret passages. When they ply him with drink he tells them everything they need to know about the comings and goings of the Royal Family. There are two of them in the Palace right now. They've been searching methodically, room by room. And tonight they've reached fever-pitch. Something big is going to happen, and I'm missing it, standing in the cold, babysitting you.'

Katie was astonished. This was a lot to take in, but she wouldn't stand around in the cold being babysat by James either. 'Well then, let's go,' she said. 'And no buts – I'm sorry to break my promise to Alice, but you need a brain with some historical perspective working on this.' A few weeks earlier Katie would have been undermined by James's tirade. But fear and friendship had changed her. She simply smiled at James's annoyance. 'I think the noise is coming from Prince Albert's private study,' she added. 'Don't just stand there looking annoyed, come on!'

Chapter Fourteen

The Queen Must Die

The door of the secret passage opened into a deep alcove containing a stuffed owl in a glass dome. Peering over the owl they could see two men masked and cloaked. They were moving through the Prince's study quietly and rapidly. They were looking for something. 'Yes,' said one, taking a red box from amongst the Prince's private papers. Katie recognized the dark hair and glinting eyes, peering fiercely through the mask. He deftly undid the red tape surrounding the box and peered inside. 'We have it. If the Prince did not walk in the night we could have got in here sooner – hey?'

Tucking the red box under his cloak, he swung around,

bumping into the replica of the Crystal Palace, back on display in the Prince's study. 'You are a folly, a silly building,' he said, addressing the miniature structure. 'But you are going to be more important than even the Prince might think!'

Turning to his comrade, he added, 'Thank God for the clockwork mentality of the Prince. The project is running on time. The completion of the Crystal Palace will mean the completion of our plan. We shall shatter the Royal Family as one… might… break… glass.' With each word he cocked his finger and thumb in the shape of a pistol and took aim at the Crystal Palace. 'The Queen must die,' he said softly. 'And with her will die the inequality of mankind.'

'The Queen must die.' Suddenly a vision flashed before Katie, one that she had seen before. The small woman in a pink satin dress, silver lace and diamonds. Her laughing happy face turning to shock and pain as blood spread across the bodice of her gown. But of course, Katie now understood. The final vision she'd had in New York – it was the Queen. Katie's teeth began to chatter. 'James,' she whispered.

'Shhhh,' he hissed furiously. But Katie knew, he was frightened too. A sound in the hall made them both jump further back into the alcove.

The cloaked men were startled as well. 'Damn the Prince,' their leader exclaimed. 'Does he not sleep? He will be back in here in the moment to check once more on the state of the nation. Well, come on,' he exclaimed to his cohort. 'Our entrance ticket should be within these papers.' And bowing mockingly towards the Crystal Palace, he stepped into the large fireplace. The marble along its side slipped inwards with a scrape and the men pushed through the narrow opening and were gone.

James and Katie stood very still, while their minds raced ahead. Trying to subdue the panic rising within her, Katie made an effort to speak lightly. James hadn't wanted to take her along, and being a hysterical girl would only prove him right. 'Now that was a cool exit – and a whole new passage we know nothing about,' she said. Her night vision wasn't that good, but she knew James was shooting her a killer look. His breathing was jagged.

'Alice slides *The Times* under your bed every day. What is the date today?' he finally asked in a strangled voice.

'Well, it's long past midnight, but yesterday's paper was dated April 16th.'

'And what day does Alice say the Crystal Palace will open?'

'The Queen is due to open the Great Exhibition to the nation on the first of May,' Katie told him.

James thought hard for a moment, and then turned to Katie. 'Don't you see what all this means? We only have two weeks to put a stop to this. The first of May. That is the day they will strike. The Crystal Palace – that is the location of the attack. And the object of the attack is…' James could barely bring himself to say it. 'The object of the attack is… the Queen.'

'We can stop them, James. We have all this information now, so we can.'

James interrupted her. 'We still don't know enough. We know why, and when, and where, and who. But we don't know how – how do they plan to kill the Queen? And without that we cannot stop them.' James gave Katie a little shake. 'Now, don't yelp at me. I know we all agreed it was too dangerous for you to tell us the future – but Katie, do you know what happens in the Crystal Palace? Could you possibly know that the Queen will be killed and you haven't told us?'

Katie didn't yelp. She stopped to think. The next words she said could change the shape of history. 'I know things both sad and terrible,' she finally said. 'But I haven't kept the murder of the Queen of England from you. In my history books the Queen lives on to reign all the way into another century. And I might have been brought to this time precisely to make sure that is what happens. But we know now that the future can change. Look at young Felix. He died when I first read those letters but now he lives. And James, I know something even worse. One of those visions I started having in my own time… it was a vision of Queen Victoria… Queen Victoria, being shot. I might return to my own time and find the entire British Royal Family was assassinated by the Black Tide in the name of equality. I can't foretell the future, because time itself has become too slippery.'

James had to agree. 'We'll have to postpone all attempts to send you back for now,' he added. 'We've only two weeks to figure out what the Black Tide's plan is, and how to stop it. We will need at least some of your knowledge of the future – you're the only one who has that.'

'Except DuQuelle,' Katie said, 'he—'

Just then the door to the study was pushed open. They had a new night visitor, Prince Albert. He was dressed in a nightshirt, cap and slippers. Tying his robe more firmly about him, he went to his desk and unwound the tape from several red boxes. Finding a specific batch of papers, he reread them carefully. 'Ah, yes,' he muttered to himself. 'Here is the letter from the Duke of Wellington. But will his answer to the question suffice? A military man is not necessarily a naturalist, and his ideas, though firm, often lack subtle detail. I will have to cross-check against my own ornithological works…' Moving across the room he clambered up the library steps to a top shelf and began to rummage through some large leather-bound books.

The door opened again – and this time it was the Queen, night-gowned and robed, her hair in curl papers. Katie remembered the advice Mimi had once given her when she was in a school play: 'If you're frightened to go onstage, imagine everyone in the audience in their pyjamas, that will make you laugh.' Well, here was Victoria

Regina – Queen of England, Scotland and Wales – in her nightie. And she was the one who was laughing.

She ran across the room and, coming to her husband on the top rung of the ladder, gave his foot a playful tap. 'When I came looking for you *liebchen*, I didn't expect to be looking up your nightshirt.'

Prince Albert came down the ladder and said something in German. While Katie didn't speak the language, she had a good idea from the way he tugged his wife's curl papers and kissed her round cheek of what he was saying. Katie stepped further back into the alcove. Next to her, James was stiff with embarrassment. Prince Albert was talking baby talk with the Queen of England and James O'Reilly was about to fall down dead from the mortification of witnessing it. Though Katie had been exposed to many a worse scene during Mimi's romantic escapades, she still felt fairly awkward. A horrible thought occurred to her: 'They wouldn't, I mean, they wouldn't…'

Finally, after a great deal of cooing, the Queen began to talk some sense. 'I woke up and you were gone, and here you are working. You give so much to this country; couldn't you reserve three in the morning for me?'

'You are right, of course, *mein liebling*, but I could not sleep. There was yet one more problem, if I could just tease out the solution.'

'Is it the Foreign Office? Is it Palmerston?'

'No, for once the man is not a problem.'

'Is it DuQuelle – such an unsuitable member of the Royal Household, far too exotic.'

The Prince smiled and shook his head. 'It is not DuQuelle. He has great knowledge and capabilities in so many fields, if only he weren't always there, at one's elbow, praising one to the skies.'

The Queen laughed and Albert continued. 'The problem is with the Great Exhibition, the Crystal Palace.'

'But everything is going so well,' the Queen protested. 'The design is magnificent, the building is on schedule, materials and exhibits from all over the world are arriving – even now, at this hour of the night.'

The Prince sat down in one of the large, overstuffed armchairs, and took his little queen in his lap. 'The problem is the elm trees,' he explained. 'Having built around them, we now discover the Crystal Palace is filled with sparrows, seeking refuge in their branches.'

The Queen threw her head back and laughed: a loud hearty laugh for such a small woman. 'Sparrows! Whatever will we do?'

The Prince was laughing too. 'I know it sounds silly,' he admitted, 'but they could be most distressing. Think of the, well, the mess they will make, the havoc they will wreak on the ladies' bonnets. They will have to be captured or killed. The Duke of Wellington has suggested we can achieve this by the use of sparrow hawks.'

The Queen was now shaking with laughter, tears running down her face. 'So we shall release hawks to catch the sparrows and then cats to catch the hawks and then dogs to catch the cats…'

The Prince gave her a little shake. 'That is not helpful, *mein Schatz*. If you will just let me get on with my work, I believe I have several very helpful studies on the habits of predatory birds…'

The Queen wiped her eyes and tried to look more serious. 'I will help. Two pairs of eyes will take half the time. We will be back in our warm bed within the hour.' The Prince began to protest, but she kissed him lightly on the lips and took a large volume from him. Soon they were sitting side by side at their matching desks, exchanging comments on what they read. 'To shoot the sparrows would be too dangerous with all the glass… and poison with the crowds of people, no, that would never do… but how to *control* the hawks once they had killed the sparrows…'

James and Katie could do nothing but stand in the dark and watch this tableau of marital happiness and political dedication. The snatches of conversation grew less frequent, and then stopped. Queen Victoria's eyes fluttered shut, her head drooped and soon she was asleep; her head resting on a coloured plate of a large bird devouring a water rat. Prince Albert tidied their desks and, picking up his small, plump, sleeping wife, he carried her from the room. 'We need to tell Alice,' was James's only comment.

*

'The Queen,' said Alice in a stunned voice. 'Not my mother, not the Queen.' Katie and James had dashed back to the nursery. News this big would not wait for sleep. Katie now wished she'd let her have a few more moments of peaceful slumber. Alice slumped in misery at the foot of her bed. Trying to rouse herself, she explained to her friends: 'If it was me, or even Leopold, the country would go on – of course there would be great alarm and mourning and tributes paid in Parliament, but the damage would be limited. To attempt to…' – she could hardly say it – 'to kill the Queen would shake this country to its roots. No wonder this Belzen has chosen the Black Tide as his earthly envoys. For what they seek might mean the end of the monarchy for ever, and universal upheaval would ensue.'

James tried to reassure her. 'We know so much now, Alice. There are just a few more pieces of information we need. And then we can put a stop to it.'

'Maybe you should go to the household guard with this,' Katie suggested.

Alice shook her head. 'They'd go immediately to Mr MacKenzie, and he'll deny the whole thing – think what's at stake for him.'

'Shall we try your father again?'

'I will try to see him – but he's so busy with the final preparations for the Crystal Palace. And we've seen that a note isn't to be trusted.'

Katie chewed the end of one of her nails. They were

over their heads; if ever they needed an adult, this was the time. But as usual, the adults were failing them.

'I think you should tell your father,' Katie insisted. 'See him alone, face to face. If anything happened to the Queen, and he could have stopped it, he would never forgive himself. You should have seen them together, Alice.'

'I wish, I wish, I wish I hadn't seen that,' James O'Reilly moaned. The tension in the room broke and Katie and Alice laughed.

'I've never seen anyone more embarrassed than James,' Katie explained. 'Goodness but he's a coy young man. You'd think he'd never seen a normal loving family before.' The moment she said it she could have bitten her own tongue. James's father hadn't been much of a husband. When his wife died in childbirth, leaving behind a brood of four, Dr O'Reilly took it as a personal betrayal. He paid almost no attention to the children.

James was looking at the floor, a face like a thundercloud. Katie tried to dig herself out. 'It's not as if *I've* ever seen a normal loving family either. At least not in my own house,' she said. 'Mimi is an absolute goddess of love. She falls head over heels, over and over and over again. It makes her feel young – and being young is the most important thing in the world to her. Me? I just make her feel old. So she either pretends we're friends, equals, the same age, or tries to forget about me completely. I mean, I miss her, but I'm pretty sure she doesn't miss me. I think one of the reasons I can't get home is that I have so little to go home to.'

Alice patted her friend's hand. 'There is no such thing as a completely happy family,' she said. 'Even ours, with Papa's perfection and Mama's great love – all the feeling she has for him… it seems to stop *with* him… it doesn't continue on to us… to the children… well, not to me at least. And then of course, the duties of a queen and wife do not leave much time for other concerns.'

Alice shook her head as if to clear her thoughts. 'How silly of me. It is wrong to say such things. Mama became the Queen when she was just eighteen. They came to her in the dead of night, to tell her. She went down the stairs in her nightdress, and they kissed her hand and proclaimed her Queen. "I will be good," she said. And she has. She has been good. As to her marriage, most royal marriages are cold and heartless, designed for the status of the country, not the happiness of the individual. We are so lucky that the Queen and my father are truly in love. And to have a ruler of such greatness… it is unworthy of me to question dear Mama.'

Katie had noticed that Alice tried always to refer to her parents by their formal titles, but being human, she often forgot.

James kicked the side of Katie's chair. 'This is rubbish. The Princess is right. I've never heard such a silly conversation. We've got a crisis of national importance on our hands and you, Katie, start whittering on about "my mama doesn't love me".'

Katie didn't snap back. She knew she'd hit a sensitive nerve with James. 'You're right,' she said. 'In my own time, all three of us would be sent to a shrink – a doctor who listens to you talk and tries to make you understand yourself.'

'A shrink,' James snorted, 'I don't need to get any smaller. I've got a better idea; let's stop talking about ourselves and try and understand the Black Tide's plot to kill the Queen. Katie, sometimes your way of doing things in the future seems very stupid to me.'

Katie opened her mouth to fight back, just a bit, but Alice interrupted. 'The first thing we need to know is what was in the papers the Black Tide took from the Prince's study.'

They were all silent. Katie tried to replay in her head the conversation she'd heard at three in the morning. 'They said the papers were their admission ticket, admission to the Crystal Palace, I suppose.'

'The papers probably have to do with the grand opening on the first of May,' James added. 'That's the day of the Queen's visit.'

'I still don't believe it,' Alice said. 'They wouldn't try to kill the Queen at the official opening. Not with the entire aristocracy, the dignitaries, the Church and the ambassadors present. And all the world's newspapers will be reporting on it. Why would they attempt this in such a public manner?'

'But that's exactly why,' Katie explained. 'They're terrorists, at least that's what we call them, and they're an even bigger part of my modern life than of yours. They want to commit the crime in the most public way, so that the largest number of people will see what they've done. If the great and the good – as well as the press – are at the opening of the Crystal Palace, this will make the strike as powerful as possible. It's a kind of sick publicity stunt, so that everyone will focus on what the Black Tide wants. And, as Alice says, so much of Britain's stability is based on the Queen, this could change the course of the world. We'll need to find out exactly what was inside that box. And time is running out.'

For the next two weeks most of the footwork was carried out by James. DuQuelle and the Black Tide had put Katie and Alice in far too much danger to move about the Palace. The night movements of the Black Tide came to an abrupt stop too. 'They must have found what they wanted,' Katie said. 'If only we could find it too.'

Alice put down her needlework. 'I've tried to see my father half a dozen times,' she said. 'I've even gone uninvited to his private rooms. But he's so busy with the last-minute preparations for the exhibition and he's never alone. Bernardo DuQuelle sticks to him like glue, except for the times he's trailing me through the Palace, asking awkward questions about you, Katie. He's bowing and smiling as usual, but I can't help thinking he's more and more anxious.'

James came in looking particularly grim. 'For a long time I didn't believe this whole thing,' he said. 'I challenged Katie's story, demanded proof. Well, now I have that proof, and I wish to God I didn't.'

'What's happened, Jamie?' Alice asked.

'They found Fräulein Bauer's body.' A chill crept through the room.

'How bad was it?' Katie asked.

James couldn't speak for a few minutes. He glanced at Alice, who seemed to read his mind. 'You'd best tell us everything,' she said quietly. 'I can take it.'

'They pulled her out of the Thames early this morning. Father was sent to identify the body. He says it's the most horrific mutilation he's ever seen of a corpse. And not just bloated from the river. Poor Fräulein Bauer…' James looked at the floor and cleared his throat several times before he could continue. 'Her eyes had been gouged out and her tongue ripped from her mouth. Strange red welts covered her whole body, like burns, or suction marks. And the worst thing is… when they opened her up… all her internal organs were missing. She was filled with a poison-ous tar-like fluid. The original doctors examining the body have been taken to hospital themselves.'

Alice had become very pale and Katie felt like she might vomit again. 'Your father told you all of this?' Alice asked.

'He's usually a more discreet courtier,' James said in the bitter ironic voice he reserved for his father, 'but he's seven sheets to the wind tonight. He came back to the Palace and bathed himself in gin, then drank a bottle for good measure.'

'It will make a sensation in the papers,' Alice commented shakily.

'You won't read a thing about it,' James replied. 'They've sent Bernardo DuQuelle to Scotland Yard – supposedly to help with the investigation, but really to hush things up. He's an authority on ancient diseases, with an outstanding knowledge of the medications of the Hebrews. He also knows anyone who counts in England, and exactly what skeletons they have in their closets. He'll call in quite a few favours on this one.'

'I think Alice needs a glass of water,' Katie said, 'and I could use some of your father's gin. Sadly, there's nothing we can do for Fräulein Bauer – but we can still help the Queen. Let's just try to keep the body count down, and figure out what's going on with the Crystal Palace.'

In the end it was Baroness Lehzen who gave them the information they needed, and only just in time. It was the very eve of the opening of the Crystal Palace. Alice tossed in her bed, while Katie fretted underneath it. Suddenly a battalion of servants descended on the nursery, Lehzen at their head. The room was bright with candles and Alice was pulled roughly from her blankets. 'Curls,' the Baroness Lehzen shrieked. 'The Prince Albert suddenly remembers "Oh Baroness, Please make certain all the princesses haf the curls, and the flowers in their hair with the curls. It will look so picturesque at the opening."' Yanking Alice's hair out of its braids she muttered under her breath, 'He is impossible that man, the silliest man, and my dearest Victoria, to be besotted with *such* a man…'

Curling tongs were heated in the fire and damp linen cut into strips to wrap around Alice's hair. In the meantime, a lady's maid had been instructed to give Alice's hair '100 strokes, vigorous strokes' from the scalp down.

'But my hair doesn't curl. It's so fine, the tongs will surely singe it,' Alice managed to protest, as her head was jerked back and forth.

'He said CURLS and I will gif him CURLS,' Lehzen snarled through clenched teeth and barked at two shivering maids: 'Run down the hall, wake up the others and start the curls with them. I will attend shortly.'

'As if I didn't have enough to do,' the Baroness Lehzen continued. 'The Queen's new dress is not ready, and I must sew the silver lace on myself, and dress her hair… and, on top of that, the Prince Albert has managed to lose his personal copy of the list of dignitaries. Several of the Ambassadors have changed these last months. And the

Queen has never even seen their faces. How can my precious Victoria greet her Ambassadors from around the world when she does not know who they are? I can see it,' Lehzen barked, 'the Ambassador from Lithorgia steps forward. He is announced "The honourable Mr Smith"? Or perhaps Mr Jones? Or maybe Prince Schlag of Creampuff? This is what the English would call the joke. Ha. Ha. Ha. But too distressing for the precious Victoria.'

Katie could smell burning hair and Alice began to complain in earnest.

'You are the most vexing of child,' the Baroness said, pinching Alice's cheek very hard. 'I must go to have my hundreds of things now. Come! Come!' she cried, clapping her hands together and the parade of servants vanished as quickly as they had come.

With a flash Katie was out from under the bed. 'It's the guest list, the Ambassadors,' she cried. 'That's what the Black Tide took from the Prince's study, that's what they wanted so much.'

'Yes,' Alice said, chewing on a burnt ringlet, 'but why?' Katie sat down on the floor to think.

'The Black Tide said the project is running on time… the Crystal Palace will be more important than anyone realizes… their entrance ticket was within those papers. That's it,' she cried, looking up into Alice's puzzled face. 'It's the missing list of dignitaries – that's their entrance ticket. Didn't you hear Lehzen talking? Some of the

Ambassadors are new. The Queen won't recognize them – no one will. The Black Tide are going to substitute one of their men for one of the unknown Ambassadors – and that's how they will get close to the Queen, close enough to kill her.'

Alice looked like she was about to cry. 'Do you remember when I pulled you out from under the sofa? I thought it was so funny, an adventure. I didn't really believe you were going to kill my mother. And now here is true evil, the real thing.' She pulled herself together, shaking her head until her damp and singed hair flew about her. 'We have only hours now to save the Queen. We must find Jamie O'Reilly immediately. The assassins have a plan of great cunning, and now we need a damned good one ourselves.'

'Damned?' said Katie, startled at her friend's language.

'Damned right.'

An hour later Katie, Alice and James sat on the nursery floor. Beside them was the blueprint of the Crystal Palace, showing the positions of all the invited guests and a timetable of events. James had filched them from Prince Albert's files. Everyone was too busy at this point to notice they were gone.

'We will be here,' Alice said, consulting the floor plan and schedule. 'It says that "the Royal Family will arrive promptly at 12.00 p.m. and progress down the central transept to a raised dais directly in front of the largest of the elm trees.

The Queen and Prince Albert will be seated under a canopy, the children behind them. Senior dignitaries will be below the Royal Family to the left, and Ambassadors will be standing behind the Bishops, to the right." The Ambassadors need quite a bit of space, since many of them are travelling with large delegations from their own countries.'

'The canopy might help,' James said. 'It will stop them from getting any kind of aim from above. But then the balconies above aren't the problem. They'll be filled with the season ticket holders. The building will be packed, but only the few chosen groups will be near the Queen. The Black Tide, should their plan succeed, will be with the Ambassadors.'

'The Ambassadors are standing really far back, though,' Katie reasoned. 'A pistol wouldn't have enough firepower from there to hit the target. They'd need a rifle, and that would be just too hard to get into the building – and really obvious when taking aim. There would be too much of a chance that someone would notice, and stop them.'

Alice was turning pale and her grey eyes were anxious.

Katie patted her friend on the shoulder. 'It feels awful to talk like this in front of you,' she said. 'It sounds so cold and brutal.'

'It's necessary.' Alice managed a thin smile.

James looked over Alice's shoulder at the timetable of events. 'You missed something,' he said. Taking the sheet of paper from Alice he read: "'12.20 to 1. The presentation of *the Ambassadors. Each Ambassador shall be announced. The named Ambassador will hence proceed up the transept to the foot of the dais, bow to Her Majesty, and salute the Royal Family."* They'll be within feet of the Queen then. That's when they'll try.'

Katie could still see the fierce-eyed assassin before her in the Prince's private study, cocking his finger and thumb like a gun, and saying in a deadly whisper, 'The Queen must die'. For a moment none of them could speak.

'Where will the Royal Household be positioned?' James finally asked.

'Here,' Alice pointed. 'Most of the Royal Household will be stationed behind the senior dignitaries. But Dr O'Reilly and the Reverend Duckworth will be directly to the left of the dais, in case there is a problem with Prince Leopold.'

'Your father might be very busy tomorrow,' Katie added. 'It's going to be a hot day, and that will cause a lot of problems in the glass structure. There will be more than one case of heatstroke.'

'I'll point that out to my father and get him to take me along to help. That will position me here, directly to the left of the platform. Is there anyone in front of the Bishops?'

Alice consulted the blueprint. 'Just a small political grouping,' she said. 'The Prime Minister, the Duke of Wellington, a few of the most senior figures from the Royal Household.'

The three of them looked at each other, thinking the same thing, 'DuQuelle'.

'Well, I'll just have to chance it,' Katie said. 'If James is on one side of the platform and I'm on the other, we can disarm the assassin as he's ready to strike.'

'You're not going to be anywhere near DuQuelle,' James told her firmly.

Alice added, 'He's right, Katie, we'll have to leave this to Jamie. The moment DuQuelle sees you, your future will be sealed.'

'Unless we can find a way that he *can't* see me,' Katie said. She looked at the blueprint again. 'I never was any good at reading a map. Now what's that cluster of red dots next to the Prime Minister again? They're really close up.'

'We told you,' James said impatiently. 'Those are the Bishops, and you will…'

'I will be a Bishop,' Katie interrupted.

'Katie!' Alice protested. 'You cannot dress up as a bishop. It's… it's heretical.'

'Alice,' Katie smiled. 'It's not, like, the church would think much of a girl in skimpy clothes who not only plays cricket like a boy but travels through time. Borrowing one of their kinky red dresses can't make it any worse. Besides, with the pointy hat and long red robe, DuQuelle won't recognize me.'

James was not much of a church-goer himself. She'd won him over. 'The Bishop of London's extra vestments are kept in the Chapel Royal,' he said. 'He's an exceptionally small man, almost the size of a girl.'

'Good,' Katie said. 'I'm an exceptionally large girl, or at least you guys think so. They'll probably be a perfect fit. James can nick them tonight. I could also use a fake beard.'

Alice sighed. 'If you are going to insist on this godless behaviour, we might as well make it work. Lehzen has an entire dressing room of wigs. You didn't think that abundance of black hair was real? She's as bald as a coot. I'll borrow one when we're done here, we can powder it grey.'

This brief bit of fun over, they were again weighed down by the task before them. 'It's not exactly Alice's "damned good plan",' Katie admitted. 'All James and I can do is try to find the assassin and then jump him.'

'What about me?' Alice asked. 'You two are risking your lives to stop the gunman, while I'm "on stage" with my giggling sisters and my burnt frizzy curls.'

'From the dais you'll have a better view than any of us,' James said. 'If you see anything, wave your arms, get our attention.'

'And Alice,' Katie added, 'if we fail, if it's too late, duck. Take cover. Please. Save yourself.'

Chapter Fifteen

God Save the Queen

May 1st dawned, a day for splendour. The Queen rode in an open carriage from Buckingham Palace, her pink satin dress laden with silver lace and hundreds of diamonds. Across her breast was the Garter ribbon, and her hair was caught up in a tiara and white feathers. She had never been so proud. Dearest Albert would be immortalized through the Crystal Palace. He had been its guiding light from conception to completion; and not only her own dear country, but the whole wide world would bow down to acknowledge his superiority.

As she left the Palace gates, a thousand bells peeled through the air. It seemed that all of London, half the country, and a good part of the world had come to witness the opening of the Crystal Palace. Among the people she could pick out the occasional turban and fez that signified a visitor from afar. The crowds were so dense; they looked like a street themselves – a jostling, cheering street paved with heads. 'They are everywhere around us,' the Queen murmured.

'Above us too,' replied Prince Albert, pointing upwards. The trees were filled with little boys trying to get a bird's eye view. They swung from the branches, cheering themselves hoarse, their skinned knees and grimy little feet just over the Queen's head.

'God save our Queen! Long live our Vic!' they roared. The Queen smiled and nodded and waved her tiny hands, twinkling with rings. These filthy urchins were as important to her as the grandest Duke in the realm.

A disturbance at their carriage wheels drew the royal couple's attention. Squealing and protesting, two women were pushed against the rails lining the street by an angry mob. The source of the crowd's fury was the women's attire. They were dressed in the most immodest fashion. Their tiny skirts ended above the knees while long pantaloons stretched to their feet. They were followers of the American feminist, Mrs Bloomer, and the British masses were in no mood for progressive women. 'So you want your own rights, do you?' one wag roared. 'Rights to vote... rights to make an ass of yourself is more like it.'

'We are not amused,' was the Queen's only comment.

Averting her face, she spied a tableau more to her liking. It was the street performers Katie had seen near DuQuelle's home. The strongman jingled the tambourine in his enormous fist, and Signor Salamander tooted the trumpet, despite a throat made sore by dining on fire. The Countess Fidelia, rougher and wider than ever, held the Little Angel by the hand. They had come, with the rest of London, to partake of the great day. 'What a lovely girl,' the Queen cried, spying the Little Angel. 'Such beautiful black ringlets, such dark pools of eyes. She is most picturesque with her curls and rags.'

The Queen's pleasure did not seem to be shared by the Little Angel. She leaned forward, gesturing to the Queen, her voice rising, almost pleading with the monarch. But her voice was carried away by the shouts of the crowds. The Little Angel burst into tears and hid her face in her burly mother's skirts.

A shadow passed over the Queen's face. 'Wasn't it strange,' she said to the Prince. 'That little girl wanted to tell me something, so very desperately.'

Prince Albert smiled reassuringly. 'Do not worry, my dear. It's the excitement; it is too much for the youngest ones.

'Look over there, my dearest,' Prince Albert continued, pointing to a large group under a chestnut tree. Three hundred rural workers stood quietly, bowing their heads before their Queen. The men were in their smocks, the women in clean but rough calico.

'It will be the entire parish,' the Prince explained. 'Their village at home will be completely empty.'

'But the cost,' the Queen questioned. 'How can they afford to come?'

'There is a special rate for the poor. The trip will come to 2s 6d per person. We have thought of those in need of aid. The exhibit will be open solely to invalids on Saturdays until noon.'

The Queen's eyes filled with tears, and the Prince patted her plump hand covered in gems. 'Now *liebchen*, this is not the time to cry. Look, my dear, the whole world is on holiday, the whole world smiles!'

The Queen and Prince Albert waved and waved at the mobs of spectators. Hawkers moved among the crowds, selling ginger beer, fatty-cakes and hardbakes. From the open carriage, the Royal Family could smell as well as see and hear. The spices of the baking cakes mixed with the tang of peppermint water and a pungent undercurrent of something much less appetizing. Yes, the entire world had turned up for the celebration, and most of them hadn't bothered to wash. But what they lacked in cleanliness, they made up for in enthusiasm. The souvenir pedlars already had engravings of the Crystal Palace and bright tin medals with its replica. 'Lord protect our gracious Queen!' one shouted, throwing a shower of bright medals into the air as her carriage turned into Hyde Park, and another half a million people took up the cry. 'God save the Queen!' they shouted. 'God save Prince Albert, the Prince of Wales! And the little Princesses!'

Following their parents in a golden phaeton, the children were equally resplendent. The Princesses were in matching white lace with wild roses twined in the ringlets that had enraged the Baroness Lehzen so the night before. Leopold was wrapped in blankets, but smiling widely. He was finally strong enough to be out of his wheelchair and could walk through the Crystal Palace. Bertie was kitted out in a tartan kilt and velvet jacket. He hadn't been very happy about this, but word had come down from his father: 'wear the kilt, or miss the opening' – and this was a spot of fun not to be missed. As they passed through Hyde Park, Charles Spencer, the celebrated aeronaut, doffed his hat and bowed. He was standing next to the basket of his famous helium balloon, and was due to go up into the sky at the exact moment the Queen opened the Crystal Palace.

'Come back,' he shouted to Bertie. 'Come back for a ride later today!'

'I will,' Bertie bellowed and the crowd roared approval. But he knew he would never come back. Bertie's gruelling regime of study and good works did not include balloon rides.

Vicky had her own carriage, as befitted her new status as an engaged woman. Frederick William sat beside her, surrounded by his Prussian entourage. While Vicky smiled and waved gamely, the Prussians were shocked at the closeness and exuberance of the British public. In their own country, the people would be controlled in such a situation. The military would surround the royal carriages, the Emperor would be protected at all costs. Any Prussian peasant who dared address their monarch in the easy way of the English underclasses would receive a sharp blow with the butt of a musket. Young Felix was particularly scornful. 'These English,' he complained to his uncle Frederick William, 'they are like savages. They howl and bay at the Queen. How dare they? They should be whipped.' Vicky looked at the child with distaste. He had always been a sweet boy, affectionate and loving. But since his illness, he had changed. Despite the blond curls and blue eyes, he had become cruel and bitter. She shrank away from him.

'Perhaps we should have left Felix at home,' she whispered to her fiancé. 'He has been so ill, after all…'

'*Nein*,' Felix interrupted. 'I must be here. My part in this is important. I must see it through to the end.'

How could the child have heard her through the noise? Vicky wondered.

Inside the Crystal Palace, James and Katie were already in place. At any other time, James would have rushed off to see the thousands of exhibitions and displays. The entire north side of the building was dedicated to inventions and machinery. There was a printing press that could produce 5,000 newspapers in one hour, a locomotive engine that laid down its own tracks, an apparatus for supplying rooms with pure warm air. He longed to see the sheet of paper 2,500 feet long, and the phosphor matches that could light themselves. There was even a medicine made from the livers of cod – a new miracle drug – and they were giving out samples. But today was not the day for machinery, medicine and invention. The Queen's very life was at stake, and James was one of only three people who could save her. He looked across the room. Just behind the Duke of Wellington he could see a short, slight bishop, Katie. 'Let's hope she can catch an assassin the way she can catch a ball,' he muttered to himself.

It was very hot – especially in a long red robe, cone-shaped hat and a fake powdered beard. Katie was dripping with sweat and the powder from her beard made her sneeze. She tried to keep her distance from the other bishops. They were staring at her. Still, she thought, I've got a good view of the proceedings and if I don't want this historical event to take on a more sinister significance, I've got to keep my eyes peeled. Outside she could hear the excited crowds – a humming and buzzing swirling around the building as if it were a giant glass beehive. The cheers moved closer and the 30,000 privileged people assembled under the glass roof shifted in anticipation. The trumpets sounded and the great bronze gates were thrown open. The Queen had arrived.

To the little sovereign, nothing had ever looked more

splendid. It was an *Arabian Nights'* structure, full of light, so graceful and yet so grand. The millions of panes of glass reflected on the sparkling fountains, the chandeliers, the opulent coloured banners and tapestries. A kind of coloured rainbowy air appeared to pervade the whole building and give it a solemn sense of majesty. The arched glass transept was over 100 feet high, yet it looked like it could float away. In the centre of the transept was a raised dais directly in front of the largest of the elm trees. The Queen progressed towards it, past the marble statues, past the cut crystal fountains, past the enormous elms, hand in hand with Prince Albert. The 600 choir boys, the 200 musicians and the fifty-foot organ burst into song as she went by.

As the Queen stepped on to the dais, Katie could see that Alice was trying to stay as close as possible to her mother. Everyone else was swivelling around, gawping with wonder; Alice was concentrating on the small regal figure in pink satin and silver lace. James was stationed next to his father at the foot of the stairs, and Katie stood on tiptoe to see past the Duke of Wellington's old crooked back. The ceremony began: an endless and tedious prayer from the Archbishop of Canterbury, followed by the Hallelujah chorus and the National Anthem. 'God save our gracious Queen,' 30,000 voices sang. Princess Alice, James and Katie sang with their hearts in their mouths. It really was up to God.

And then came the salutation of the nations and colonies. As they were called in alphabetical order, each Ambassador came slowly down the great transept to bow to the Queen. Abkhazia, Abyssinia, Anguilla… The European delegates were dressed in full court regalia, their long white embroidered silk waistcoats covered in ribbons and medals. Others had come in the splendour of their national costume. The Japanese delegates in full kimono, the maharajas in silk turbans and diamonds. The Americans had included a native Indian in their retinue, complete with ceremonial paint and feathers.

The glass ceiling was sealed and in the heat of midday, the Crystal Palace was becoming very warm indeed. Next to Katie, the Bishop of Rochester was beginning to wheeze. He was *not* a thin man, nor a young one. He swayed, stumbled and then fell to the ground with a resounding crash. Dr O'Reilly was there in a flash, carrying him into an anteroom. Towards the back of the hall, one of the Swiss delegation also fell victim to heatstroke, and then one of the Queen's own ladies-in-waiting. James tried to stand his ground, to guard the Queen, but his father dragged him away by the arm. People were dropping like flies – he needed help – this was not the time for James to stand around taking in the sights.

The delegates continued to move forward: 'Azerbaijan, Bhutan, Bolivia, Braunschweig.' Katie scanned their ranks. In their elaborate costumes it was nearly impossible to get a good look at them. Would she be able to recognize the killer? She could see James across the room, helping an elderly woman towards an open window. He had his hands full and Alice was out of reach. It would be up to Katie.

Suddenly a silk-robed Indian pushed through the ranks of dignitaries. 'I will come now,' he said, 'when I choose. What I am giving the Queen cannot wait.' Katie sprinted forward, knocking over the Bishop of Durham in her wake. She'd almost reached the Indian, when the Duke of Wellington caught hold of her.

'I say,' he cried in the very loud voice of a very deaf man. 'Pushing and shoving at a royal ceremony? This is not appropriate, Bishop.'

Katie found herself tangled in his sword.

The Indian proceeded directly up the steps of the dais. Katie could see Alice, struggling to reach her mother. With a sudden dramatic gesture, the Indian unfurled his magnificent turban and, taking something from it, pointed directly at the Queen. 'This is what you deserve,' he said.

It wasn't a pistol in his hand. It was a diamond. 'The Koh-i-noor,' the Duke of Wellington roared. 'The largest diamond in the world. Well, I'll be damned. Who would have thought the Maharaja of Punjab had it in him. Splendid chap! Capital fellow, eh Bishop!' He slapped Katie on the shoulder and shook her by the hand. Smiling weakly, she slunk back to her place.

The Queen was clapping and dimpling. There was nothing she liked more than a big, bright gem. Alice looked as if she might faint. The roll call of dignitaries continued. 'The Sultan of Burkina Faso, the Governor of the Cape Colony…' and on came the delegates. The false alarm had left Katie feeling both foolish and frightened.

'He must be here,' she muttered. 'It has to happen, but when?' Her eyes moved frantically, scanning the crowds. And still they came forwards, 'Sir Edmund Walker Head, Governor General of Canada, Hee Sing, the Ambassador of Imperial China…' A man moved up the aisle, his black and scarlet cap, blue tunic and gold chains making a fanciful tableau. Katie looked again – he was surprisingly tall – and then she knew – this was no Chinaman. It was the eyes that gave him away: fierce, black ignited eyes, the eyes of a fanatic, a killer. Before the assembled crowd stood the anarchist, the assassin, the leader of the Black Tide – stepping forward, to kill the Queen.

Katie made a spring towards him, but suddenly her head jerked back, her feet were in the air. She was lying on the ground, staring up at Bernardo DuQuelle, who, with one shining black shoe, had pinned down the hem of her robe.

'Tisk, tisk,' he said, smiling. 'This is unusually aggressive behaviour from a bishop. Even a bishop from the twenty-first century has better manners than that. And now – you are coming with me. Excellent costume, my dear.'

Katie scrambled to her feet. 'No – no – help!' she gasped. 'The Queen… the Black Tide… the Assassin… the Chinaman… look… please… help!'

DuQuelle's smile was gone in an instant. Taking Katie by the arm, he ran through the startled Ambassadors and towards the dais. The leader of the Black Tide had prostrated himself on the floor in a long ceremonious bow. Getting to his feet, he reached into the long sleeves of his silk gown, searching for something in the folds.

'We're too late,' Katie thought, and DuQuelle looked frantic. But then she saw Alice break forward, to stand directly in front of her mother's silver throne. 'Mama, it's too beautiful,' she cried. The Queen tried to smile, but looked nettled by this break from protocol.

'Thank you, Alice dear,' she said. 'Now please return to your position, the ceremony has yet to finish.'

A furious Baroness Lehzen was moving forward to take Alice away, but Alice climbed into her mother's lap and put her arms around her neck. The Queen's smile froze as she tried to unclasp the child, but the assembled dignitaries were laughing quietly and murmuring their approval. What could be more appealing than a child's natural fondness for her mother?

Prince Albert bent down to his wife.

'Let her stay, *liebchen*,' he said. 'Yes, she is over-excited and it is inappropriate. But to move her would interrupt the beautifully planned ceremony.' The Queen did not look happy, but she did as Albert said.

'What is Alice doing?' Katie puzzled anxiously.

'She is being very brave,' DuQuelle answered. 'She is

using herself as a human shield. If he shoots now, she will literally stop the bullet with her own body.'

Katie looked from the Queen to the assassin. It was his move next. Alice's appearance had unsettled him. The Black Tide's glittering prize, the target – the Queen – had been within his grasp, and now this girl was in the way. In a split second he made his decision, he'd have to make do with the target on offer. His hand found the cold metal hidden under his robes.

'I don't think so,' came a voice next to him. 'I too have a pistol, and you can feel it against your back. Now, bow nicely to the Queen and withdraw.' The Queen looked annoyed. First Alice's unforgivable behaviour, and now what was DuQuelle doing with the Chinese Ambassador? She would have to talk to Albert about that man.

After a flicker of hesitation, the assassin obeyed Du-Quelle and, bowing yet again, walked backwards into the crowd of dignitaries. DuQuelle led him through the Great Transept. With one arm he had the assassin, with the other he held Katie. 'Two at once,' DuQuelle murmured. 'That is an excellent catch.' They passed the assembled guests and DuQuelle lifted a velvet curtain, ushering them both into the small waiting room.

Katie exhaled deeply. 'I think I'll be going now,' she thought. But it wasn't DuQuelle that stopped her. The assassin whipped around and struck DuQuelle a blow to the stomach. Grabbing Katie, he made a dash for the door.

She could just see DuQuelle, doubled over in pain and surprise, before she was dragged into the labyrinth of the Crystal Palace.

A French bureau, a Greek urn, a threshing machine and a stuffed elephant. They all whizzed by as Katie was hurled through the empty corridors. Everyone else was in the Great Transept. She struggled against him, shoving the assassin with her elbows and trying to kick his ankles. 'Do you want me to shoot you here and now?' he spat, aiming a vicious blow at her head. She ducked, but it caught her just under the jaw. The pain was so great it broke through her fright. She cried out, only to receive another blow to the head. 'One more sound and I will kill you,' he shouted in fury. 'We need to find some quiet place, and then you will have to start talking. I want explanations.'

The sculpture hall was far from the ceremony. The hundreds of statues were still covered in their long trailing dustsheets, waiting for the grand unveiling. The assassin pushed Katie behind a particularly vast drapery and pulled off her hat and beard. 'I haven't got to the bottom of this,' he panted, 'but I know you are involved. Pivotal.' He twisted her arms behind her back and held his gun to her head. 'And what do I see – a mere girl? Are the great of England to use the little girls to do their dirty work? But yes, in a society so unequal, to sacrifice the poor girl would be nothing. At least we are *men* doing the *men's* jobs.'

'It's true, what you say. She is nothing to us,' DuQuelle's

voice echoed through the empty hall. 'She is just a little girl – as you said – a little girl who dressed up in disguise hoping to see the Queen. Go ahead, kill her.'

Had she always known it would come to this? She had hoped DuQuelle might help her, send her home. But now he was sending her to her death. She thought about Alice, about James. But mostly she thought about Mimi. She was glad her mother would never know what had happened.

Katie heard the click of the gun as the assassin cocked the barrel. A second sound made her look up; just in time to see a large sparrowhawk swoop overhead and catch a tiny bird in its beak. 'So Prince Albert went for the sparrowhawks,' she thought, feeling strangely detached from her own death. 'It's the last thing I will ever see, another predator with another victim.' And then the shot rang out. She braced herself for the tearing of her flesh, the fall, but instead she saw a look of frozen surprise, almost irritation cross the assassin's face. He clutched Katie tight, as in an embrace, then fell to the floor.

'Well, he looked up too,' DuQuelle explained, almost apologetically, pocketing his freshly fired pistol. 'Thank God for the elm trees, and the sparrows and the sparrowhawks. I will drink a toast to the Duke of Wellington tonight. Sparrowhawks, what a capital idea it was.'

The anarchist was still alive, though only just – with a mortal wound to his chest. He was lying on his side, a warm dark pool of blood forming around him on the wooden flooring. 'The anger is gone,' Katie thought. His face had a look of intense concentration as he tried to fight off pain and death. DuQuelle took his ebony walking stick and pushed the man on to his back. A bubble of blood formed in his open mouth as he tried to speak.

'There's nothing to say now,' DuQuelle murmured in a low soothing voice, 'you've failed, the plot has failed. And now you are leaving us – goodness, but I *do* have an idea of where you will be going.'

The assassin was losing his fight for life – the look in his eyes was changing into the fear of a small child. He whimpered.

'There, there,' said DuQuelle, again in that eerie soothing voice. 'I will tell you something to ease your way. You are right. What you wanted was right.' DuQuelle laughed gently. 'You looked surprised to hear that from me. Well, there are many things about me that would surprise you. But in the very last moments of *your* life, it would be supremely rude to talk about *mine*. And it is a particularly uncomfortable way to die; drowning in one's own blood. So I will be brief. Why shouldn't all people be equal? Why should some live in squalor and ignorance, while others wallow in the soft folds of opulence? Why should we subjugate entire nations to our imperial will? What right have spoilt monarchs to dictate the lives of millions?

'You are right,' he continued, 'but you will fail; because violence will never succeed. Killing breeds more killing, and each generation hates more than the last. It is never the means to equality. Instead of liberating us all, you will bring a war that destroys the world.'

The anarchist's eyes glazed over and the bubble of blood burst in his mouth.

'The life and the lesson are over,' DuQuelle mused, 'but has anything been learned?' Picking up the end of the dust-sheet, he peered up at the statue underneath – 'Ah, the admirable Albert on a rearing steed – heroic, indeed – though perhaps a bit overblown? But it will do as a hiding place for our dead friend. The Black Tide, for now, is at low ebb.'

And taking the end of the trailing dustcloth, he pulled it over the dead man. 'I wonder if the other sculptures are as horrid as this,' he added. 'Though I hear the French have quite a racy Bacchus in their display.' Even as the light banter continued, Katie winced as DuQuelle gripped her arm like a pincer. 'You are coming with me, Katie Berger-Jones-Burg,' he said. 'We have much to discuss. And I've been waiting quite some time for this conversation.'

Chapter Sixteen

Half Moon Street

'F or once I'm inside a carriage,' Katie thought, as they bounded around the Serpentine and towards Piccadilly. She would have paid more attention but she'd been too frightened for too long and couldn't concentrate.

'Better than being rolled up in a blanket, choking on dust, I assume.'

Was it possible that DuQuelle could read her mind? If so, she was in an even weaker position than she'd thought. She looked over at DuQuelle, unnaturally still in his corner of the carriage. More like a wax effigy than a man, except for his glittering green eyes. 'I don't care how comfortable the carriage is. I'm not exactly happy about where it's going.'

'Thankless child. I've just saved your life,' DuQuelle laughed a mirthless laugh, while Katie moved as far as possible from the pale man before her. This wasn't really the time to laugh. Yes, he had just saved her life, but he'd also just killed a man.

'Why did you tell the anarchist that all peoples and nations should be equal? You don't believe that. You're employed by the Queen, and she's very big on empire. You know, she even becomes Empress of India…'

'Really?' said DuQuelle, 'fascinating. What a marvellous idea. When does this happen – sometime… in… the… future?' With each word he prodded Katie with his walking stick with a force that was more than playful. Katie winced and squeezed into the corner. 'To answer your questions – as I hope, my dear, you will answer mine – I do believe that the independence of nations is the best hope for peace. This is my personal belief. But my *job* – as you might call it – is to ingratiate myself with the Queen. And the Queen *likes* ruling things – such lovely new toys with which to play. Toys like India. Look how her eyes lit up when she saw the Koh-i-noor diamond? So prudent of the Maharaja of Punjab to hand it over. Though it wasn't his choice of course, the East India Company strong-armed him. I must have it reset in a crown for her. Perhaps you could tell me which design to choose?'

The carriage came to a stop and Katie recognized the dark timbered house on Half Moon Street. 'Now, come along,' he said. For a fragile-looking man his grip was unbreakable. 'As I said, we have so much to discuss. And so very little time.'

They went quickly down the carriage steps and into the townhouse. A wave of fright rolled over Katie as the door closed behind her.

'Do not disturb us,' DuQuelle said to the manservant in the hall. 'Oh, but what rude manners, I almost forgot – are you hungry, my dear?' Katie shook her head. 'Chocolates, ices, cakes? I believe these stay the favourites of the young throughout time.'

Katie was silent. She remembered what James had said: 'Anything you say can be a clue.' She could have kicked herself for talking about Queen Victoria becoming Empress of India. 'I must be careful,' she thought. She took courage from the fact that DuQuelle didn't seem to know she had been in his townhouse before. His ability to read her mind must be limited. She stood in the hallway – uncertain. It was best to let him make the first move.

'This way,' DuQuelle said, stepping aside for her to walk up the stairs. Was this a trick to see if she knew the way? She paused at the top of the stairs, feigning confusion. He ushered her into his dark study at the top of the house and shut the door. It had been tidied since Lucia's whirlwind visit. 'Don't look so worried,' he said with a forced smile. 'I believe I can be of great help to you. My sole desire is to protect you. I will not harm you.'

'How well he lies,' Katie thought. ' His face is like a mask, so white and so lined – it's hard to read.' She feared her own face was telling the whole truth – fright, loneliness and total distrust. DuQuelle sighed as he looked down at her, a sad sight in her tattered bishop's robes. This might take him time – time neither of them had.

'Please sit down,' he said, gesturing to a sofa near the fire. Even on this warm day flames leaped in the grate. 'What a very dark horse the Princess Alice has turned out to be,' he added. 'With those wide grey eyes and silky tresses, she looks as passive a doll as the best of them. And yet *she* was the one who sized up the situation, seized the initiative – saved her mother's life in fact. She provided me with just the pause I needed. If the assassin hadn't hesitated, we would be in the middle of a most serious crisis. Prince Albert would have had quite a battle on his hands to continue to rule. And with a weakened England, any foreign power might have struck – Russia, France or even the newly emerging Prussia. And then the war might come, the one that destroys all. Bravo for the Princess Alice. She may be the saviour of the *Empire,* as you call it.'

Katie's eyes lit up at the praise of her friend, and she began to hope. But DuQuelle continued. 'Don't even think, though, that she is on her way here to save you. No, no – Princess Alice's heroics are over for the day. I suspect she is locked in the nursery; being punished by the Baroness Lehzen. And knowing the Baroness as I do,

Princess Alice is probably far less comfortable at the moment than you are.' Katie felt as if all the air had been let out of her body. To make things worse, DuQuelle added: 'That young James O'Reilly, such an irritant. There's no bend to that boy... stubborn... determined. Well, the fates were with me today, or at least the bright sunshine was. He was so busy with the victims of sunstroke that he hasn't a clue what's happened or where you've gone. And with Princess Alice under lock and key, he's not likely to find out.'

'Don't panic and keep your mouth shut,' Katie said to herself. She tried to think about anything other than the situation she was in, to count the beams in the ceiling, to recite the alphabet, but she couldn't help hearing DuQuelle's low drawling voice.

'I know you have come from another time,' he finally announced. 'I can quite possibly send you back home. Do you miss your family?'

'Do I?' Katie asked herself. 'Do I miss my family?' She thought of Mimi, so utterly selfish, so totally absorbing, leaving no space in the room for anyone else. And then there was Dolores, talking endlessly, grumbling over the slap-slap of the iron. And why didn't Katie have any close friends? Katie realized she'd kept the kids she'd grown up with at a distance, so they wouldn't know the truth – the truth that no one really wanted Katie. For Mimi she was a reminder of her own youth ebbing away. For her father, she was dollars disappearing into private schools, ballet, piano lessons. For Dolores, she was school uniforms to iron, sandwiches to make – yet another set of chores. Yes, Katie might miss her family; but she didn't believe her family missed her.

Perhaps the only people who had ever cared for Katie were Alice and James. For the first time in her life she had friends, real friends, and she could not let them down. She stiffened her resolve. She would have to beat DuQuelle at his own game. Suddenly it hit her. It was so simple and yet so complicated. Bernardo DuQuelle knew the three children had travelled through time, but he didn't know which of the three children Katie was: the child who brings peace, the child who brings war and peace or the child who brings the war that ends the world. If she could convince him that she was the child who brings peace, her life would be saved. 'What he'll do with me afterwards – I'll think about that later. But right now I have to think peace, breathe peace... look peaceful... like I'm supposed to act in yoga class... if only I could remember my mantra...'

Katie breathed in deeply several times and exhaled slowly through her nose. Unclasping her hands and relaxing her posture, she looked up to DuQuelle and smiled. 'Yes, I do miss my family, my lovely mother. She is tireless in her care of me and will be so distressed at my absence. And my dear father, so dedicated to our well-being. In my time children are completely safe. We often sleep with the doors and windows open to see the stars. And the skies are so clear, there are millions of stars!' Katie could see the interest quicken in DuQuelle's eyes, but he leaned back in his chair and feigned nonchalance.

'How very nice for you all,' he said. 'Tell me more about your time. It will help me to send you back there.'

Katie reached into the corners of her imagination, searching for that perfect world. 'The children are the centre of everything,' she began. 'The family, the community, the government – their first priority is to raise happy, healthy children. We have fewer things than you do, but we don't seem to want as much. We fix broken things. We share a lot. We want to protect the planet and everything that lives on it.' Was DuQuelle buying this? She didn't dare look at him, but stared at the tips of her pointy bishop shoes instead. This was a whopper of a lie, and she had to make it convincing. What were those things that politicians said when they were running for election – the things that always sounded so great, but then never happened? 'Better health and education,' she continued, 'safety, opportunity for all. These are the things we strive for. We believe in the future.'

DuQuelle pondered this utopia. 'And what happens in times of war?' he asked.

Katie knew this was the pivotal question, and she lied through her teeth. 'War? There is no war,' she said. DuQuelle smiled to himself, absorbed in this image of Katie's world. Gradually the smile faded, and his face hardened. His skin had become so white, it developed a greenish-blue tinge. The deep creases around his nose and mouth deepened into crevasses. Lucia and the Verus were losing patience, Mr Belzen could be here any moment, and this child was playing with him. He would not be manipulated.

'Aids,' he said. 'I can see you recognize this word. All right my dear, let's try some other words. Global warming, fanaticism, terrorism, famine, weapons of mass destruction, nuclear capability...' With each word he played his favourite new game, tapping Katie with his walking stick, slightly harder each time, until she winced with pain. 'I have been in contact with many worlds, Katie, but the one you talk of does not exist. You overstepped the mark by creating something too beautiful, too perfect. You come from one of the most greedy, selfish, brutal societies of all time. Harbinger of peace! You and your people are planting the seeds of destruction.'

'No!' Katie cried. 'No!' She knew she was pleading for her life. 'We are trying, honestly we are. We are trying to learn, trying to find a way to stop wars, to feed the world, to house and educate the poor, and cure the ill. We have prizes for peace and global groups with thousands of doctors who help the sick; educational projects that span the world. We are trying, trying to do the right thing. And yet...'

'And yet,' DuQuelle said, 'it isn't working, is it? What a

mess you've made of things. And it's not the type of mess that can be cleaned up easily. I'd make an educated guess that there are two or three hotspots in your world that are about to implode. And this type of explosion might be terminal for us all. If you want to save anyone, Katie, I suggest you start telling the truth.'

Katie tried to look completely bland, but even as she struggled, her mind was betraying her. DuQuelle sat down next to her on the sofa. Taking her chin between his hands, he turned her face towards him and looked directly into her eyes. His pupils were strangely black, surrounded by deep green, and drew her in. The tenseness left her body. She felt drugged, hypnotized. Images of her world, her real world swam before her – could he see them too?

She was in her own time, her own city. It was late at night in New York and an elderly woman was walking down an empty street. In her shopping bag she carried dinner, just enough for herself and her cat. She turned a corner, into darkness. Shadows leaped towards her. Hooded boys, a half dozen of them, jeering and cursing. They pushed the old woman to the ground and grabbed her handbag. They swung her shopping against the wall. 'Not my dinner!' she cried out, 'and the little kitty's dinner. You must give it back. We'll have nothing to eat.' Laughing, the boys kicked her hard, again and again, in the head, to make her shut up. She pleaded and cried and then was silent.

Katie wanted to turn away, but DuQuelle kept a firm

grip on her. His pupils widened, and grew even darker, sending her mind forward to the twenty-first century. And now she was in a foreign land, on a new continent. A tall black woman walked towards Katie, one weak footstep after the other, through a landscape blasted and desolate. It seemed a hopeless journey, but the reason the woman continued lay in her arms. It was a baby – a sick baby, a baby who had not eaten for many days. As the woman walked past, the dust circling her bare feet, Katie knew that her search for food and medicine would be of no use. The baby in the woman's arms was already dead.

In front of Katie's eyes swam an army of the damned: dictators and thugs, prisoners and orphans, the violent and the hopeless. Above them all loomed the image that had defined Katie's childhood: the enormous mushroom cloud that could bring death to millions of people across thousands of miles. The cloud that could destroy everything: not only across space, but across time. The nuclear cloud of Hiroshima. Tears streamed down Katie's face.

DuQuelle wiped the tears from her cheeks with his fingers. His hands were soft and very dry, like old velvet. They smelled of musk. His touch seemed to further sap her will. 'You do not like what you see?' he questioned gently.

'I do not like what I see,' Katie repeated dully. DuQuelle stroked her cheek with one hand and reached for a sofa cushion with the other. He addressed her quietly, almost as if having a philosophical debate. 'And yet, just by being alive, this is the future you will create,' he explained. 'Just by being here. Just by being alive. Is this really what you want for your friends, for your family? Now tell me, tell me the truth about your world. And once you've told me, you will not have to return. You can rest, let go – you can be free of it. You can be free of everything.'

Katie longed to tell him all: from the loneliness, the bland uncaring isolation of her own life to the far greater terror of hunger, disease and ignorance that surrounded her. She felt it would be a relief to be gone, not just from this time, but from all time – to relieve the world of a reminder of dreadful things to come. DuQuelle seemed to understand. He knelt in front of her and placed her head against his shoulder, the pillow against her back. 'All you have to do is tell me. And then we can say goodbye to it all. It is a terrible world, Katie, and I promise you will leave it.' He rocked her back and forth like a baby.

As Katie opened her mouth to speak there was a sharp rap on the door. She sat up and shook her head. The visions blurred and faded. The spell was broken. DuQuelle sprang back, his look of soft sympathy turning to fury. Wrenching open the door, he glared at his manservant. 'What… do… you… want?' he spat.

'I know, sir, you said, sir, not to disturb you, sir,' the servant sputtered. 'But… but… the Princess, the Prince… they are here – and they would not go. No sir, they would not take no for an answer.'

The door pushed open and there stood Princess Alice, followed closely by James O'Reilly and Prince Leopold leaning on the arm of the Reverend Duckworth. 'I do apologize for this intrusion,' the Reverend Duckworth bumbled, nearly faint with embarrassment. 'You see, the Princess and then the Prince – they…'

Alice waved him away, a pint-sized Queen Victoria. 'That will do, Duckworth. I take full responsibility for our actions. Now I suggest you step into the hall while I speak to DuQuelle.'

'Absolutely not,' the Reverend Duckworth protested. 'It is bad enough that three children have the impudence to intrude upon the privacy of an outstanding member of the Royal Household, but to think that you would then…'

'Duckworth, I suggest you reflect on the threats of the Prince Leopold,' Alice said with great dignity.

'Yes,' Leopold piped up, a look of satisfaction spreading over his face. 'Leave the room or I will throw myself out of the window and bleed to death. Truly I will.'

The Reverend Duckworth led Leopold to a sofa near the window. 'It is only to preserve your life that I yield to your request,' he muttered, bowing his way out of the room.

'More likely to save his own skin,' Leopold said, looking more pleased with himself every minute. 'Just think of the trouble he'd be in if I died on his watch.' Leopold took in the room. Staring at Katie and DuQuelle he added, 'Now which of you is the time traveller and which of you is the devil? Alice was in such a state, I couldn't half understand what was going on.'

Alice put her arms around her brother and kissed him on the top of his head. 'The important thing is that you believed me,' she said.

Katie began to come out of her trance. The starvation, the ignorance and the violence she had seen would never quite leave her. But they were fading into the background, and as they lessened, her desire to leave this world lessened with them. 'No,' she said, more to herself than anyone in the room, 'it is not the best of times. But I can't believe that my own world is beyond saving. To abandon my time would be just like destroying the world. And I cannot believe I am the child who does that. I need to go back, to live. I count. And I can make a difference. Whether there's anyone there who knows or cares, that doesn't matter. What matters is that I choose to do it.'

It was as if Katie had been filled with light and air. She turned to talk to her friends – only to find James O'Reilly attacking Bernardo DuQuelle. He had seized the ebony walking stick and was raining blows upon DuQuelle's head and shoulders. 'A girl!' James was screaming, 'you attacked a girl! She's thoughtful, clever, funny and a loyal friend. She fixes things, she mends people, she cares. She's not going to destroy anything. You stay away from her, you, you...'

Alice shrieked, Leopold tried to rise from the sofa, and

Katie darted forward to grab James's arm. Yes, she had things to do in her own time, but at this moment she was needed in the here-and-now.

Chapter Seventeen

The Verus and the Malum

'Tea?' said Alice, pouring from a large silver urn. 'Milk?' They were all seated in DuQuelle's study around a cloth-covered table laden with scones, sandwiches and cakes. 'This is the first normal meal I've had in ages,' Katie said, giving James a reassuring look. 'That is if you can call all this sugar, cream and caffeine normal. James, doesn't your father have any idea how terrible all of this stuff is for your health?'

Leopold's normally thin tight lips stretched wide to fit in a scone, covered with whipped cream and jam. 'Are you really one hundred years old?' he asked Katie.

'More like over one hundred and fifty, or kind of minus one hundred and fifty,' she replied. 'And that one there,' she added, jerking her head towards DuQuelle, 'he seems to be, like, beyond age.'

The situation was out of DuQuelle's hands. He'd accepted this as he tried to ward off the blows from his own walking stick. The silver top, with its engraved letters and symbols, certainly made it an effective weapon. He rubbed one of the many bumps rising all over his head. He'd have to work with these children. Once Katie had pulled her hot-headed friend off him, DuQuelle had suggested tea. Youth of this age had a constant need for nourishment. If he could keep their mouths and stomach's full, this would give him time to think.

Leopold was helping himself to a slice of fruit cake. Alice had never seen him eat so much. 'What about Duck-worth?' he asked DuQuelle. 'He might knock down the door and rush in any moment.'

'I've sent him to the downstairs drawing room. He's looking over a portfolio of drawings I am considering purchasing for the Queen's collection,' DuQuelle replied. 'I've concocted an explanation for your visit; told him we are planning a charade on the theme of the Crystal Palace as a surprise for the Queen and Prince Albert. That is why you rushed over here. You are young and excitable and couldn't wait to get started.'

DuQuelle turned to James and smiled ruefully, still rubbing his head. 'Have a piece of cake, or a glass of Madeira,' he offered. 'Here is your Katie, safe and sound.

Now tell the boy, Katie. Tell him I did not harm you.'

'It's the truth,' Katie said. 'DuQuelle *was* planning to kill me, but he didn't even hurt me, or at least not very much. But I really could have lived without these last few hours. When I was up here alone, and I saw him coming at me with the sofa cushion, I thought my time was up. How did you three get to me?'

'I was frantic,' Alice said. 'But you can imagine the trouble I was in. They bundled me into a carriage with Leopold for the ride home. I told him everything. Before we reached the Palace, we'd ambushed the Reverend Duckworth.'

'Yes,' said Prince Leopold excitedly. 'I told him if we didn't turn around and drive immediately to Half Moon Street, I would throw myself under the horses.'

'And you,' said DuQuelle, turning to James. 'How did you end up in the carriage?'

'My father was supposed to ride with Prince Leopold,' James said stiffly. 'At the last moment he was called away to a medical emergency. They put me in the carriage instead.'

Of everyone in the room, James was having the most trouble adjusting to the change of atmosphere. Instead of flight, disguise, mayhem and murder – tea and conversation were the mode of the day. He was more comfortable with the mayhem and murder.

'Young man,' DuQuelle said, giving him an unpleasant wink. 'I suggest you cheer up. No one has been hurt, yet. Now,' he added, looking at the young people before him.

'How would one turn the phrase? What is to be done about Katie? An ever-widening circle of people know her real identity – Princess Alice, James O'Reilly, Prince Leopold, myself – and the Reverend Duckworth must have some suspicions. This cannot be good.'

'It's good for me,' Katie said. 'It makes it harder for you to kill me.' They all laughed uneasily and then silence fell around the table. What *was* DuQuelle going to do about Katie?

'If you lay another finger on her,' James said.

'Oh, do stop,' interrupted DuQuelle. 'Youthful heroics can be so tiresome. No – I'm not going to lay even my pinkie finger on her.' He turned to Katie and bowed his head, as if saluting an equal. 'If we cannot eradicate you in this century, we must send you back to your own.'

'But how?' Alice asked. 'We've been trying and trying – reading every possible book on time and space.'

'We've put her under every sofa in Buckingham Palace,' added James. 'We think that books somehow have a lot to do with this. We've tried to use the book that originally sent Katie here.'

'I've read and reread that damned book until I know every word by heart,' Katie chimed in. 'Sometimes I've felt as if it were working – as if I was flying through time. But when I've opened my eyes, I'm still under the sofa, and still in the wrong century.'

DuQuelle walked over to a shelf and, reaching behind

several books, brought out *The Daughters of Victoria: Royal Correspondence, 1848–1860.* 'So you think this is the key to your travels,' he said, handing the book to Katie. 'Don't look so startled… just a quick search of the nursery… you are not the only clever ones here. You're right about the words. They are vital. And Katie probably has been travelling through time, but quite naturally ends up back in the same place. This is a nineteenth-century book and can only lead you back to the nineteenth century.' DuQuelle opened the book and sniffed delicately, withdrawing his long, curved nose with distaste. 'Ugh,' he exclaimed, waving his handkerchief in front of his face. 'I can smell interference all over this. Someone has tampered with the book. But I no longer believe it was meant for you, Katie.'

DuQuelle paced the room. 'What you really need, my dear, is something similar to this book, but from your own time, and in your own words. We must act quickly, before you influence this time any further. Your thwarting of the assassination attempt on the Queen could have disastrous consequences for the future – though somehow I think not. What I do know is that the newly departed assassin was not working alone. His accomplices are looking for Katie. If they find her first and kill her in our time…'

'They would have to kill me first,' James said.

'And me,' Alice added.

'Yes,' DuQuelle replied drily. 'I've noticed that the three of you are quite a loyal little band and I simply cannot afford to entangle the Princess Alice in this.' He looked at James O'Reilly. 'It's a pity film has yet to be invented,' he mused. 'You'd make a rugged, if slightly awkward, movie star.'

James turned to face DuQuelle. 'Why have you changed your mind about killing Katie? Unlike the Black Tide, you would be able to cover your tracks. She doesn't exist in this time. No one would question her disappearance. All this talk of "keeping Princess Alice out of it" is just a front. We're children. We don't count. No one would believe our story.'

'I would,' piped up Leopold, still glowing with his new-found role. 'I believed Alice right away.'

'Yes,' said Alice, 'you did. But then Leopold, you are exceptional.' Leopold never looked happier.

'We know there's more to this than Katie, that there are two other children who travel through time,' Alice told DuQuelle. She couldn't help smiling at DuQuelle's astonishment. 'Katie's even seen the other two. A boy and a girl. They've appeared to her over and over again, both in her own time, and our time. Of the three, I am certain Katie is the child who brings peace. It was silly of you to frighten her so much when you should be protecting her with all your might. And maybe the best thing is to keep her here, with us, to bring peace...'

For the first time ever, Katie saw DuQuelle's face relax, and soften, real colour appearing in his cheeks.

'He looks almost human,' she thought, as he bowed his head again, this time to the Princess Alice, and spoke slowly, as if finding new words.

'It is not in my make-up – friendship, love and devotion. I have passed too much time in this and many worlds. It has been burnt out of me. But I can recognize these qualities in others, and I salute them in you, Princess Alice. Your friendship for Katie is so true that you do not even consider the possibility that she might bring evil as well as good. Your love of your little brother gives you patience with his illness. For him, you are a greater tonic than any medicine they can administer. And your devotion to your mother, the Queen, is such that you have risked your life to save hers.' DuQuelle smiled, a true smile. 'What a pity,' he murmured, 'that you will not ever reign as Queen. You are more than fit to lead your country.'

DuQuelle turned to James O'Reilly with a very different tone. 'Why is it that good people are so often stubborn and difficult? Just because right is on your side, doesn't mean you can't loosen up and enjoy life a bit. The world is not as black and white as you think. But your loyalty is to be admired. I observe that *you* are not as certain about Miss Katie as the Princess Alice is – yet you will bend your formidable will to the Princess, just as you would bend your knee to the Queen… And yes, you are right to question Katie, as am I.'

DuQuelle looked at the tiny group gathered around the

tea table. 'So you know about the children of time, the Tempus?'

They all nodded, except Leopold. 'I don't,' he cried. 'Tell me.'

'Is there anything else you wish to share?' DuQuelle asked quietly. The little group was silent. Somehow it seemed insulting to voice their suspicions of him, to his face.

James finally spoke up. 'We know you are not human.'

DuQuelle laughed. It was a quite human laugh. 'You don't need to look so sheepish. I might not wish to be human. I might be something far superior. Any more marvellous revelations?'

'I've seen Lucia,' Katie said. 'And Mr Belzen,' she added in a low voice.

DuQuelle gave a soft whistle. 'Belzen!' he said. 'And you live to tell me? Katie Berger-Jones-Burg you grow in my estimation with every minute. Are you familiar with the Verus, and the Malum?'

They hesitated at this, but Leopold cried out again. 'You really should tell me, now that we all know how helpful I can be.'

Alice added gently, 'Leopold should know. He is one of us now. And there's so much we all don't understand. I think you should tell. It's only fair.'

DuQuelle sighed wearily. 'Fair,' he said. 'Yes, that would be your word, yet another of your quaint notions. But I will explain as a courtesy to the Princess. And I will start at the beginning. Lucia, Belzen and I; we were once part of a civilization, not unlike yours. More intelligent and refined, naturally, and certainly better-looking; but the similarities were striking.'

'Remember, I've seen Mr Belzen,' Katie said. 'Something's gone wrong with that civilization of yours.'

'Quite,' said DuQuelle. He paused again, sniffing the air, searching for the words. 'But what did go wrong? I've often wondered. Were we ambitious, or did we simply want to be better? Did we wish to live on a higher level, or were we driven by power? The motivation could even have been as low as vanity.'

DuQuelle seemed to forget his visitors as he stared into the distance, reliving the past. He face was still, as always, but his eyes glowed dark with anger and sorrow. It was an uncomfortable sight. Alice coughed slightly, to draw his attention, and asked gently. 'Your people, what terrible thing did your people do?'

DuQuelle laughed, short and sharp, more of a bark than a laugh. 'People! Well that is rich. We felt we were far above people. We had to keep refining, you see. We couldn't leave well enough alone. The goal of our civilization was to evolve the body and the mind. Our medical, astrological and technical abilities progressed. We learned to shed the parts of ourselves we scorned and expand those we valued. But it wasn't enough to prune and transplant, to tinker with ourselves. Everything within our reach had to be modified. All species had to be brought together as a super species. Even the elements had to be harnessed, contained, and then absorbed. To put it into your terms, we became man, animal, vegetable, air, water, fire and earth – all in one.'

James was fascinated. Here was science, set free by a superior race. The questions spilled out of him. 'Which were you able to do first? How did you do it? How did you survive without the interdependence of other species? If the elements were within you, what was outside you?'

Katie cut across James. 'We've done a couple of these things in my own time, not in such a big way, but it's where we're going. So why did it go wrong for you? What was the problem?'

'Ah Katie, you have a great ability to come to the point,' DuQuelle smiled. 'It all went very wrong. Each time we implanted and grafted, absorbed and spliced, we gained some gift, but we lost something too. We didn't know it, but each addition was diluting the essential thing that made us different from everything else.'

'Your soul?' Alice questioned.

'Your feelings?' Katie guessed.

'No it has to be reasoning,' James said.

DuQuelle shrugged. 'Call it what you will. Once it was gone, we had no name for it.' Again he stopped, looking through them, into the past, trying to find an explanation.

Katie remembered the first time she had seen DuQuelle, in the New York City subway entrance. He had spoken to her, silently. The word had been 'SEEK'. He had sought, and found Katie, but still his search went on, for the words and for the answers.

Shaking off the past, DuQuelle tried to smile again. 'We finally overstepped ourselves when it came to the body. It had become cumbersome, ill-adapted and very unhygienic. Why would we need a body when we had everything else? So we gradually shed it. Many of its functions were transferred to highly developed systems. Amongst these transferred functions was our ability to communicate. To put it mildly, this was a mistake.'

James was nodding his head vigorously, trying to take it all in. 'Systems? Are you talking about machines? Did they talk for you? Were they all one kind, or were there many different machines to control the different functions performed by the body? Who manned the machines? If none of you had bodies, who kept them working?'

DuQuelle shot him an irritated glance. 'You're just the type that got us into this scrape in the first place. No, I won't answer your questions. You might try the whole thing over again, here. And it would end, again, in disaster. It is a relief though, that your questions are so rudimentary. Machines! Really. You have a long way to go; though as time progresses, to Katie's time, there is more to worry about.'

James's cheeks flamed with anger, but Alice put a

restraining hand on his arm. 'These systems, why were they a mistake?' she asked.

DuQuelle shivered and seemed to shrink within his black frock coat. 'It was catastrophic. We had gone too far. There was no technology, no system that could live up to our ambition.' DuQuelle began to perspire and sniffed the air anxiously. 'I can't even begin to find the words.'

'Melt down,' Katie said. 'I think that's what you're looking for. It must have been bad.'

'Did you all die then?' James asked. 'Or at least most of you, I mean, you are here.'

'We were nearly extinct,' DuQuelle said. 'Those who survived had lost something vital. We had no language, written or verbal, no speech. That had disappeared. Our ability to communicate in any way was fatally impaired. And it turned out that words were our meat, our drink, our water and our air. Communication was our primary means of survival, what is the term Katie might use? Our major source of energy? Without it we could not live.'

'What did you do?' Alice asked.

DuQuelle looked almost apologetic.

'We remembered you – a primitive civilization, yes, but you could communicate, and that was crucial. By this time you had evolved, past the initial symbols and grunts and gestures to a series of quite sophisticated dialects. The Babylonians and the Hebrews were particularly impressive. Today you speak over 5,000 dialects.'

'You mean languages,' James corrected.

'No,' said DuQuelle. 'I mean dialects. You all speak the same language. But it is a marvellous resource. We have been importing it ever since. It's what keeps us alive.'

James's anger was mounting. 'You take our language, against our will?' he said.

'Really James,' DuQuelle responded. 'It's not that different from what England does in India, Africa or China. You take gold and diamonds, silk and tea. We take words. Think of yourselves as one big colony, overseen by a benevolent if unknown imperialist.'

Katie thought James might slug DuQuelle. 'So you feed off our words,' she said.

'Yes,' DuQuelle replied, 'we need a constant supply. We can only speak through your words; our own thoughts and ideas must be lifted from *your* thoughts, *your* ideas. Sometimes I have the most terrible trouble finding the right word. I think on such a higher level, you see.'

Katie chose not to be annoyed, she was too curious.

'But what about Lucia, and Belzen?' she asked. 'Why are they here? I know now it's not just to find me, or even the other two time travellers. And what is the Verus? And the Malum?'

'It all relates to communication,' DuQuelle answered. 'We were so dependent on this resource, we couldn't let you squander it. We had to watch you carefully. But as we watched, we began to judge, and our judgements differed.'

DuQuelle's affected dandyism had long ago deserted him. He shifted slightly towards the fire, always seeking warmth. 'Some of us wished to make you better,' he continued, 'or at least better by their own lights. They wanted to interfere in your world to bring about their notion of morality. The continous "refining" we value so highly. One might call it moral colonization.' He smiled weakly at Katie. 'You have said you've seen Lucia?' he asked. Katie nodded. 'She is the leader,' he said drily, 'of the Verus. She sees herself as the guardian of all that is *right*. Not that right is always related to good, but then nuance has never been Lucia's strong point.' DuQuelle lost himself in the fire.

'Why is Lucia here?' Katie asked.

'It was one of her brilliant ideas to keep the precious commodity of communication safe – she would change mankind,' he continued, a note of bitterness in his voice. 'The Verus discovered that while we could not stay in your world, we could use humans to carry out changes. It's known as the Great Experiment.'

Alice looked hurt, and very shocked. This defied everything she had ever been taught. What was progress, or goodness or faith if humankind were nothing more than puppets? She wished Leopold was not hearing this. 'You've been experimenting with us?' she asked quietly.

DuQuelle moved his walking stick out of James O'Reilly's reach.

'Yes, but please do understand: I am not a member of

the Verus. I never agreed with the Great Experiment, and now my doubts have been justified. There was also a selfish side to the actions of the Verus. Lucia was certain you would start a war that would destroy your world. With you would go our ability to communicate.'

DuQuelle glanced briefly at Katie. 'I'm certain this is very strange, and frankly, quite foreign to you. But now we will talk, of what is familiar, and should be comforting. We will talk of *you*, Katie.' Katie looked away from DuQuelle. Nothing he said was ever comforting.

'The central idea of the Great Experiment was to send a child from another time to this century. You see, a child would be so much easier to manipulate, to carry out the changes the Verus wished.'

'Katie isn't a child,' James interrupted. 'We are all much older than that.' DuQuelle sighed. The young were always in such a hurry to shed childhood. They wouldn't make such haste if they knew what was to come.

'No, Katie is no longer a child,' he conceded. 'And that's part of the flaw in the Verus's plans. The key to the Great Experiment is the written word. The Verus has the ability to take your words and transform them. The words can be used as a form of travel. And when the right child reads the right words, they can fly through time. These children are exceptional, gifted. They are known as the Tempus Fugit.'

Katie couldn't help but feel ever so slightly pleased. 'Exceptional, gifted' – she never thought of herself that way.

Alice looked at her with new admiration. James though had his suspicions. 'So what's this flaw in the Verus's plans?' he asked. DuQuelle gave his short, barking laugh.

'The Great Experiment is still in its early stages. The Verus's powers are limited,' he explained. 'They can choose the words, but cannot choose the child. The child must choose, have the ability to travel, to fly through time, the gift of the Tempus. The Verus don't always get the type of child they want, or even a child at all. There have been a few botched attempts.' He looked at Katie, who chose to ignore the look.

'What about the child who destroys the world?' James asked. Katie could have kicked him.

'One cannot pin that upon Lucia,' DuQuelle said. 'The Verus wants peace. But there is a splinter of our society who desires the exact opposite. They think they have found an alternative resource to communication. They have located huge quantities of brute force. They think we can live off this. They wish to destroy this world and make us all dependent on the Malum. They have tampered with the Verus's Great Experiment. They have sent their own child, not a Tempus Fugit, who flies through time, but a Tempus Occidit – one who falls through time. This is the child who brings the war to end the world.'

'Who leads this other group? It's Mr Belzen, isn't it?' Katie asked.

'Yes, Belzen. He rebelled from the Verus, bringing other

discontents with him to form the Malum. It was a terrible time for us. One didn't know whom to trust, and I learned to trust no one. Obstinate and domineering as Lucia is, she at least does stand for good. A rather one-dimensional good, but good none the less. Belzen – he is corrupt, swollen with greed and ambition. You've seen the shape he takes?'

'Only from the back,' Katie said.

'That explains why you survived. He can take human shape briefly, but the moment he is angered or excited he becomes what is within him. I don't believe a human can survive seeing that.'

For Katie this was too much. Over the past months she, James and Alice had gathered the parts of this puzzle, but it was a horrifying thing, piecing it together. Yet DuQuelle hadn't answered the question that had haunted her day and night. She took a deep breath. 'Which child am I?' she asked.

James moved quickly, to stand between Katie and DuQuelle, and Alice put a protective arm around her friend. 'You can't possibly think Katie is that evil child,' she protested. 'She is not bringing a war to end the world.'

Katie looked to DuQuelle. 'I just can't be,' she said, almost pleading.

DuQuelle patted her hand, a rare and gentle gesture. His smile was weak, but reassuring. 'I don't think you can be, my dear. When we were alone, I saw the mushroom cloud within your eyes, but I also saw your defiance of it. Your world might be on the brink of destruction, but you will fight it to the end. You have great potential, Katie: intelligence, clear-sightedness and a longing to give and get friendship and love. These are not the traits one finds in the destroyer of the world. Plus, you are quite good company. I find I do not have it in myself to smother you with a pillow. You are not to be sent off into eternity. But neither can you remain here. You all must see how great the danger is. My apologies to the Princess, but her little friend must leave this time as soon as possible. Katie's destination must be her own time, though I do dread the fallout when it's discovered.'

'But we told you, we've tried to send Katie back,' James cut in.

'Yes, you've tried, and a jolly good try for a boy your age too.' DuQuelle patted James on the head, knowing how much he would hate it. 'Let's just say I have capabilities that tiny bit beyond yours. I will meet you tonight at the Palace – midnight – at the spot where Katie first appeared. I have some planning and searching to do first.'

'Will you be alone?' Katie asked. It was still very hard to trust Bernardo DuQuelle. Again, he seemed to read her thoughts. She did wish he would stay out of her head.

'I will try to keep my more unsavoury acquaintances away from our midnight tryst… but time is not with us… we can but hope.'

Chapter Eighteen

Katie Finds Her Voice

It was almost midnight. Katie stood with Alice in the north corridor of Buckingham Palace, shivering in her school uniform. She'd grown so used to her petticoats and pelisses that the short grey pleated skirt and dark green knee socks didn't seem like real clothes, but just another layer of underthings. 'Knees are ugly,' Katie thought, 'especially mine – knobbly and scaly and bulbous.' She pondered how the girls in her class at school rolled up the waistbands of their skirts to expose even more scabby lank leg. 'I used to think you looked like a piece of upholstered furniture in all those clothes,' she said to Alice, 'but now I feel almost naked in my own things.'

James, as he turned the corner, obviously thought so too. He stopped in his tracks, turned bright red and spun around to face the wall.

Alice wrapped her cloak around Katie.

'It is a bit of a shock at first,' Alice conceded. 'Jamie, I've wrapped Katie up, you can turn around now.' James turned slowly, but still couldn't look at Katie.

Katie sighed. 'Yes, you've seen my legs, and I know they're not the greatest sight in the world. Think of me as a cadaver. You're perfectly OK with those, and they're usually naked.'

'You're bony enough to be one,' James grinned, 'and there were several times over the past months when I've thought you were certain to become one.'

Katie's eyes filled. 'Without you, without Alice, I probably would be one. You, like, believed in me, protected me; put your own lives in danger. I never thought I would have a friend like this – ever – and now I have two!'

Alice, clutching Woolie Baa Lamb, was a picture of misery. She put her arms around Katie and held tight. 'I don't see how I can let you go,' she whispered.

James put a hand on both their shoulders and firmly, but gently pulled them apart. 'Oh blast, I've been dreading this. The girlish protestations, the waterworks. Katie has to go back. That's that. As much as I detest Bernardo DuQuelle, he seems to be the only person who can do it. So let's just say goodbye rationally.'

Alice burst into tears. 'How can you be so heartless? I thought Katie was your friend?'

James sighed and fished out a rather grubby handkerchief for Alice's use. 'I am Katie's friend,' he tried to explain, turning to Katie in exasperation. 'You're as good as a girl gets, Katie. You have some fairly funny ideas but you're brave as they come and can catch a ball better than anyone I have ever met. If you had been a man, you could have done great things.'

'She can still do great things,' Alice said, mopping her eyes and trying to regain her dignity. 'She can be a loving wife and mother.'

'You forget,' Katie said drily, 'in my own time I can be a wife and mother and I can also be the President of the United States of America. Maybe there are some good things to go back to after all.'

James and Alice looked rather astonished, but this did dry Alice's tears.

'Where is Leopold?' James asked. 'I can't believe he'd miss this, not after proving such a star today.'

'He's standing watch at the end of the hall.' A voice echoed down the corridor. It was Bernardo DuQuelle. 'I had to convince him it was really me, and not an impostor. It took me a good five minutes of hard talking, and really, these were five minutes we could not afford to lose. There's something up in the Palace – lights and movement where there shouldn't be. The Black Tide might be afoot – or something even worse – all looking for Miss Berger-Jones-Burg.' His eyes rolled to the ceiling. '*What* a name, so arriviste.'

Katie was feeling decidedly shaky. 'If I'm going to take the plunge, I might as well do it quickly,' she said. Du-Quelle scanned the many sofas lining the corridor. Bending down, he sniffed one, and taking his chiffon handkerchief from his waistcoat pocket, rubbed in against the sofa's leg. The handkerchief stuck to the side of the sofa.

'This will be the one,' he said.

'How do you know?' James asked.

DuQuelle walked over to Katie and, taking the hand-kerchief, held it above her head. All her hair stood up on end. She felt little popping sparks above her. 'Static electricity,' DuQuelle explained. 'One picks up a vast amount of excess energy when one travels through time.'

'Now that is interesting,' James said, 'because I read in the Reverend Chauncy Hare Townshend's treatise *Mesmerism Proved True* that…'

Just then, Leopold's reedy voice could be heard down the corridor. 'Quick, hide. Someone is coming.'

Everyone dived for the nearest hiding place, as two sets of feet ran from opposite ends of the hallway, and met in the middle.

'At last, there you are. I haf to look everywhere.' A splat-tering of carraway seeds announced the arrival of Baroness Lehzen.

'Really Baroness, what is this urgency. I was asleep. It was a long day and it is almost midnight.' James squirmed further under the sofa. It was his father.

'We haf not the time to hear of your tiring day. There has been an accident, no, a crime so serious within the Palace. It is Mr MacKenzie. He haf been hurt, badly hurt, battered and bruised till the speaking he cannot do – and when he does speak, oh! You would not want to hear the words. "He came to me in the dark of the night," he screams. I couldn't answer. I couldn't say. And then, "The arm," he screams, "the arm – it did whip out, snatching at me, oh the oozing pus-like tentacles. It spat and hissed," and then MacKenzie he does cry and bab-ble of Beelzebub and Belzen. He is insane with the terror, is Mr MacKenzie. I do not know that he will live past the night this is.'

Dr O'Reilly shifted nervously. 'Perhaps we should call the household guards?' he suggested.

'No!' Baroness Lehzen barked. 'We must keep *stumm*. I do not wish to disturb the precious Queen. We must learn more before we act. You must go to his bed. *Mach schnell!*'

As the two hurried down the hall, DuQuelle slid from under a sofa, looking with distaste at his dusty trousers. 'If only that woman would put half the energy into house-keeping that she puts into court intrigue,' he lamented. 'But my trousers will survive the night, while Katie might not. Here's trouble in the worst shape of all. Mr Belzen has been here. He obviously wanted information from

MacKenzie, and almost killed him trying to get it. I don't believe he could tell him what he wanted, as it had to do with you, Katie.'

'Will MacKenzie live?' Katie asked.

'If he saw what I think he saw,' DuQuelle replied grimly, 'he will wish for death the rest of his life. Now quick – say your goodbyes and it's under the sofa for you. We have even less time than I thought.'

This was goodbye then. Katie turned to James O'Reilly. 'Being a doctor is a great thing,' she said. 'I know you will be the one who changes the world. Give Riordan a hug and kiss for me.'

James looked her briefly in the eye then, looking down, punched her in the shoulder. The only sound was a derisive snort from DuQuelle.

Alice began to cry again and Katie held her close. 'You have made me understand about family by being the sister I never had. I will miss you every day of my life.'

DuQuelle handed Katie a battered notebook. 'My diary!' she exclaimed. 'No one knows about my diary. Where did you find it? Was it under my bed? Did you go to my own time? To my own room?'

'What would I do in your silly pink room,' DuQuelle replied. 'The diary was right here, in the side pocket of your rucksack. It was discovered by a housekeeper. I picked it up early on. I believe you'd been unleashing some grievances against your mama before you decided to join us in the nineteenth century. A most amusing read.'

Katie was trying hard to understand. 'So what have you done to my diary?' she asked. 'Is it magic now? Or scientifically modified?'

DuQuelle laughed. 'No, indeed, and that's the beauty of it all. Though you travelled here through our abilities, you will travel back through your own. You are the Tempus, chosen by some force beyond us, to understand the power of the written word. And now you must harness that ability to your own writing, your own words. It is your thoughts, from your own time, that will send you home. Katie, find your own voice. That is the key to all the travels of your life.'

Katie took off Alice's cloak and, hitching the rucksack over one shoulder, slid under the sofa. DuQuelle got down beside her. 'Turn to the 1st of May,' he ordered.

'But that is today,' Katie protested. 'Or at least the bit of today that's left. I haven't written in my diary since I arrived. I didn't even know it was here.'

'You'll be surprised,' DuQuelle responded. 'Now open the diary and try to concentrate. Dig your heels in. Put that wilfulness of yours to good use.'

Katie opened her diary to find all her feelings and actions lay before her. There in its pages was the friendship and fear, the kidnap of Riordan, the Crystal Palace, and the attempt to assassinate the Queen, Lucia, Belzen, DuQuelle... How could it all have got there? 'Find your own voice,' Bernardo DuQuelle had said. This was her own voice.

DuQuelle peered under the sofa, 'You certainly don't think much of me,' he said, poking the diary with his walking stick. 'But that will change with time. I somehow think that we will meet again.'

Katie looked up at DuQuelle. His eyes glittered, but his face was sphinx-like. He was still the greatest mystery of all. 'What is your universe called?' she asked.

'I do not know,' he said. 'We have lost our words and can only use yours. You think of a name for us. Though limited in many ways, you have great powers of communication. I will abide, Katie, by your choice of words. Now go back,' he commanded. 'Go back in your diary to the time before you came. Read up to that date. Concentrate on what is happening, feel it, live it.'

She bent her head to the diary to meet – again – her own life. There was her school, Neuman Hubris, and the babble of her classmates. Tiffany sprang up from the diary cooing adoringly at baby Angel. Her father exhaled through his nose in exasperation and Dolores grumbled 'You think you're so smart, but you don' know nothin…' And there was Mimi, sitting in the kitchen, smoking by the open window so that Dolores wouldn't know. Head tipped back, blowing smoke rings, her speciality.

'How can you let those girls get to you?' Mimi was saying to Katie after some playground fiasco. 'I've seen them in endless school plays. Cheyenne is certain to run to cellulite and Amber has a very iffy chin. Neither of them has your long legs or cheekbones. Tell them to go to hell.'

As Katie reread her diary, Mimi seemed so different. Why? Could it be that Mimi had changed? Or was it Katie? It had only been a few months since Katie had appeared under the sofa at Buckingham Palace, but she felt years older. One hundred and fifty-something years had given her a bit of distance from her own life. 'Look at Alice,' she thought. 'The Queen spends so much time as the mother of the Empire, that she has little time to mother her own children. And then there's James, so secretly hurt, wanting his own mother so much – a mother who can never come back.'

As Katie turned the pages, she could hear her own voice, telling her what really counted. It was Mimi, looking up from the diary with a face that expressed so many emotions at one time. There was anger, resentment, boredom, frustration – and love. And not just 'Hey, girlfriend, call me Mimi' love, but mother love. Katie turned to another entry. 'I cried myself to sleep,' she had written, 'and when I woke up Mimi was lying next to me, her arm across my chest.'

'She doesn't know it most of the time,' Katie realized, 'but I am the love of Mimi's life. The men will come and go, but I will always be there. Hey, I'm the only stability she has. I haven't been truthful with myself about Mimi. She'll be frantic when she realizes I'm gone. And yes, it will be drama queen, over-the-top, cry on prime-time news frantic, but her pain will be real enough.'

Something was happening in the corridor at Buckingham Palace. Katie could faintly hear Leopold's excited voice and then a cry from Alice. There was shouting and shuffling, a full-scale brawl. Someone was pulling her rucksack out from under her... trying to reach her... but Mimi was reaching out too... becoming stronger and louder... insistent that Katie return to her... asserting herself as a mother... demanding her daughter... Katie was flying, or was she falling?... all she could see now was Mimi... with her complex face of love and anger... and then there was nothing.

Silence. And then the growing murmur of suppressed, excited voices. 'It's all gone wrong,' Katie thought. 'Oh my God, is it Mr Belzen? I don't believe DuQuelle is strong enough to fight him off. Alice and James: they need my help. We must abort the time travel attempt. Now that we know how to do it, we can try again, I can always go back tomorrow.'

She turned her head and felt the scratchy shag of carpet beneath her cheek. She sneezed. Dust. Dolores hated getting out the vacuum cleaner. The slap of the iron came to her. The excited voices were a Spanish soap opera. She was home, and whatever was happening in Buckingham

Palace would have to go on without her. She could be of no help.

Katie crawled out from under her bed. There was no panic in the apartment. No police cordons and no screaming Mimi. It looked the way it always looked, with the vomit pink carpet and wallpaper fairies. It sounded the way it always did, what with the ironing and the TV and the New York traffic many floors below. 'But it's not the same,' Katie said to herself, 'I can prove it.' Feeling around under the bed, she found her diary.

Flipping through the pages she looked for the day's entry. There was no 1st of May or 1st of April or 1st of March. The last thing Katie had written was on the 1st of February, the day she had fallen asleep over her book and travelled through time. There was no Alice, no James O'Reilly and certainly no Bernardo DuQuelle, no Verus and no Malum. It was as if her adventures had never happened. Searching under her bed again she found the book, the letters from Queen Victoria's daughters. She carefully looked up Princess Alice. There were dozens of letters from Alice to her sisters, but not one of them mentioned Katie Berger-Jones-Burg. Katie shook her head at the book. 'I'm sorry I teased you about writing boring letters,' she told the printed words. 'Because this is all I have of you now.' She carefully closed the book, as if saying goodbye to a best friend, and giving it a hug, put it in the cardboard box with her other treasures. '*It was not a dream,*' she said as loud as she could. '*There is a world beyond my world. Many worlds. We are still in danger.*'

'Is that you, sleepy head?' Dolores yelled from the kitchen. 'You've been dozing under that bed for the whole afternoon,' she added, without taking her eyes from the small television perched on the counter. 'She's got a nice comfy bed with Gucci sheets and pillows, a down comforter, the works. But does she sleep on it? No, she does not. She sleeps under it, like an old stray dog,' Dolores confided to a very sexy nurse on the television screen. 'Mimi called,' she added.

Katie knew this final comment was not meant for the nurse. She stumped into the kitchen and opened the refrigerator. There was nothing new inside.

'So she's married, huh? Well, mazel tov to her.'

'She is *not* married,' Dolores said. 'She did not make it to the altar. She didn't even make it to Acapulco. Seems there's already a Mrs Fishberg, and that Dr Fishberg is not planning a divorce. So much for Mimi's soulmate. My guess is that soulmates and alimony don't get along too good.'

Katie took a banana from the bowl and peeled it. 'Katie Berger-Jones-Burg-Fishberg,' she said tentatively. 'That was a narrow escape.'

Dolores finally looked up from the television.

'Mimi was crying,' she said, taking up a white silk shirt to iron. 'Crying to beat the band. When she gets home she's gonna cry all night long, and you're gonna have to be the shoulder she cries on.'

'That's OK,' Katie said. And she really did mean it.

'There's a package for you,' Dolores added. 'It arrived some twenty minutes ago. The doorman says be careful. It was a kind of weird guy dropping it off. I said, don't worry. You've had some pretty weird daddies. Maybe one of them remembered your birthday or something.'

Katie took up a very long, narrow parcel. It was wrapped in stiff brown paper and tied up in cord.

Katie Berger-Jones-Burg

was written in the most elaborate penmanship, the many flourishes and swirls made it difficult to read. There was no address, no stamp, no date. Her heart skipped a beat. It was not from her time. With shaking hands she cut the cord and undid the paper, exposing an ivory and gold box. She lifted the lid.

Dolores harrumphed and returned to her ironing. 'That's no gift for a child,' she said to the nurse on the television.

Inside the box was a walking stick of ebony with its elaborate silver head engraved with strange letters and symbols. Katie could still see Bernardo DuQuelle. Still feel the walking stick poking her in the chest as the carriage rolled along. An embossed card fell from the folds of tissue. The card read:

Aide Memoire

To help her remember! Katie shivered, and then smiled. As if she could forget.

Dear Reader,

This is a story filled with both fact and fiction. Queen Victoria did have a daughter named Alice, but there is no record of Alice finding a twenty-first-century time traveller under the sofa in Buckingham Palace. Baroness Lehzen did exist; though Fräulein Bauer's grisly death is pure imagination. Prince Leopold did suffer from haemophilia. Joseph Paxton did create the Crystal Palace. And the Queen did love Prince Albert dearly.

If you're interested in the Victorians and the 1800s, the Victoria & Albert Museum in London is a good place to start. Its collection of drawings, reporting and memorabilia on the Crystal Palace is wondrous. I also recommend The Museum of Childhood and The Foundling Museum, also in London. They often have moving and fascinating exhibitions on Victorian childhood.

There are so many interesting facts about the Victorians, but occasionally the 1851 in The Queen Must Die is at odds with the 1851 in your history books. Every once in a while I've tinkered with the ages, temperaments and actions of some of the real people

involved. I don't think it's enough to affect any of
your exams...

    One fact is rock solid though. Katie, Alice and James
are as real to me as if they were my own sisters and
brother. They were alive in my head, and I was truly sad
when I finished writing this book. Luckily for me, The
Queen Must Die is the first of three books, a trilogy
called 'Chronicles of the Tempus'. It was a great joy to
begin writing the second book: The Queen at War.
Katie, Alice and James will be back, along with many
new characters, such as Florence Nightingale. I'm
particularly fond of Miss Nightingale, though she
probably wouldn't have cared for me. She didn't suffer
fools gladly.

    I'd really like to know what you think of this story.
And do you have any questions? I'll try to answer
them. You can talk to me on my Facebook page
(Chronicles of the Tempus), or through my website:
www.chroniclesofthetempus.com. It would be very
exciting to hear from you.

Respectfully yours,
K. A. S. Quinn

The
Queen
At War

Chronicles
of the
Tempus

K. A. S. QUINN

The Darkened Room

A single candle flickered on the bedside table, casting the faces of a boy and girl into light and shadow. The boy bent over the bed, and wiping the girl's forehead with a damp cloth, spoke with a roughness meant to mask his anxiety. 'I am surprised at you Grace; you're supposed to be the obedient one. Yet you've gone against father's orders and returned from Florence. The climate there was helping you. Father says you were gaining strength each day and were on the road to a good recovery. How do you expect to get well in London's damp and fog? You had to take to bed from the moment you stepped off the mail steamer.'

The candle caught the girl's eyes, bright with something beyond the tears that filled them. 'James, I couldn't stay away. I begged to return. I longed for the mists and rains, the soft green of England. I even yearned for the smoke and bustle of London. And I had to see you and Jack, to be with my dear wee brothers. You're growing so fast, the only truly little one left is Riordan. And then war is coming. Jack's regiment will soon be off to the East. I know father says I was getting better in Florence, but each day I woke, feeling I'd lost something, and knew I would never get it back. I so fear—'

A hacking cough sent the girl bolt upright in bed, struggling for breath. James rubbed her back vigorously, propping the pillows behind her. He busied himself, warming a liquid over the candle, and then measuring drops into a glass. 'Don't talk Grace,' he said. 'It tires you so. Here, take this, it will help you to rest. Now do as your "wee brother" instructs, he's a good foot taller than you now.' James tried to smile, but it was a thin-lipped effort. Grace smiled back, and taking the glass, drank it down to please him.

'You take such good care of me James. You and Jack, such strapping fine young men now; I want so much to see you grown, to—'

James interrupted, placing a finger against her lips. '*Rest*, I said. Not talk, but rest. When did you become such a chatterbox? Father says there's nothing wrong with you except exhaustion, too frantic a social life, too much dancing in crowded ballrooms. He thinks the waltz is the source of much evil.'

'Father says even worse. Don't you know it's all due to books? He says I read too much and it's brought on a hectic fever. The lectures I've had on "over-stimulation of the female brain".' James and Grace both laughed, but hers was cut short by the persistent hacking cough.

'Rest,' was all James said, but his eyes said much more as he made her as comfortable as possible. 'I've left a bell next to the bed, and I'll move the candle over here onto the dresser. The palace has arranged that I can sleep next door. Ring if you need me. Goodnight dear Grace. Sleep well. I am certain you will feel better in the morning.'

'You are sweet to hope James, but I doubt it will be so,' Grace murmured. The drops were beginning to take affect. She closed her eyes, breathing more evenly.

In the next room another girl waited for James, a girl with silky brown hair and serious gray eyes. She moved quickly across the room, holding back her long skirts with one hand. 'How is she James?' Princess Alice asked. 'Do I need to call your father?' James looked bitter and weary, older than his years.

'My father continues to pretend that Grace is simply "delicate". I try to go along with this, but you know as well as I do what the truth is – Grace is an intelligent person and can see through the pretense as well. She's losing hope, and we're losing vital time.' Alice drew a chair up next to the fire and coaxed James into it.

'If your father could put aside his pride, admit he was wrong about Grace's illness, could he cure her?' she asked.

James stared at the fire. In his mind, Grace's frightened eyes glittered back through the flames. 'I hate to say it Alice, but Grace's illness is beyond my father's capabilities. Yes, I know he's at the peak of his profession, physician to the Royal Household. But that position was achieved through good looks and a glib tongue. I'm afraid his ability to charm the Queen holds more sway than his medical talents.' James blushed. 'I'm sorry Alice. I would never be disloyal to your mother, and I wish with all my heart I had more faith in my father, but he is more likely to harm Grace than cure her.'

Alice stood behind James, staring into the fire as well. 'Is there anyone else who could help – any other physician?' James shook his head.

'There are doctors who have had some luck treating this type of illness. But that's the problem, it is just luck. Sometimes patients recover, yes; but at other times they waste away, or are gone within hours through a galloping fever. I've been reading everything I can; doctor's notes, university lectures, medical treatise. Each one contradicts the other. The only certainty is the no one in this world knows enough to cure Grace.'

He slumped in the chair, and Alice looked down on her friend's bent head. 'If the answer isn't in this world, it might be in another,' she said. 'There's only one thing I can think of to do, and I'm going to go do it now.' Patting James lightly on the shoulder, Alice went out of the room and into the corridor. Up the stairs and down she went, stumbling slightly on her skirts – they'd only just been let down to suit her years. 'It is a nuisance,' she mumbled to herself, '*she* was right about our clothes.' Moving aside a tapestry, she knocked softly on the low door behind it.

'Ah yes, do come in,' said a low, foreign voice from within, as if she were expected. It was a small room, more like a closet, with stone walls curved upwards to an arched ceiling. It had a strangely medieval feel, a forgotten room in the midst of a modern, bustling palace. Inside she found a tall man of striking pallor, sitting at a desk, poring over a manuscript. He stood as Alice entered, bowing deeply.

'You are up late princess.'

'I come from a sad vigil,' Alice replied. 'James O'Reilly's sister Grace. She is deathly ill.'

The tall, pale man offered his chair. 'It is indeed sad,' he said, 'when one so young is found in such a hopeless, helpless state. She has my sympathy.' Alice did not sit, but stared at his desk absently, hardly noticing the strange symbols etched on the manuscript before her. She looked up, into the man's creased white face.

'It is hopeless for Grace,' she said. 'Because no one in this world can help her. But you have other means, other ways. You know what brings me here?' He smiled slightly and nodded. '*She* must be called,' Alice added. He smiled again, but this time shook his head in dissent.

'Grace knows her time has come,' he said. 'She has returned to her family to die. She has resignation and fortitude. She has faith,' his lips gave an ironic twist at the final word. Alice pressed her hands against the desk, palms down. She needed to remain calm.

'Grace can live,' she said. 'You, by making the call, by bringing her here, you might give Grace life.'

Talking up a long black walking stick, the man turned it slowly, examining the curious shapes engraved on its silver tip. 'You do remember the last time? The trouble? And though it's really not something we can discuss, I can tell you in confidence – that trouble is still brewing, building in fact.' Tapping the walking stick lightly against the floor, he shook his head as if to clear it. 'You talk of giving Grace the gift of life? I doubt the Archbishop of Canterbury would approve,' he said in an attempt at a lighter tone. 'Me? Creating life? A collective shudder would run through your church.'

The princess would not be put off by his banter. Circling the room, she came before him again, holding out her clasped hands. 'Bernardo DuQuelle, you can help, and you must help,' she cried, finally losing patience. 'How can you tease me in the face of death? Grace will die, and James' heart will break. If you make the call, Grace might be saved.' The tall pale man looked down on the small princess.

'You know I can not interfere,' he said. 'To save one life you could endanger thousands.'

'I've never believed that of her,' Alice replied. 'She can only bring good. She is our friend, our companion. You think so too, I know. She can help. Please.' Alice took the man's long, cold hand. She had never touched him before.

The touch seemed to affect him strangely. He looked at her hand. It fit into his palm, delicate and warm as a newly baked pastry. Sighing and shaking his head, he went to his desk and shut his books. He wrapped his cloak around his shoulders, and taking up his black top hat and walking stick, bowed to Princess Alice. 'As I've always said, you are a true daughter of Queen Victoria. Such a will, but pressed with great gentleness.' The creases in his face deepened, but it wasn't a face to show much emotion. 'I shall do as you wish. I shall send the message. But there is no need to dimple and clap your hands. I will call, but whether she hears it, that I can not say.'

Chapter One

The Stranger in the Bed

A fire engine tore down 82nd Street, its blaring sirens ricocheting across a canyon of skyscrapers. The sound bounced upwards, finally reaching the 11th floor bedroom of Katie Berger-Jones-Burg. The many windows in Katie's apartment had no double-glazing. 'Who needs the expense?' her mother Mimi asked. 'It's perfectly quiet this far up.' But then Mimi took so many pills at night, she was dead to the world. King Kong could come crashing through the windows, and Mimi would sleep on.

Katie didn't take pills. She had, according to her mother, a drearily non-addictive personality. Mimi was the lead singer of Youth 'n Asia, a fading all-girl pop band. Her life had been filled with adventure, drama and a fair share of hallucinogenic drugs. By contrast Katie was, well, bland. Mimi had once complained that she was the only mother amongst their acquaintance who hadn't checked her daughter into the Betty Ford Clinic. 'Don't you have any obsessions?' Mimi goaded her. 'Addictions make a person interesting.'

'I read,' Katie countered. 'I read a lot.'

'Reading,' her mother sighed. '*So* outmoded. Couldn't you text or tweet instead?'

An ambulance followed the fire engine, throwing its wail up through the apartment windows. 'New York,' Katie said to herself, 'the city that never sleeps – well that makes two of us.' Getting out of bed, she went to check on Mimi. Her mother was splayed across her beige cashmere duvet. On the wall above her, a multitude of Mimis were reproduced, in block colors on canvas. Was it a real Warhol? Katie had her doubts. The real Mimi was wearing a pink velvet eyeshade and ear-plugs with purple tassels. 'Good night, sleep tight, don't let the bed bugs bite,' Katie shouted into Mimi's tightly plugged ears, and was greeted with an answering snore.

Tucking Mimi in firmly, Katie headed back to bed. There was a glow coming from her room, which was strange, since she didn't have a night light any more. Something made her stop at the door, and looking in, she practically leapt out of her own skin. The ridiculous storybook words rang through her head, 'somebody's been sleeping in my bed – and they're still here!' But she didn't believe Goldilocks could have been as scared.

Lying in Katie's bed was a stranger, a girl, an extremely beautiful girl. She sank back on Katie's pillows, her chest rising and falling in the effort to breath. She was so thin and pale, her eyes started out of her face, glowing eyes, frightened eyes. She leaned forward to cough, pulling back the ruffles of her muslin nightdress and pushing her long damp red hair from her face; anything to stay the cough and force that precious element, air, into her lungs. It was a desperate, but silent struggle. No sound came from the girl in the bed. As she turned her eyes towards Katie, words slipped like a fog from her mouth, circling round her head and dissolving into the darkness.

'Can you help?'

And then she was gone. As vivid as the girl had been, nothing remained. Katie rubbed her eyes hard. She too was struggling for breath. Taking a pink shawl from the rocking chair, she crept into the living room and lowered herself, shaking, on to the big cream sofa. For the life of her, she wasn't getting back into that bed.

The visions were appearing. Again.

To be continued...